THE THIEF AND THE GANGSTER

Firsts & Forever Stories Vol. 7

ALEXA LAND

Dedication

Contents

Acknowledgments

I'm so grateful for my amazing, talented team—Kim, Melisha, Anita, and Kelly. Thank you for all you do to make my books the best they can be. Special thanks to Amy, Valerie, and Jamilla for your help along the way.

Adriano

The blond at the bar was trouble. I knew it the moment I saw him.

There was mischief in his smile, and in this coy game he was playing. Two men were vying for his attention, and even though he'd been encouraging them and letting them buy him drinks for the better part of an hour, his gaze kept straying to me.

He had my full attention as I circled like a shark. The bar was a free-standing island in the center of the room, so I did a slow lap all the way around, weaving through the Saturday night crowd while closing in on the only man in here who'd captured my interest. It allowed the anticipation to build, so by the time I reached him it was palpable.

I slid in between this guy and one of the douchebags in a cheap suit, who'd been trying and failing to seal the deal. Finally, I got a good look at my quarry. He'd been cute from a distance, but up close he was perfection. He had the face of an angel and was almost too pretty, but his short, scruffy beard provided some balance.

Just because I liked figuring people out, I tried to guess his age. I would have said late twenties, except for those big, green eyes of his. It wasn't the delicate lines at the corners that drove the number up. Instead, it was that tinge of skepticism, which suggested he'd been around the block a few times and learned some hard lessons along the way. I placed him at maybe thirty-three, thirty-four.

A flirtatious smile curled his full lips and drew my attention. That was one hell of a mouth. Luscious, that was the word for it. I really wanted a taste, but not yet.

I looked away long enough to order two shots of top shelf tequila from the bartender before turning back to this guy and asking, "Want to get out of here?"

This amused the blond and annoyed Cheap Suit Guy in equal measure. Blondie asked, "Just like that? Aren't you going to buy me a drink first?" Meanwhile, the second douchebag who'd been hitting on him—probably with a pipe dream of a three-way—had already given up and wandered off.

I handed him one of the shots and said, "I just did." Then I picked up the other one and clinked our glasses together before tossing it back.

He downed his without so much as a flinch and smirked at me, holding my gaze so steadily that it felt like he was issuing a challenge. I grinned at him and tossed a hundred-dollar bill onto the bar top, then turned toward the door and held my arm out.

My kid brother would call dropping that C-note a flex—needlessly showing off, in twenty-something speak—and he'd be right. But I figured this guy would notice and appreciate it. He seemed the type, someone who didn't grow up wealthy but was ambitious and looking to upgrade his station in life. It was written all over him, from his expensive haircut and artfully subtle highlights to that aspirational blue suit—probably the very best quality he could afford, but not quite in the big leagues.

Sure enough, he glanced at the hundred and reached some conclusions about me, the same way I'd reached some conclusions about him. Then he linked his arm with mine.

Cheap Suit Guy wasn't giving up easily, though. He got in our way and asked me, "What do you think you're doing?"

He had balls, I'd give him that. At six-two and with my big build, it was obvious I could crush him like a bug, but his arrogance and sense of entitlement bolstered his courage. I shot him a look that a smarter man would have heeded as a warning and said, "I'm taking doll face home with me. What does it look like I'm doing?"

Cheap Suit turned his attention to the blond and tried another tactic. "You're leaving with this asshole, just like that? After I bought you three vodka tonics?"

The blond bristled at that and growled, "What the fuck did you think, that you were buying me for the price of three cocktails? That's not how this works, you self-important, entitled prick! Besides, I paid for those drinks—not with money, but with the hour of my life I spent listening to you droning on and on about yourself. Newsflash, investment banking isn't that interesting, and if you were any good at it you wouldn't be wearing that polyester atrocity you're trying to pass off as a suit. Want some advice? Stay away from open flames, because that cheap-ass fabric would go up like a fucking dumpster fire."

I was grinning ear-to-ear as we stepped around the shell of a man Blondie had just eviscerated. Cheap Suit Guy muttered, "You two assholes deserve each other."

"It's your fault, you know," my companion told me, as we headed for the exit. "If you hadn't taken for-fucking-ever to make your move, I wouldn't have had to spend my evening listening to that douchebag talk about himself."

"It looked like you had a good thing going there, so I wasn't sure if I should cut in. Who am I to stand in the way of a nice, old fashioned spit-roasting?"

"Ha! In their dreams."

I held the door for him, and once we were outside, I handed my ticket to the valet. While we waited for the car, he asked, "So, do I get to know your name? Or are you cultivating a whole man of mystery vibe to impress me?"

I produced a business card and handed it over as I said, "I'm Adriano Dombruso. My friends call me Reno."

He barely glanced at the card. Instead, he pinched it and ran his thumb over the surface. I almost laughed. He was checking out the paper quality and feeling for the embossing. He might as well have asked for my bank balance at that point, since that little move was clearly meant to gauge how successful I was. Maybe my five-thousand-dollar bespoke suit was too subtle. In fact, it probably was. I'd selected the top quality, black wool fabric not for flash but for substance.

He stuck the card in his pocket and shook my hand. "Jack O'Donnell. Why is your nickname a tacky little city in Nevada?"

"It started because my kid brother Romy couldn't say my name when he was a toddler. The best he could do was Reno, and somehow it stuck. I like it, because it makes me think of him."

"Sounds like you two are close."

"We are, and I couldn't be prouder of him. He's an EMT back home in Vegas, and all about helping others. The kid's basically a saint." Not that he'd asked, but I couldn't pass up an opportunity to brag about my baby brother.

Those intelligent green eyes held my gaze as he teased, "And what about you, Reno? Are you a saint, too?"

I smirked and told him, "No, Jack, I'm definitely a sinner. Once we get to my apartment, I intend to illustrate that point vividly and repeatedly."

He raised a well-groomed brow. "Repeatedly? You sure your mouth isn't writing checks your dick can't cash?"

That little brat. "What are you suggesting, that I'm too old to get it up more than once?"

"I'm just saying, once a man hits forty, the plumbing isn't always up to code."

"I'm thirty-seven, thank you very much."

"Apologies. That's obviously a huge difference."

"That smirk makes me want to put you over my knee. Just saying."

"You love this smirk. It's what drew you to me."

He wasn't wrong. "So, now you know how old I am. What about you?" He was going to lie about his age. I'd put money on it.

"You want to know how badly you're robbing the cradle? I'm twenty-seven, Gramps." He knit his brows at my snort and asked, "You don't believe me?"

"Sorry, doll face, but you're thirty-three if you're a day."

"You know what? Fuck you. I'm going to go see if I can get that spit roast back on track." He was joking, but he was a little insulted, too. To make his point, he took a step toward the bar, and I caught his hand and pulled him back to me.

"It wasn't meant as an insult. You're a man, not a boy, and that's a good thing."

"Whatever. I'd already been considering Botox. I think you just made up my mind."

"Don't you dare." I tilted his chin up with two fingertips and told him, "This face is a work of art. You don't fuck with something so beautiful."

He frowned as he met my gaze. "You think you can tell me what to do?"

"I doubt anybody can. But maybe someone should try."

Before he could reply, the valet joined us and said, "Pardon me, Mr. Russo. Your car is ready."

After I thanked the kid and slipped him a twenty, Jack turned toward my ride and exclaimed, "You absolutely ancient prehistoric fossil! Of course this is what you drive!"

I grinned at that and ran my gaze down the length of the convertible as I informed him, "This gem is a 1962 Cadillac De Ville. If you say one bad thing about her, I'm driving off without you." It really was gorgeous—about a mile long with a pristine black paint job, white wall tires, and a red leather interior.

"No, don't do that. I'll asphyxiate in a thick, black cloud of exhaust fumes if I'm standing here while you drive off. What does this get, a mile a gallon? Every time you turn the key in the ignition, you can probably hear polar bears weeping."

I walked over to the car and shot him a look as I opened the passenger door. "So, are you going to stand there and rant, or are you going to get in my gas guzzling, ozone depleting relic and come home with me, so I can fuck you into oblivion?"

"The latter." He flashed me a smile as he hurried past me and climbed into the Caddy.

As I slid behind the wheel and put the car into drive, I said, "You know what I'm looking forward to? A nice, long blow job."

"So, it's been a while, huh?"

"It's been about six hours." Why did I say that? My most recent blow job had happened months ago, not earlier this evening. But I didn't like his assumption that I hadn't gotten any in a long time. "The part I'm looking forward to is you not talking because your mouth is full."

Jack burst out laughing and called me an asshole. Then he said, "Joke's on you though, because I'm fluent in ASL. That means I can keep talking even with your cock down my throat."

He signed something in what really did look like authentic American Sign Language, and I asked, "What did you just say?"

"I said poor, weeping polar bears."

I chuckled at that and pointed out, "Okay, yes, this car does have a big engine. But it's all been modernized, so it's not as bad as all that."

"Uh huh."

"Why do you know ASL?"

"So I can communicate with my best friend." He turned to look at me and abruptly changed the subject. "Why'd you give the valet a fake name?"

"Because I'd like to keep a low profile while I'm here in San Francisco."

"You blew it when you handed me a business card with your real name on it."

"You weren't someone I wanted to lie to." Except about the blow job, apparently.

"But that's what you're supposed to do with guys you pick up in bars."

I frowned and asked, "Lie to them?"

"Of course! Create a whole fantasy for them."

"So, for example, tell them you're twenty-seven instead of thirty-five?"

"Thirty-four, and once again, fuck you. But yes, exactly. I'll be lying about being twenty-seven until I'm forty. Fifty, if the Botox works."

I grinned and told him, "It's good to have goals."

"Agreed."

"So tell me, Jack O'Donnell, what do you do for a living?"

He waved a hand dismissively and said, "I'm in acquisitions, but let's not talk about work. I'd much rather talk about who was blowing you a mere six hours ago."

Shit, he wasn't letting that go. I deflected by asking, "Jealous?"

"Cautious. If there's a husband or boyfriend in the picture, then—"

"There's nobody," I assured him. "I just got lucky earlier this evening when I stopped off for some coffee." Fuck, this was getting worse by the minute. And this was why lies were such a bad idea—they usually spiraled out of control.

"Hey, we all need hobbies. If yours is being a man-whore, more power to you."

"So judgmental! How long's it been since the last time you had sex?"

"A nice, respectable twenty-four hours, thank you very much."

"And that's *so* much better," I muttered.

"It is! Call me hopelessly prudish, but one sexual encounter a day is generally my limit." He turned to look at my profile and added, "Plus, if it's only been six hours, I'm not even sure you'll be able to get it up again."

"I didn't finish earlier. He had to go back to work." Still spiraling and becoming more ridiculous by the minute. It was too late to back out and admit I was full of shit though, so I just had to roll with it.

"Well, that's what happens when you let random Starbucks baristas blow you in the parking lot. They only get fifteen minute breaks, you know. That's usually not enough time for the extra frothy cappuccino treatment."

I chuckled and told him, "You have a way with words."

"Thank you."

"He didn't work at the coffee house though, and it wasn't a Starbucks." Please let this topic die soon!

"I'm glad you clarified that. Those details are obviously important."

"They are."

After a beat, he said, "I suppose I should actually be thanking Mr. not-a-Starbucks-employee. If he hadn't left you with a case of blue balls, maybe you wouldn't have been out cruising for ass tonight, and I'd have been forced to resort to the matched set of douchebags."

"You wouldn't really have let either of them take you home, would you?"

He clicked his tongue and asked, "Now who's being judgmental?"

"I'm just saying, neither of those men were good enough for you." We'd pulled up to a stoplight, so I turned to meet his gaze and added, "Not by a long shot."

2

Jack

This guy was smooth. He knew all the right things to say, like that last comment about those men not being good enough for me. He was right, but we'd met all of fifteen minutes ago, so what was he basing that on? It was obviously just an attempt at buttering me up, same as calling me beautiful.

Annoyingly, I was starting to let my guard down with him, and it was so important not to do that. He was a player, no doubt about it. The fact that I'd found him in a total pick-up joint just a few hours after getting his dick sucked confirmed it.

Okay, yes, I'd been in the same sleazy bar, but that was different —I was there to work. The fact that I'd told this guy I was in acquisitions made me grin. Uh, no. I was a thief, plain and simple, and I'd been out looking for my next score.

It never ceased to amaze me how many men were perfectly willing to allow strangers into their home. Forget bypassing alarm systems or breaking and entering—all I had to do was find some douchebag with a hard-on, and I was in. We'd have a few drinks, and then I'd tell him I was going to use the bathroom. Instead, I'd pluck a few valuables and slip away before he had a clue what was happening.

I didn't even feel bad about it, because fuck rich people and all their excess. Hell, I'd make like the Grinch and rob them of every single thing they had if I could, right down to their last can of Who Hash.

This guy—Reno, of all things—was different, though. For one thing, he was fucking gorgeous, and that was a problem. I didn't think clearly around men I was attracted to, and he had that whole tall, dark, and Italian thing going on, which was my kryptonite.

I'd decided as soon as I spotted him that this was just going to be about sex, and not a score. And why not? It'd been a while since I'd gotten laid, even though I'd claimed it had been twenty-four hours.

Well, what was I supposed to do after he told me about that BJ, admit I hadn't gotten any in months? Hell no. I should have said I'd had a cock in my ass two hours ago, just to one-up him.

But even if he was a total player, deciding to fuck him instead of robbing him was a good call, and it let me relax a little. Not that he wasn't loaded. I knew what collector cars like this land yacht went for, and that suit was clearly custom-made, given the way it fit his big, muscular body.

He was hard to figure out though, because that black wool number was the most understated suit I could imagine, while the car was anything but subtle. Then again, a vintage ride like this was all about a certain image and lifestyle rather than the flash, and it was a lot more interesting than, let's say, dropping a hundred grand on a new Mercedes-Benz.

But then I didn't know what to think when we got to his place. What he called an apartment was actually a two-story townhouse. It was expensive, immaculate, and utterly generic. What it reminded me of was a hotel, from the beige-on-beige color scheme to the completely unremarkable artwork on the walls.

In fact, it was so strikingly bland that I had to ask. "What happened here? Did you hire an interior decorator, or maybe a design student, and tell them you hate color?"

Reno smirked at me as he took off his suit jacket and tossed it over the back of his beige sofa. "If you're asking whether I chose any of this boring shit, the answer is no. This place came furnished.

It's one of those by-the-week executive rentals, since I don't know how long I'll be staying in San Francisco."

"So, you're in town for work?"

"No."

"Then why are you here?"

He took off a pair of cufflinks and rolled back the sleeves of his impeccably tailored white shirt as he told me, "I needed to get out of Vegas for a while, and this was as good a place as any to pass the time."

"What'd you do, piss off a mob boss?"

I'd been kidding, but Reno shrugged his broad shoulders and muttered, "Something like that."

"Do you think the trouble might follow you here, since you're giving out fake names?" Not that this was any of my business, but I was nosy.

"Actually, no. I have relatives here, and I don't want to draw their attention."

"Now that I get," I told him. "Aside from my mom, all the rest of my relatives can fuck right off."

He went over to a bar cart in the corner of the living room and changed the subject with, "Can I make you a drink?"

"Sure. I'll have whatever you're having."

He unfastened the top button of his shirt and loosened his tie before pouring two shots of something from a decanter. Then he crossed the room and handed me one of the glasses. It was heavy cut crystal. I wondered idly if it had come with the furnished townhouse.

Reno lightly tapped our glasses together and said, "*Salut,*" before tossing back what proved to be a high-quality scotch. After I finished mine, he took the glass from me and put it with his on the coffee table.

When he moved a little closer, my heart started pounding. Why was I nervous? It wasn't like one-night stands were new to me.

This guy though, he was intimidating. In part, it was because he was fucking huge. It wasn't just that he was about six-two to my five-foot-nine, he was also built like a tank. If he wanted to, he could hurt me. Badly. Usually, when I went home with men I felt like a fox in a henhouse. Right now, I felt more like a bunny in a lion's den, and that didn't sit well with me.

I looked up into his eyes. They were light brown with flecks of green and gold, and they crinkled at the corners when he smiled at me.

He reached out, slowly and deliberately, as if he sensed my nervousness and was trying not to startle me. His hand looked big and clumsy, but his touch was gentle as he traced my jawline and murmured, "You're so beautiful, Jack. My god. You take my breath away."

I reached for him too and ended up placing a hand over his heart. It was beating as rapidly as mine. That was probably because of anticipation rather than nerves though, since this guy oozed confidence.

He raised my chin with a fingertip and brushed his lips to mine. It was sweet and tender, but I was already feeling vulnerable, and I wasn't going to let this guy strip away any more of my defenses. Instead, I pressed myself against him and deepened the kiss, and he instantly responded.

Everything happened really quickly after that. We made out wildly and pawed at each other as one article of clothing after another got tossed onto the floor. Just a couple of minutes later, we landed on the couch, and I began sucking his cock like my life depended on it.

After a while, he mumbled, "I need to be inside you," which was really fucking hot.

I sat up and pushed my hair out of my eyes. "Where do you keep your condoms?"

"There are some in the guest room."

We both got up, and he tucked his hard-on into his briefs and straightened his unbuttoned shirt, which was all that I was wearing, too. Then he took my hand and led me down the hall. Along the way, we passed a half-bath and a kitchen so pristine that it looked like it had never actually been used for anything. Opposite it at the back of the townhouse was a small bedroom that also looked like it had never been used, except for the large shopping bag on the tan and white bedspread.

I was surprised when he dumped the bag's contents onto the bed. Apparently he'd recently visited a sex shop, and I asked, "Did you impulse buy everything you saw on this little shopping excursion?"

In addition to a huge box of condoms and two types of lube, there were three dildoes, a butt plug, a pair of handcuffs lined with red fake fur, and a silk blindfold. He sighed and told me, "I'll admit I got a little carried away. I recently got out of a relationship and thought…I don't know. That maybe my sex life needed a reset?" He placed the condoms and lube on the nightstand and asked, "Any of this stuff grab you?"

I picked up the handcuffs and tugged them to check the strength of the chain. They were heavy and good quality, despite the fuzzy sasquatch fur lining, which just made them look silly. I removed the key and the tag, and then I tested them and said, "Oops, sorry. I shouldn't have taken off the price tag, because they're defective. The quick release button doesn't work." I tried the key and added, "They do still function as regular cuffs, though."

"I wouldn't have bothered to return them anyway." He glanced at me curiously and asked, "Would you let me put those on you?"

"I have something else in mind." To make my intentions clear, I flicked open one of the cuffs and smiled at him while I waited to see what he'd do.

He glanced at the restraints before looking me in the eye and asking, "Can I trust you, Jack?"

"Hell no, not even a little."

That was the truth, but he assumed I was kidding. He even chuckled, and then he asked, "How do you want me?"

I gestured at the bed. "Naked on your back, with your hands above your head."

Horny men should absolutely not be allowed to make decisions. Ever. Reno rushed to clear away the toys before doing exactly as I asked. After his shirt and briefs hit the floor, he stretched out on the bed and grasped the headboard's wooden slats.

Once I threaded the cuffs through the slats and fastened them around his wrists, I could finally relax. There was no way he could do anything unexpected now, and I was right where I wanted to be —totally in charge of the situation.

I turned on the small beside lamp and shut off the harsh overhead lighting, and I ran my gaze down his body while I undressed. He was perfection, from his muscles and hairy chest to his thick cock. It was rock hard and leaking precome onto his stomach, which made it perfectly clear how he felt about being tied down.

I climbed between his legs and ran my tongue up his shaft, which made him shudder with pleasure. Then I took my time sucking him, until he rasped, "I need to be in you, Jack."

He watched like it was the most fascinating thing he'd ever seen as I grabbed the lube and worked myself open. After that, I wiped my hands with some tissues and tried to pry open the box of condoms.

In my haste, I ended up ripping the box in half and flinging rubbers all over the bed, the nightstand, and Reno. I muttered, "Oops," as I quickly swept them onto the floor. Then I unrolled one over his cock and slicked it with lube.

I said, "Hold still," as I straddled his hips and took a breath. He planted his feet on the mattress and grasped the headboard's slats again, as if he was steadying himself.

I tried lowering myself onto his cock and met with all kinds of resistance. It felt like a personal triumph when the tip finally slipped inside me, but then it was slow going to take the rest of him, because he was so thick.

"It's like trying to fit a can of pop in my ass. Not that I've ever tried that," I muttered. After a beat, I added, "Okay, so there was that one time. But none of us should be held responsible for the things we do when we're drunk, super horny, and in our early twenties."

He chuckled at that, and I frowned at him and said, "Focus. If you lose your hard-on before I take all of you, I'm going to be pissed."

"Oh, believe me, there's no way that'll happen. Not with this incredible view."

Finally, the last couple of inches slipped inside me, and my ass made contact with his hips. I held still for a few moments to get used to the intense stretch and told him, "You need to send a gift basket to every guy that ever let you fuck him, Girth Brooks. I realize that's probably hundreds of men, but maybe you can get a bulk discount at 1-800-I'm-fucking-sorry. I'm going to look like the Holland Tunnel when we're done here."

He grinned and said, "You're a strange man, Jack O'Donnell."

The fake name made me wince. The first part was real, but I always made up a last name for the men I met in bars. Why feel guilty, though? I didn't date, so it wasn't like I was ever going to see this guy again.

Instead of dwelling on it, I concentrated on rocking Reno's world. I rode him hard and fast, then slowed down again—back and forth like that, so he wouldn't finish too quickly.

He was so sexy, especially chained up like that. A couple of times, he got so caught up that he forgot about the cuffs and tried to reach for me. When the restraints pulled him up short, he growled like a wild animal, his muscles flexing as he fought to break free. It made my cock throb, and I began jerking off as I bounced on his lap.

Eventually, he decided he was done letting me set the pace and started thrusting up into me. He happened to be at the perfect angle to graze my prostate, and my higher brain functions shut off as intense pleasure and sensation reverberated through me.

I started jerking off faster as I braced myself with a hand on his shoulder. A minute later, he threw his head back and yelled as he started to come. His thrusts were so forceful that all I could do was wrap my arm around him and hold on. He nailed my prostate even harder with me in that position, and I ended up shooting all over both of us.

The orgasm was so intense that it left me shaking. I reached behind me and held the condom in place as I climbed off of him. Then I unlocked the cuffs and dropped onto the mattress.

Reno kissed my shoulder and told me he'd be right back before heading to the adjoining half-bath. That gave me a chance to catch my breath and try to get myself together. When he returned, I took a turn in the bathroom, where I did a half-assed job of cleaning myself up.

Normally, I'd get dressed and make a hasty departure at this point. I was still feeling shaky though, so after I put on my briefs, I curled up next to Reno. He looked happy and relaxed, and he pulled a soft blanket over both of us as I told him, "I'll be out of your hair soon. I just need to rest for a minute."

"Why don't you spend the night? In the morning, I'll try to impress you with my epic Eggs Benedict."

The last thing I remembered was muttering, "So fancy."

Sometime later, I woke from a dead sleep feeling more than a little disoriented. When I sat up, a large figure beside me stirred. Then Reno turned on the small lamp on the nightstand and mumbled, "You okay, doll face?"

Fucking hell, had I actually fallen asleep in a stranger's bed? That wasn't something I did—ever. It made me feel way too vulnerable.

On top of that, I'd been having some sort of vivid dream that mostly eluded me now, and it just added to the state of confusion I found myself in. I told him I was fine, and then I quickly climbed out of bed and began gathering my clothes.

He glanced at his phone and told me, "It's two a.m. You should come back to bed."

"Can't." I went with the first lie that came to mind. "I have to be somewhere early." That sounded a lot better than the truth, which was that I'd never intended to fall asleep in the first place and was pretty freaked out.

I found my phone and the rest of my things in the living room. Reno appeared a moment later dressed in just a pair of briefs, and I shifted the bundle of clothes in my arms as I asked him, "What's your address, so I can tell the cab company where to pick me up?"

He answered my question and added, "But you don't need to bother with a taxi. I'll drive you home."

Oh, hell no. Like I wanted this rich guy to see the shithole I was currently living in? "There's no need. It'll be here soon."

Damn it, the message on my screen told me it would actually be about forty-five minutes, probably because the bars had just closed. I really didn't think I was capable of making small talk at this point, so to kill time—and because I felt gross and sweaty—I asked, "Would it be okay if I take a shower while I wait for the cab?"

"Of course. It's on the second floor, through the main bedroom."

"Thanks. I won't be long." Ideally, forty-four minutes, leaving just enough time for a quick goodbye.

The huge suite I found upstairs was really nice. It had high ceilings, a fireplace, and a set of glass doors that led to a balcony. Even though the room had the same bland color scheme as the rest of the place, it looked better in here. It was more white than beige, so it felt light and airy.

The wood furniture was all in honey maple, so the dark mahogany chest on the dresser stood out. Reno must have brought it with him from Vegas, since it didn't match his current digs at all.

I was far too nosy to walk by that chest without taking a peek inside, and what I found when I raised the lid made my breath catch. The box was lined with black velvet, and its upper tier was divided into eight compartments, four of which held watches.

They were all striking, but one stood head and shoulders above the rest. I shifted my clothes bundle and picked up the vintage platinum Rolex. The metal was cool to the touch, and the watch was heavy in my hand. I went through my mental checklist and examined it to see if it was a fake, but this was clearly the real deal.

I whispered, "Holy shit," as I ran my thumb along the edge of the elegant watch face. This wasn't just any Rolex. It was a sought-after collector piece, and it was easily worth fifty grand—maybe more with the right buyer.

I'd had no intention of stealing from Adriano, but this watch was a once in a lifetime score. It would make a huge difference, not just for me, but for my mom. I sent money home every month, since she was barely making ends meet. With this, she'd be able to put a down-payment on a house, and I could move into a nice apartment.

It wasn't an easy decision though, not by a long shot. I liked this guy. Plus, robbing someone I'd just had sex with really wasn't how I operated.

While I was trying to make up my mind, I pulled open the drawer in the bottom half of the mahogany chest. It was divided into smaller compartments, which held a few pairs of expensive cufflinks.

It would take no effort whatsoever to fill my pockets with these and the watches, but I didn't want to clean Adriano out. In fact, I didn't want to take from him at all, but how could I pass up that Rolex, knowing how much it could help both me and my mother?

In the end, I rationalized my way around my guilt by deciding to only take one thing, instead of being greedy and taking all of it. As soon as I made up my mind, I began moving very quickly. The Rolex was so big on me that I ended up fastening it just below my elbow, instead of around my wrist. Then I got dressed as fast as I could.

The safest way out—in terms of not getting caught—was probably climbing off the balcony, so I crossed the room and opened the double doors. It occurred to me that I really should have ducked into the bathroom and turned on the shower, because the sound of running water might have bought me some time.

The hairs on the back of my neck stood on end when a deep voice behind me asked, "What are you doing, Jack?"

My heart rate was already quick. Now it started beating in double time as I turned to face Adriano. I noticed randomly that he was wearing nothing but a pair of gym shorts, and he was watching me curiously. Then I did something stupid—I glanced at the chest, which I'd left open on the dresser.

He followed my gaze, and then he rushed to the box and looked closer. When he turned back to me, there was barely contained fury in his eyes. He said, in a dangerously low voice, "No. Not the Rolex."

I swallowed hard as my heart pounded. I'd never been caught in the act before, and I wondered if there was a chance I could talk my way out of this. I couldn't think of a single thing to say, though.

"If you need money, I'll help you. But I can't let you take that watch." The deceptively calm way he said that was unnerving, and so was the way he held my gaze with all that anger in his eyes. I took a step backwards, over the threshold and onto the balcony, and he growled, "No! Don't you fucking do it."

I took two more steps backwards, bumped into the metal railing at the edge of the narrow balcony, and grasped it with both hands. Then I quickly glanced down, judging the distance to the ground.

In response, he yanked open the top drawer of the dresser, pulled out a giant fucking gun, and pointed it at me as he yelled, "Stay there!"

And just like that, the situation went from scary to terrifying.

I didn't even think about what I was doing. With my heartbeat thundering in my ears, I vaulted over the railing and landed in some bushes in the compact front yard. I turned my ankle, but that didn't matter right now. Nothing did but getting away from that gun, so I took off at a sprint.

From somewhere behind me, I heard a yell of frustration but no gunshot. That was followed by a loud thud and the unmistakable sound of branches cracking. Fucking hell, he'd followed me off the balcony!

Even though I was confident in my ability to outrun someone as big and bulky as Reno, I didn't put it past him to shoot me. The look in his eyes right before he reached for the gun suggested he was capable of it.

In my panic, I'd started running right down the middle of the street, like I wanted to get shot or something. Delores Park was to my left, but it was mostly just an open, grassy area with no place to hide, so I kept going until I reached the next neighborhood.

Then I had an idea and quickly climbed over a fence, which put me in someone's back yard. If I did that a few more times, I'd come out at the other end of the block, and then I'd probably lose him. Sure, I could also just hide in the yard until I was sure he'd passed, but I was exhausted and afraid, and I really just wanted to go home.

I crossed the yard and climbed over another fence, then repeated the process. It was all going according to plan, until I cleared another fence, landed on something uneven, and twisted the ankle I'd messed up when I jumped off the balcony. I yelped with pain as I fell face-first into a lavender bush. It smelled like a funeral.

My yell had alerted whoever lived here, and a moment later a bunch of lights came on in the house and yard. I tried to scramble to my feet, but pain shot up my leg, so I sat back down again. There was no way I was going anywhere on that ankle.

Instead, I brushed some lavender flowers out of my hair and took a look at my surroundings. The pretty yard belonged to a hot pink Victorian. If it was possible for houses to look friendly, that one did. I just hoped the homeowners weren't armed, because one gun a night was more than enough.

A moment later, a bunch of people rushed out the back door. A petite brunette in a red silk camisole and shorts was in the lead. She was armed with a baseball bat, and it looked like she had every intention of using it on the intruder in her flower bed.

"I'm so sorry," I blurted, as I held up my hands to show them I was unarmed. "I didn't mean to trespass. I was on a date and it all went horribly wrong. I had to get away from him, so I ended up climbing over your fence." There was actually a lot of truth to that. I just left out the fact that I was the reason it went wrong.

The woman with the bat relaxed her posture slightly, but she still looked wary. Meanwhile, the curvy blonde at her side rested a hand on her companion's arm and asked me, "Are you okay?"

"I think I sprained my ankle when I landed in your yard."

A tall, muscular Black guy and a cute twink with dark hair had followed the women outside, and the tall guy stepped forward and said, "Here, let me help you up. Don't put any weight on your ankle."

His confidence and the way he took charge of the situation made me ask, "Are you a doctor?"

"No, I'm a retired firefighter. My name's Dylan, and this is my boyfriend Lark." He indicated the twink with a nod as he hauled me to my feet. "Yolanda's a nurse, so maybe she can take a look at that ankle. She's the one with the bat. And that's JoJo, her wife."

Hallelujah, I'd managed to land in an LGBT household. "I'm Jack," I said, as I balanced on one foot and leaned on Dylan. "Again, I'm so sorry about this. I can only imagine how it must look."

"I'm just glad you escaped your date from hell," JoJo said, as Dylan began to guide me toward the back door. "There are a lot of jerks out there." Truer words were never spoken. In fact, they were currently helping one of them.

They ended up bringing me into their kitchen. It was pink, white, and purple, and it looked like its last remodel had been in about 1975. I absolutely loved it.

While Lark made me some tea, I took a seat, pried off my loafer, and put my foot up on a chair so Yolanda could examine it. "It's starting to swell up pretty good, but there's no way of knowing if anything's broken without an x-ray," she said. "Would you like a ride to the ER?"

"No thanks. I don't have insurance. Even if I did, I hate hospitals and would only go if it was a matter of life and death. I think I'll just give this a day or two and see if it starts to improve."

"It's your call," Yolanda muttered, as she studied me carefully. She was the smartest one of the bunch, because she was the only person who seemed suspicious of me.

Not that she had a reason to worry. These were decent, working class people, like my mom. I'd never steal from them, not in a million years. As a matter of principle, I only stole from rich people. I was like Robin Hood in that respect, except that I kept the loot for myself. I was poor, so it still counted.

Yolanda tried a different approach for getting rid of me. "After I bandage your ankle, I'll find you some crutches. We have a pair in the garage. Then I can give you a ride home."

"It's okay, I can just call a cab. I don't really know what I'm going to do when I get home though, because I live in a third-floor walk-up." The bit about the apartment was true. I just left out the fact that I didn't want to go outside because a huge guy with a gun was hunting me.

Lark put a mug of herbal tea on the table beside me, along with a bear-shaped squeeze bottle of honey. Then he turned to Yolanda and said, "Jack should just spend the night here, because he's injured and there's no way he'll make it up three flights of stairs. Plus, it's really late."

JoJo nodded. "I agree. He's had a rough night, and I don't think he should go anywhere."

Yolanda caved under the peer pressure and asked me, "Would you like to spend the night on our couch?"

"I'd love that," I said. "Thank you."

Sometime later, I found myself tucked in on a comfortable, plum-colored couch in their cozy living room. I was dressed in a pair of Lark's flannel pajamas, which had cartoon unicorns on them, and my bandaged foot was sandwiched between a towel-wrapped bag of ice and a stack of pillows. Even though my ankle was throbbing, the fistful of ibuprofen I'd taken was dulling the pain, and the herbal tea was making me feel warm and relaxed.

Everyone had gone to bed, but I was pretty sure Yolanda was sleeping with one eye open and totally prepared to clock me with her bat if need be. All the housemates were great, but I was a fan of hers because she was such a little bad-ass.

I shifted a bit to settle in. Then I pulled up the sleeve of my absurd, soft, and very comfortable pajamas and took a look at the watch around my forearm. I instantly felt a pang of guilt, but I shoved that aside and tried to concentrate on the watch itself. It was classy and elegant, and the kind of thing I could never hope to own in this lifetime.

I slid it off and examined it closely. There were three initials engraved into the back in a diamond shape: a large D surrounded by a smaller P and A. It was common to put the initial for the last name in the center, so two of those letters fit. I didn't know what the P stood for, though.

I turned it over and ran a fingertip along the edge of its face. Okay, so maybe I'd hang onto it for a week or two. There was no reason I couldn't enjoy it a little before I sold it. As gorgeous and expensive as the Rolex was though, I still couldn't quite believe Reno had pulled a gun on me over it.

After returning the watch to my arm, I reached for my jacket. One of the sleeves had gotten torn, probably from the bushes in front of the townhouse. That was a shame, since it was my best suit.

I dug through the pockets and located Reno's business card. I found myself with a lot of questions about him, but it didn't tell me anything. The only two words on the card were Adriano Dombruso, above a phone number with a Las Vegas area code.

Who did that? Who made super expensive cards for themselves with almost no information on them? Players, maybe, to impress people in bars. That fit with what little I knew about him. Aside from that though, who else?

Well, a gangster might have a card like that. What else would they do, have stationery printed up announcing themselves as a crime boss? Hell no.

Actually, that fit with what I knew about him, too. It could explain not only the huge handgun, but how perfectly at ease he'd seemed when he was wielding it. Then there was his noncommittal reaction when I asked if he left Vegas because he'd pissed off the mob.

Maybe it would also explain why he'd leave a box of valuables sitting out like that, because who'd be stupid enough to…

Fucking hell, had I just robbed a mafioso?

If so, I was seriously screwed. They weren't exactly the type to forgive and forget, and they had a lot of resources at their disposal when it came to tracking people down.

Okay, so maybe I was being paranoid. I was obviously going to avoid the bar where we'd met, so how could he possibly find me? He didn't even know my real name, and I'd only been here for a few weeks, so it wasn't like anyone knew me and could point him in my direction.

Then again, it also wouldn't be the worst idea to get the hell out of Dodge. It wasn't like I had any ties to this place, so once my ankle healed maybe I'd pack my suitcase and pick a new destination—another big city to get lost in, the latest in a very long line. I'd spent my entire adult life totally adrift, moving every three or four months to stay ahead of the law and the men I'd robbed. San Francisco wouldn't be any different.

Even so, I couldn't shake the feeling that Adriano Dombruso and I were destined to cross paths again someday.

3

Adriano

That little asshole! I couldn't believe he'd stolen from me. And of all the things to take, of course he'd chosen my most prized possession. Well, why not? It was the most expensive thing in that chest by far, though I really didn't get why he'd left the rest of my watches and cufflinks behind. It made no sense.

Also, he'd chained me up—and I'd fucking let him!—just a few hours earlier. Why hadn't he robbed me while I was incapacitated? He could have slapped some duct tape over my mouth and taken his time completely wiping me out. But instead, he'd set me free, slept by my side for a while, and *then* he robbed me.

Okay, so maybe it had been a spontaneous thing. Maybe curiosity got the better of him on the way to the shower, so he'd looked in the chest, seen the watch, and made a snap decision to take it.

I was almost as mad at myself as I was at Jack, because leaving the mahogany box sitting out like that was totally on me. Usually, it was kept in a safe. But I'd brought it out earlier this evening, so I could select a watch and a pair of cufflinks. It was my first night at a singles bar in almost five years, and I'd wanted to look good.

Then my fucking ex-boyfriend called, and I'd gotten so wrapped up in fighting with him that I'd forgotten all about locking up the box again. In fact, I hadn't given it a second thought—not until I saw it sitting there wide open, with an empty slot where the Rolex should have been. How could I be that careless?

With a sigh, I turned and started trudging uphill, back toward my rental. I'd been out here for what felt like hours, combing the neighborhood, but Jack had disappeared. He'd only had a few seconds head start too, which was the time it took for me to chuck the unloaded gun in the drawer, follow him off the balcony, and untangle myself from the hedge.

He was really fast though, and I just wasn't. The only reason I even knew which direction he'd gone was because I'd caught a glimpse of him in the distance. He'd been running down the middle of the street, but as soon as he reached the neighborhood beyond the park, he'd ducked into the shadows and that was that.

It was time to pack it in. If some cops should happen to roll up on me, I'd definitely be questioned. It was beyond late, and I was sweaty, barefoot, and in nothing but a pair of shorts, which I'd ripped on the bushes that had failed to cushion my fall. Looking like this was bound to attract attention.

Not that I was giving up. I'd track down that little thief if it was the last thing I did, but not like this.

Once I got back home, I tried the front door. It was locked, of course. With a dramatic sigh, I plucked the plastic trash can from the side of my neighbor's house and tried to use it as a step to help me climb up onto the balcony. On my first attempt, it rolled out from under me, and I ended up landing back in those fucking bushes. During attempt number two, the plastic lid folded inward, and I dropped into the bin like a huge bag of trash. The fact that there was something squishy under my bare feet made me shudder.

This was Jack's fault. I was already furious with him, and this just added fuel to the flames.

Finally, I managed to brace the can against the building and climb up onto its rim. From there, it was just a matter of swinging my leg up high enough to get a foothold on the edge of the balcony, then heaving myself up with a death grip on the metal railing.

The whole time I was doing this shit, I kept waiting for the sound of police sirens. If any of my neighbors saw this, they'd definitely report it as an attempted break-in by the world's most inept cat burglar.

Somehow though, I managed to flop onto the balcony without a SWAT team arriving on the scene. Then I crawled through the open doors and collapsed in a heap, breathing heavily and sweating onto the beige carpet. Even though I worked out religiously, I obviously needed to add more cardio to my routine. I wasn't nearly as fit as I liked to think I was.

Eventually, I got up, closed and locked the double doors, and pulled the curtains. When I crossed the room, I expected to find the mahogany box totally emptied out. After all, I'd left the doors open and this place unguarded for the last couple of hours, and there was plenty left to steal. Everything else was still there, though. Surprisingly, Jack hadn't doubled back and finished the job.

I closed the chest and stuck it in the closet. There was no hurry to lock it back in the safe, since the most important thing I owned had already been stolen. The rest was just stuff.

Next, I went into the bathroom, stripped down, and stuffed my torn shorts into the trash can before stepping into a hot shower. I took a long time scrubbing myself down, since I was a grimy mess. Afterwards, I toweled off and spent some time dressing my cuts and scrapes with antibiotic cream and bandages.

There was one more thing I needed to do before bed. I pulled on a pair of black cotton pajama pants, went downstairs to the home office, and took a seat at the desk, which I'd never actually used before. Then I began to sketch Jack on a sheet of copy paper, while the memory of him was still so fresh in my mind. I'd always been good at drawing for some reason. My mom called it a gift, but so far it had proven to be useless. Maybe now it'd finally pay off.

It took four attempts, but after I finished a sketch that captured his likeness, I wrote down everything I knew about him. It wasn't much. Under the (probably fake) name he'd given me, I noted his approximate height and weight, age, hair and eye color, and where we'd met. Beneath that I wrote in big letters: $2000 reward for any information on the whereabouts of this man. It was tempting to offer a huge amount to really motivate people, but I figured I could end up with multiple tips and might have to pay several people, so it was best to keep the amount manageable.

I added my phone number and looked it over, and decided that was about the best I could do. Then I ran off a bunch of copies on the combination printer/copier/fax machine in the corner and stacked the papers neatly on the desk. Tomorrow, I'd visit the bar where we'd met, and every other place like it in the city, and I'd leave those with bartenders, bouncers, valets—anyone who could potentially have some information.

Jack had seemed perfectly at home in that singles bar, so this was probably a good way to find him. I just hoped it happened quickly, before he sold the watch for pennies on the dollar and it was lost forever.

Now that my little art project was done, I left the office and went in search of my phone. It was right where I'd left it—on the night-stand in the guest bedroom. I picked it up and scowled as I looked around. The bed was rumpled, there were condoms all over the floor, and the shopping bag had tipped over and spilled sex toys onto the rug. What a fucking mess.

I took one of the pillows and held it to my nose. The faint smell of sex and Jack and his cologne still lingered. Damn it, I'd really liked this guy, before he proved to be a snake. I'd even planned to ask him out, take him somewhere nice for dinner, maybe see if this could turn into something. But he just had to go and betray my trust.

Before leaving the room, I untangled the handcuffs from the headboard and put them in my pocket. If and when I found that little shit, they might come in handy. Then I shut off the lights and closed the door behind me. I'd have to remember to clean up in there before the maid service was in on Tuesday, but there was no way I wanted to deal with that tonight.

I went back upstairs and climbed into bed, and then I tried searching the name Jack had given me on my phone. There were about a million Jack O'Donnells on social media. I wasn't even sure of the right way to spell it. Besides, it was probably an alias. Why wouldn't it be? He'd said as much, something along the lines of lying to the men he met in bars, because that was what you were supposed to do.

Eventually, I gave up and put the phone down. My mind was still racing, though. By the time I finally drifted off, the light of dawn was filtering in around the curtains.

Just a few hours later, I was jarred awake by my ringing phone. I grabbed it from the nightstand, saw my brother's name on the screen, and answered with, "You okay, Romy?"

"I'm fine. It's ten a.m., time for breakfast."

I sat up and pushed my hair off my face. "Shit, sorry. I overslept. Can I call you back in five minutes?"

"Of course. Take your time."

My brother and I had a long-standing tradition of getting together every Sunday morning and catching up on our week over a big breakfast. We'd promised to keep it going during my temporary exile in San Francisco, so I was usually sitting in a diner by ten and waiting on his call. Not today, though.

After a quick visit to the bathroom, I went downstairs and got the coffee maker going. Then I sat on the kitchen counter with my tablet and placed a video call.

Romy was all smiles when he popped up on my screen. He was seated in his favorite diner, which was just a few blocks from where we'd grown up. I said, "You changed your hair again."

"I did. Do you like it?"

He was a handsome kid, no doubt about it. We looked nothing alike since we had different dads, apart from our hazel eyes. That was the only feature I'd inherited from our mom, while he looked a lot like her with his light brown hair, slim build, and fair complexion.

He'd just gotten a haircut, so it was very short on the sides and longer at the top. "It looks great," I told him. "Very hip. Do the kids still say that? Or has hip gone the way of groovy, keen, and bitchin'?"

Romy laughed at that and shook his head. "Where are you getting those expressions? You're only ten years older than me, not some old fossil." I grimaced at that word, and he asked, "What's wrong?"

"A guy called me that last night. It was surprising to hear it again."

He asked, a little too hopefully, "Were you on a date?"

"No. I picked him up in a bar."

"How did it go?"

"Great at first, then absolutely terrible."

"What do you mean?"

I sighed and condensed it down to, "I took him home with me, and after we had sex he stole my dad's Rolex, jumped off the balcony like Spider-Man, and disappeared into the night."

My brother's eyes went wide. "Oh no. That watch means everything to you, Reno."

"I know, but don't worry. I have a plan for getting it back. I'm going to spend the day emailing every jewelry broker, pawn shop, auction house, and so on in the Bay Area with a description of the watch. Then I'm going to visit every bar in San Francisco with what basically amounts to a stack of old-timey wanted posters, and I'm going to find this guy."

Romy asked, "Can I help? Maybe make a few calls?"

"Thanks, but I've got it. I have pure, unadulterated rage to fuel me."

"Are you going to file a police report?"

"No, I'm handling it myself."

He frowned and told me, "I'll never understand your distrust of law enforcement. I get that you've been known to break the rules from time to time, but you're the victim here. They could help you find this guy and recover your watch."

Saying I broke the rules occasionally was the nicest possible way to describe me. In reality, I was a criminal who made my living in illegal gambling. Or I used to, until a thug named Mario Greco decided to move in on my territory. When I pushed back, he came after me so hard that I ended up bailing out to San Francisco, just until I could figure out what to do about Greco and his crew of sociopaths.

"You have a point," I said, "and I'll think about filing a police report."

Romy was still frowning. "You won't do it, but whatever. It's your choice. And I'm really sorry this happened to you." He paused before asking, "You've hooked up with other guys since you and Ford broke up, right? It's been six months. Please tell me that wasn't your first time back out there."

"Sadly, that was the first guy I'd slept with since my four-year relationship crashed and burned. I think the universe might be trying to tell me something. I know it's not demented enough to try to get Ford and me back together, so I guess the message I'm meant to take from this is to give up and die alone."

My brother sat up straighter and shook his head. "No! Absolutely not. You've just had a setback, but that's not enough of a reason to give up on love."

"That's awfully optimistic, since you told me you yourself had given up on dating."

"We're not talking about me," he said. "We're talking about you, and it's a totally different situation."

"Uh huh."

He ignored that and told me, "Even though the guy from last night ended up being a terrible person, I'm still proud of you for putting yourself out there and giving it a shot."

"He wasn't a terrible person. At least I don't think he was. I definitely have some questions for him, though. Mostly, I need to know if he came home and slept with me while fully intending to rip me off afterwards. Or was it that he saw the watch and made an impulsive decision? I can maybe understand the second one. But if robbing me was premeditated, then god help this guy once I find him."

"You wouldn't really hurt him, would you?"

I'd almost forgotten who I was talking to, until I looked at the screen and saw my kid brother's worried expression. He tried so hard to believe I was a good person, despite all evidence to the contrary.

Of course, I'd normally beat the hell out of anyone who screwed me over the way Jack had, just as a matter of principle. But I meant it when I said, "I don't know what I'll do once I find him. It depends on his answers to my questions."

"Maybe it really was an impulsive decision. Or maybe he desperately needed some money," Romy said. "I'm not condoning theft, obviously, but there may be extenuating circumstances that you should consider."

A waitress arrived with my brother's breakfast just then, and I poured myself a cup of coffee and kept chatting with him while he ate. At the end of the meal, we promised to do it again the following weekend. Then I disconnected the video call and went to get dressed.

I had a thief to find.

4

Jack

I liked to think of myself as a pretty self-sufficient guy, someone who really didn't need a lot of people in my life. There was my mom, and my best friend Wyatt, who I'd known since high school, and that had always been enough for me.

But after spending nearly a week in the pink Victorian with this amazing group of people, I started to think that maybe my life was a little lonely. It would probably wear off once I was back in my world, but for now it was weighing on me.

Not that the self-proclaimed Pink Victorian Crew excluded me or anything. Just the opposite. Since I'd taken up temporary residence on their couch, they'd let me be a part of their game and movie nights, cocktail hours, late-night conversations, and family dinners—because that was what they were, a family.

A couple of them were actually related, but mostly they were a family by choice. In all, seven people lived in the Victorian. Another couple and their young son were part of the family, too. They lived in the house directly behind this one, shared the big back yard, and joined the Crew for dinner several nights a week. It was sweet, the way they all cared about and supported one another.

At the same time though, it made me feel like maybe my life was a little empty, especially since the two people I cared about most were back home in Kansas.

I'd told Hal, the newest member of this household, that it was going to feel strange going back to my empty apartment after being around so many people. "I know what you mean," he said. "I've only been here a couple of months, but I can't imagine ever going back to living alone after this. You're going to stay in touch though, right? We're friends now, and the door's always open."

I really liked Hal, even though he was obscenely young at twenty-three and far too pretty, with his perfect dark hair and flawless skin. I'd assured him I planned to stay in touch, but it didn't seem all that likely. I had little in common with Hal, or with any of them, really. They were all normal people leading normal lives. Meanwhile, I'd lived on the fringes of society for so long that I barely knew how to behave in polite company.

I had some truly atrocious habits, like the fact that I automatically cased every room I entered. Even though I had absolutely no intention of robbing these people, I had a running inventory in the back of my mind of every valuable thing they owned—which wasn't much.

Aside from a minor antique here and a so-so collectible there, the only things of real value could be found in JoJo's little studio at the back of the house. She was a jewelry designer and kept a small selection of precious and semi-precious gems and metals on her workbench. In all, it was probably worth fifteen-hundred dollars. I hated myself for mentally totaling it up while I'd sat in her studio and chatted with her one sunny afternoon.

It made me feel like a wolf in sheep's clothing, and like I wasn't worthy of their friendship. Especially not JoJo's, even though I adored her. She was lovely and stylish and smart, and she'd treated me with so much kindness from the moment we'd met.

Case in point, here she came with two cups of tea and a plate of cookies. It was around four p.m. on Friday, and she was taking her usual mid-afternoon break. Everybody else was either at work or out living their lives, so she was left with me for company.

I set aside the ebook I'd been reading on my phone and shifted around so my wrapped foot was on the coffee table instead of on a stack of pillows. After I thanked JoJo for the refreshments, I told her, "I've decided to head home this afternoon. You and your family have been wonderful, but I can't keep taking advantage of your hospitality."

It had felt good to be here and to pretend I was part of a family. But my ankle had ended up being more of a twist than a sprain and was feeling a lot better, so I didn't really have an excuse to keep hanging around.

"Are you sure? You're still limping, and I don't know about attempting the three flights of stairs in your apartment building."

"I can take it slowly," I said, "and once I get to my apartment I'll plan on staying put for a while."

"It's up to you, but just know you're welcome to stay here as long as you'd like."

"I appreciate that." After a pause, I met her gaze and added, "I want to say something, just because I really like you, JoJo. Please don't take this as an insult, but I think you're too trusting. You allowed me into your home even though I was a complete stranger, but not everyone is kind and well-intentioned, the way you are."

She grinned and asked, "Do you think I don't know that? I'm trans, Jack. Can you even begin to imagine the cruelty I've endured over the last two decades, ever since I started to transition in my late teens?"

"I hadn't thought about that."

"Don't look so sad," she said. "I didn't tell you that because I wanted pity. I was just trying to make the point that I'm not naïve, and I don't automatically see the best in everyone. If anything, I'm actually pretty jaded. I also think I'm an excellent judge of character." I must have looked skeptical, because she asked, "Do you disagree?"

"I do, because you trusted me, and you really shouldn't have." Hell, I was leaving soon anyway. Might as well put my cards on the table, in case it kept her from trusting the wrong person in the future. "I'm not a good man, JoJo. Not by a long shot. I lie and steal and screw people over, and I don't even feel bad about it…usually."

I broke eye contact, and she repeated, "Usually?"

"I've been off my game recently. Right before I met you, I took something from a man I actually kind of liked, and I regret it. In fact, I wish I could go back in time and change things, but that's obviously not an option." I glanced at her and added, "Don't worry though, I've never had any intention of stealing from you or your family."

JoJo seemed remarkably unphased by my confession. "That doesn't make you a bad person, Jack. It just means you've made some bad decisions in the past. And even if you can't go back and change things, maybe there's still a way to make things right. Can you go see that man and give back whatever you took from him?"

"I thought about that, but there's a good chance he'd shoot me on sight."

"For real?"

I nodded, and after a moment I said, "You know what I could do, though? I could mail his watch back to him with an apology, and then go and see him once he's had a chance to calm down a bit. I don't know why he'd forgive me, but it's worth a try, right?"

"Definitely. And if it's just a watch, maybe it's not even that big a deal to him."

"No, it's a big deal." I pushed back the sleeve of the oversized unicorn sweatshirt Lark had loaned me, unfastened the Rolex from my forearm, and handed it to her across the coffee table.

"Oh wow," she murmured, as she examined it closely. "This is platinum."

"It is. It's also a sought-after vintage design, and worth as much as a car." She handed it back to me, and I stared at it as I said, "When I spotted this watch, I knew it was a game changer. The goal was to sell it and use the money to improve things for both myself and my mother."

I looked up at JoJo and quickly added, "Not that I'm trying to justify stealing it. I'm also not trying to make myself sound like a good person with noble motives. I'm a two-bit thief, and there's no point in sugar-coating it. But I regret taking this, and I want to give it back."

"You can. I think the idea of mailing it back to its owner with an apology is a good one."

I returned the watch to my arm and pulled the sleeve over it as I said, "As long as I'm finally being honest with you, I should mention I was running from the watch's owner when I climbed over your fence. He pulled a gun on me when he caught me robbing him, and then he chased me. I thought cutting through all the yards on this block would help me get away from him."

"Thank you for telling me the truth."

I picked up my phone from the coffee table and said, "Anyway, I'm going to call a cab and get out of here. I'm really sorry if I made you uncomfortable."

"Spend one more night," she said. "The whole family's getting together this evening for that taco feast I told you about, and I know you were looking forward to it."

"You don't have to keep being nice to me," I muttered. "You know what I am now, and this obviously changes everything."

"What you are is my friend, Jack." When I met her gaze, I saw nothing but compassion in her eyes. "Nothing's changed, and even when you're no longer sleeping on my couch, I fully expect our friendship to continue."

I was feeling uncharacteristically emotional, and I ducked my head as I mumbled, "I don't deserve you."

"Come on. Like I'm a saint? We've all done things we're not proud of, and it's impossible to rewrite the past. The best any of us can do is learn from our mistakes moving forward."

"But in my case, I feel like it goes deeper than that—like all those mistakes merged over time, and they're just who I am now."

"That's only true if you let it be," she said. Then she picked up the plate of cookies and held it out to me. "Now would you please have some of these before I eat all of them? I can't resist homemade chocolate chip."

I got the hint—she was ready for us to move past this. As I helped myself to a cookie, I smiled at her and said, "Thanks, JoJo." That thank you was for a lot more than just some baked goods.

As a compromise, I decided to head home after dinner, instead of occupying their couch another night. First though, I stuffed myself full of fried fish tacos and chips with homemade guacamole, and then I spent the evening hanging out with JoJo and the rest of the family.

This included Logan and Lucky, the couple who lived in the house directly behind the pink Victorian, along with Owen, their toddler. Kids usually got on my last nerve, but Owen was adorable. He was also a bad judge of character like the rest of them, because he kept bringing me toys and climbing on me and acting like I was his new best friend.

Meanwhile, the conversation turned to Halloween, which was in three weeks, and everyone started brainstorming costume ideas. Lark was extremely excited about getting to dress up, and each idea he came up with was more elaborate than the next. His brother Logan kept trying to talk him down, but then he said, "Sure. If you want to dress like a merman in a giant aquarium, I'll help you build it. You're not going to be able to dance in a tail, though." That was what finally made Lark reconsider that idea.

I was surprised when someone asked, "What about you, Jack? What will you dress as?"

I looked up from my spot on the living room floor, where I was helping Owen put together a wooden puzzle, and said, "I don't know. I haven't dressed up for Halloween since I was ten or so." All the attention was on me, so I deflected it by asking, "The real question is, what's this little cutie dressing as?" I nodded toward the toddler, who flashed me a big smile.

Logan shrugged. "Who knows? Lucky's bought him five costumes so far. We'll theme ours around Owen's, but I don't know how we're going to narrow it down, especially if Lucky keeps shopping."

"He can always play dress-up with the extras, and you know I can't help myself, not when each costume makes him so happy,"

Lucky said, and Logan snuggled closer and pecked his cheek. That immediately evolved into a passionate kiss.

I was usually fine with being perpetually single, but those two were so in love that watching them together was almost painful. It didn't help that Lucky was tall, muscular, and dark-haired, which brought Reno to mind.

How far was his townhouse from here, maybe six blocks? I hadn't been running very long when I decided to hop that fence. I wondered what he was doing. It was Friday night, so was he out at the bars, finding someone to bring home with him?

And why did I care?

A few hours later, the dinner party started to break up, so I called a cab, changed back into my clothes, and draped my torn suit jacket over my arm. After I said goodbye to everyone else, JoJo walked me out.

"Text me soon," she said, "and you should plan to join us for Halloween. After we take Owen trick-or-treating, we're going to head to the Castro. The whole neighborhood turns into one huge party."

I murmured, "Sounds good," and shifted the crutches, which I was borrowing until my ankle fully healed.

My new friend pushed a platinum blonde curl out of her eyes as she asked, "Are you going to be okay, Jack?"

"Definitely." The cab pulled up just then, so I gave her a hug and said, "Talk to you soon," before making my way down the stairs and into the street.

Once I was situated in the back of the cab, I told the driver, "I'd like to make a slight detour on the way home." Then I directed him to Reno's townhouse.

As we pulled away from the curb, I turned to take one last look at the pink Victorian. JoJo was still standing on the porch, watching me go. She looked like she was worried about me.

Not sixty seconds later, the cab pulled up across the street from

Reno's townhouse. I'd told myself I was only doing this to verify the address for when I sent back the watch, but I knew I'd had it right.

And there he was, talking on the phone and pacing in his living room. He seemed angry about something, judging by his emphatic hand gestures. It also looked like he was yelling. Even if I'd wanted to walk up to the door right now and return his watch in person, this clearly wasn't the time.

His pacing brought him to the bay window at the front of the townhouse, and he glanced outside. Then he looked again when he spotted the taxi idling in the street. I quickly leaned back—not that Reno could see me through the cab's tinted windows—and told the driver, "Let's get out of here."

The guy muttered, "Not a problem," as we started rolling down the street. "In fact, if you got any more boyfriends you want to stalk, just say the word. The meter's running, and I got nothin' but time." I just sighed.

We drove across town, and when the cab driver pulled up in front of my rundown building, he muttered, "Jesus," and locked the doors.

"This is a really fucking expensive city, so it's the best I can do right now," I said, as I handed him a few bills and unlocked my door so I could get out.

"Yeah, no shit. That's why I live in the East Bay and commute in, but whatever. You do you." I fought an eye roll as I untangled myself and the crutches from the back seat.

When I reached the lobby, I took a look at the steep staircase and frowned. This was going to suck, no doubt about it. I just hadn't fully realized how true that was until I started to climb.

It hadn't been bad at all when I'd gone down the stairs in front of the Victorian, but going up was another thing entirely. My bad ankle was still too sore to take my full weight, so I basically did a push-up with the crutches on every step and then awkwardly hopped up with one foot.

By the time I reached the first landing, I was sweaty and exhausted. I tied my ripped suit jacket around my waist, then leaned against the wall and caught my breath while I unbuttoned my cuffs and turned them back. Okay, so this had been a terrible idea. I couldn't stay on JoJo's couch forever, but maybe a couple more days would have been the way to go.

After a minute or two, I made myself press on. It felt like this was taking hours. My arms and my good leg were weak and shaky by now, and all I could think about was making it to my shitty little studio apartment, falling into bed, and staying there for the next week.

I was five steps shy of the third floor when I positioned a crutch too close to the edge of a step. When it slid off, it sent me crashing painfully onto the stairs. Even worse, the fall knocked Reno's watch off my arm. It slid over my hand and tumbled down to the second floor landing, along with one of the crutches.

I winced as I shifted around to sit on the steps, and then I began scooting my way down to the watch. A moment later, a kid of maybe eleven or twelve with buzzed blond hair came jogging up the steps, and I asked, "Can you give me a hand?"

The boy paused on the second floor handing and took a look at me. Then he scooped up the watch and exclaimed, "A Rolex, cool!"

"That's mine."

An evil grin spread across his freckled face. "Then come and get it."

"Come on, I'm obviously injured here. Just give it back."

"Yeah, right! Finders keepers!"

"That's not a thing!" I started to do a combination crab walk and butt scoot toward him, and he grabbed the other crutch and took off down the stairs. I yelled, "Come back here, you little shit!"

His maniacal laugh rang through the lobby. A moment later, I heard the front door slam, and I yelled, "This is why I hate children! You're a bunch of fucking sociopaths!"

Fucking hell, that kid was karma personified.

I slumped in a defeated heap on the second floor landing and tried to catch my breath. I'd hit my knees and an elbow when I fell, and they were throbbing. But all that mattered right now was that I'd just lost Reno's Rolex, and I needed to get it back. The only way

I could ever see him again was if I returned the watch, and even then the chances of him forgiving me were slim.

While I sat there sweating, I tried to come up with a plan. I'd seen that kid around the building a couple of times, so if I staked out the lobby he'd probably show up eventually. The only problem was how to catch him. There was no way I could chase him with my ankle like this, and it wasn't like he'd come close enough for me to grab him.

Maybe I could pay someone to find the brat and retrieve the watch…but who'd be dumb enough to give it back to me, once they saw what they had? Even if they didn't know it was platinum or a collector's item, they'd see it was a Rolex, and if I was willing to pay to get it back, it obviously wasn't a fake.

I swore under my breath and lightly bonked my head against the wall behind me. Then I waited around for a while to see if the kid came back. Maybe he had a curfew and would need to come up these stairs to get home.

Or maybe he was completely feral and being raised by wolves. That started to seem likely when there was still no sign of him an hour later.

Finally, the need to pee set me in motion. I shifted around, sat on one of the steps, and started a reverse butt-scoot up that last flight of stairs. There was no way I was getting the watch back tonight, that much was clear. Might as well get some rest and try to regroup.

It took a while, but eventually my one crutch and I reached my apartment. I let myself in with my key, then deadbolted the door behind me and put the security chain in place. "Home sweet shit-hole," I muttered, as I limped to the bathroom.

Fifteen minutes later, I fell into bed freshly showered, wearing a clean T-shirt and a pair of pajama pants. I'd taken a bunch of ibuprofen, but it didn't eliminate the pain in my knees, elbow, or ankle. I was so tired that I almost fell asleep anyway—until the straight couple next door started having sex.

He kept shouting, "Yeah, baby, yeah," like he was Austin Powers or some shit, while she started screaming, "Yes, Daddy!" That scintillating bit of dialog was punctuated by their headboard slamming into the wall so hard that I half-expected them to come crashing through it.

Not to be outdone, the people across the hall started blasting some truly vile death metal. As loud as it was, it didn't manage to drown out the fornicators.

I pulled the pillow over my head and summed it all up with three words. "Fuck my life."

5

Jack

I spent the next week trying to catch the mini weasel who had Reno's watch. I'd learned three things about the kid—his nickname was Buzz, he lived somewhere on the fourth floor, and he was Satan incarnate, though to be fair, the third thing wasn't really news to me.

Since the stairs were so tough on my ankle, I decided to lie in wait and moved a chair onto the third floor landing. I almost caught the little jerk on day one, and that was when I discovered he was actually wearing the watch. Lord knew how he kept it from sliding off his scrawny wrist. I also couldn't figure out why no one had mugged him for it in this shitty neighborhood, though everyone probably assumed it was a fake.

He'd slipped out of my grasp like a greased pig when I lunged at him. Then he'd grinned and flipped me off with both hands before turning and running back down the stairs. I didn't try running after him because I knew I had zero chance of catching him, with or without a bum ankle. He was a fast little shit.

The next day, the building manager asked me what I was doing when he saw me camped out on the landing. I was dumb enough to tell him I was waiting for an eleven-year-old boy, and another tenant overheard me. Now the whole building thought I was a pervert. It was surprising they hadn't all banded together and come after me with pitch forks and torches. I was definitely moving, right after I got that watch back.

After a couple more days, I was thoroughly demoralized. The kid had discovered some way of getting to his apartment without using the stairs. I knew that because I kept hearing his hyena-like laughter echoing down from the fourth floor, taunting me.

That was when I decided I needed some help, so I hired the drunk guy who hung out in the lobby to watch for Buzz and call me if he spotted him. I didn't think he had the wherewithal to mug the boy for the watch. Apparently he didn't have it together enough to call me, either, so that went nowhere.

On Friday, I sprawled out on my twin bed, stared at the big water stain on the ceiling for a while, and found myself wishing I was back at the pink Victorian. My time there had pretty much ruined me. I used to be okay on my own, more or less, but now I was sad and lonely.

That wasn't okay, though. I had to get used to being by myself again. I'd be leaving this city sooner rather than later, and no matter where I landed next, I'd be all alone.

So, instead of texting JoJo and inviting myself over, I rolled out of bed and got dressed. I went with my second-best suit, since I'd ruined the best one the night I'd run from Reno. It was a nice marina blue number that wasn't custom-made, but it had been tailored to fit well and I felt good in it.

Then I went into the bathroom and spent some time styling my hair, while I tried to decide on tonight's objective. I didn't want to go home with anyone, that was for damn sure. Mostly, I just wanted to sit in a clean, comfortable bar, eat pub food, and drink too much. I also wanted to be around people, without actually interacting with them. Basically, I wanted to be people-adjacent.

I called a cab, then slowly made my way downstairs, since my ankle still wasn't a hundred percent. At the same time, I browsed for bars on my phone and found one that seemed promising, as long as it wasn't perpetrating any crimes against humanity like karaoke night.

Best of all, I'd never been there before, so the probability of running into someone I'd screwed over in the past was low. That was always a good thing, but especially tonight. I was off my game and just really wanted an uneventful evening.

The bar turned out to be exactly what I'd hoped for. Okay, so the fact that it was trying to look like an English pub was hokey, but the extensive menu made up for the faux Tudor beams glued to the walls, as well as most of the overall cheesiness.

Because it had been a shitty week, and since I'd been subsisting on gross protein bars in my depressing little apartment, I decided to treat myself to a sampler consisting of five different types of fried foods. This culinary masterpiece arrived heaped in a red plastic basket, which was lined in paper printed to look like an old-fashioned British newspaper. It was greasy and terrible for me, and I loved every minute of it.

Since my diet had already gone straight to hell by that point, I decided to wash it down with three vodka martinis with extra olives, soon to be followed by extra regret. There was no doubt I was going to feel like death in the morning, but tonight I was full, satisfied, and a little drunk, so what the hell—instant gratification at its best.

To prove to myself I wasn't a total lush, I decided against a fourth martini. Instead, I paid my bill, then took a moment to eat the little bits of fried batter that had collected at the bottom of the basket. After that, I daintily dabbed my mouth with a napkin, as if I hadn't just eaten everything in sight like a rabid wolverine.

All of a sudden, someone grabbed my wrist and slapped a handcuff around it. My reaction time was so slow from the alcohol that by the time I tried to jerk my arm away, it was already a done deal. I assumed I was getting arrested—I'd always figured it was just a matter of time. But why was the cuff lined with fake, red fur?

My breath caught when I looked up into Reno's eyes, which were glinting with anger. "Hi there, Jack," he said with a smirk. "Let's talk."

———————————

6

Adriano

———————————

Finally, after two weeks of repeatedly visiting every bar in the city, handing out my wanted posters and talking to what felt like hundreds of people, I got the call I'd been waiting for.

The number on the screen was unfamiliar, and when I answered a man asked, "Is your flyer for real? The one where you say you're giving two thousand dollars to anyone who can help you find some guy?"

"Absolutely. In fact, if your information pans out, I'll double the reward."

"Okay, awesome. My name's Dewey, and I'm the bartender at a pub called The Queen's Quarters off Union Square."

"And you've seen the man on my flyer?"

"I'm looking right at him. He's sitting at the bar."

I leapt to my feet and exclaimed, "Do anything you can to keep him there! I'm on my way."

"He's plowing his way through a mountain of fried food, so he's not going anywhere for a while," the man said. "I'll definitely keep an eye on him, though."

I sped across town, and when I got to my destination, there was no place to park. Typical. I ended up parking the Cadillac in an alley behind the pub, which seemed like a terrible idea, but what choice did I have? Then I unlocked the glove box and removed a gun, an envelope of cash, and the fuzzy handcuffs before hurrying inside.

And there he was, sitting alone at the end of the bar. Jack looked small and vulnerable, and he was eating crumbs from an empty basket like a goddamn orphan.

All of that started to tug at my heartstrings, but I shoved those feelings aside and focused on my anger. I couldn't forget what he'd done to me.

As I strode through the pub, I fastened one of the cuffs onto my wrist. I wanted to make sure that little thief had no chance to escape.

When I reached him, I slapped the other cuff around his wrist. There was confusion in his eyes when he turned to me, and I smirked and said, "Hi there, Jack. Let's talk." What a satisfying moment, after all that effort to find him over the last two weeks.

It wouldn't have surprised me if he'd tried to make a scene. He did try to pull away, but he quickly realized it was too late. At that point, he relaxed his posture and said, like we were old friends, "Hi, Reno. How've you been?" Was he fucking kidding me with that?

A skinny guy behind the bar approached us cautiously, and I turned to him and asked, "Are you Dewey?" When he nodded, I tossed the envelope onto the bar top and told him, "There's a little over five grand in there. You earned a bonus."

Dewey quickly pocketed the envelope and said, "Thanks, man." Then he glanced at my prisoner and asked me, "What're you going to do with him?"

"That all depends on Jack, and how cooperative he's feeling." I started to walk away, and since we were fastened together, he had no choice but to leap up and follow me.

There was still a chance he might make a scene, so I decided to get out of the bar as quickly as possible. I headed for a door marked "Employees Only," and we cut through the kitchen before exiting out a back door into the alley.

In the minute I'd been gone, some dumb-ass with a death wish had decided to try hotwiring my car. I didn't have the time or energy for this shit, so I pulled the gun from my waistband, pointed it at him, and said, "Hell no." He stumbled from the driver's seat and took off at a sprint.

When I felt a tug on the cuffs, I turned to look at Jack. He'd stepped back as far as he could on his short tether, and he definitely seemed concerned. I returned the Baretta to the back of my waistband and told him, "As long as you play nice, you have nothing to worry about."

I led him to the car and bent him over the front fender. Then I kicked his feet shoulder-width apart before giving him a thorough pat-down. Okay, so I'd had this done to me a time or two in the past, and I knew the routine.

After confiscating everything I found on him—which only consisted of a slim wallet, a phone, and a set of keys—I asked, "Where's the watch, Jack?"

He straightened up and fixed his hair as he said, "I don't currently have it in my possession. It was taken from me, but I spent this whole week trying to get it back. I actually planned to return it to you, not that I expect you to believe that."

I didn't, not even a little. The fact that he held my gaze steadily when he said it just proved he was an excellent liar. "Okay. Then tell me who has it, and we'll go get it from them."

"I can't do that."

"Why not?"

"I just can't."

I asked, "Do you fully understand how much trouble you're in right now, and that giving me the watch is the only way to get out of it?"

"I really fucking do."

"So, what do you propose?"

"Let me go, and I'll bring you the watch. Scout's honor. I know I can get it back, but I just need more time."

I rolled my eyes and asked, "Do you think there's any chance whatsoever I'll agree to that?"

"I figured the odds were slim, but they're never zero."

"Oh, believe me, they're zero." I led him to the passenger door and opened it. Then I found the keys to the handcuffs and unlocked my end.

When I went to fasten the cuff—and therefore Jack—to the door handle, he made a move so quick and smooth that I didn't have time to stop him. He snatched the Baretta from beneath the hem of my suit jacket, and both of us froze. He looked at me, then at the gun in his hand. But instead of pointing it at me, he threw it as hard as he could at a blue dumpster, which was maybe fifteen feet down the alley.

Thank god he missed. The gun bounced off the side and fell to the ground, and he muttered, "Shit. I was hoping it'd land inside."

It was all I could do to hide my smile. What an awful idea! Anyone else would have used the gun to negotiate their release, but not Jack. I told him, "That was a terrible throw," and fastened the cuff to the door handle before going to retrieve the weapon.

"Well excuse me for not being LeBron James."

"I'm not complaining. In fact, I'm thrilled you missed," I said, as I picked up the Baretta and returned to the car with it. "I would have been fucking pissed if I'd had to climb into the dumpster."

"In that case, you're welcome. And for the record, I probably would have made it if my right hand was free."

"You're left-handed. I remember that about you," I said, as I slid behind the wheel and stuck the gun under my seat.

"Fine. I'm left-handed and just can't throw. Happy?"

"Ecstatic," I muttered, as I pulled everything from his wallet. "Now let's see what we have here." It contained about a hundred dollars, three condoms, two lube packets, the business card I'd given him, a punch card for a coffee chain called Dutch Bros, and a Nevada driver's license. I held the ID toward the security light on the back of the pub and read out loud. "Jack Murphy, from Reno, Nevada of all places. This is a high quality fake ID. It must have been expensive."

"What makes you think it's fake?"

I shot him a look. "It says you're twenty-seven, when we both know you're thirty-four." He scowled at me, which made him look like an angry kitten. "What's your real last name? Because it sure as hell isn't Murphy."

"Why not?"

"You picked the most common Irish surname on the planet. You might as well have gone with John McDoe."

"There's no proof I made it up."

"You did, though." I returned everything to the wallet and stuck it in my pocket before starting the engine. "You went through a lot of trouble to get a fake ID. Why would you put your real name on it?"

"By the same token, do you think I'd actually tell you my real name, just because you asked nicely?"

"I think you have a lot of incentive to try to stay on my good side," I said, as I put the car in gear and began to drive down the alley. "Telling me your real name would prove you're willing to cooperate."

"Pass."

"Suit yourself."

We drove in silence for a minute or two, until he blurted, "Fine. It's Sullivan."

"No, it isn't."

"Why don't you believe me this time?"

"Because you gave it up way too easily."

Jack tried to cross his arms over his chest, but he only half-succeeded, since his right wrist was chained to the door. "Oh, you're right. My bad. You'll only believe what comes out of my mouth after you've been beating me for an hour or two."

That definitely wasn't the plan, but I decided to remain silent and let him stew. After another minute, he asked, "Where are you taking me? Some undisclosed location, where no one will hear me scream?"

"Undisclosed location? Where'd you get that, some cheesy detective novel?"

"Probably. Really though, where are you taking me?"

"My apartment."

He tried to let it go, but after a pause he asked, "Why do you insist on calling it that, when it's clearly a townhouse?"

"Do you really think arguing with me is the way to go here?"

"I'm just saying."

My phone beeped, and I pulled it from my pocket. The text from my brother said: *I thought you should know two guys smashed up Mom's bar and told her it was a message to you. She's fine, we're both in my apartment.*

I muttered, "Fucking hell," and pulled to the curb.

"What's wrong?"

I ignored Jack and called my brother. When he answered, the first thing I said was, "Is Mom really okay?"

"Yeah, she's just a little shaken up."

"Tell me exactly what happened."

"Two thugs came into her bar with baseball bats this evening and started breaking things. They said, 'This is for your boy Adriano. Tell him Mario Greco says hello.' One of Mom's customers called the police, and the men ran off when they heard the sirens. As far as I know, they haven't been caught yet."

"Please tell Mom I'm sorry that happened, and I'll be there in the morning. This might sound paranoid, but don't open the door for anyone, and don't go anywhere tonight."

"Will do, but are you sure coming here is a good idea? You left to keep yourself safe, and the situation clearly hasn't gotten any better."

"I don't care what happens to me. I just need to make sure you two are safe, and I can't do that from San Francisco."

"Maybe Mom should come and stay with you instead," he said, "just until things calm down a bit."

"You can pitch that idea to her, but watch, she'll refuse to leave. You know how stubborn she is. In fact, I don't even know if I can stop her from opening up the bar tomorrow and acting like it's business as usual."

My brother sighed and muttered, "You're right."

"I'd better go, so I can grab a few things and get on the road. Call me if you need anything, and I'll see you in the morning."

We said goodbye and disconnected the call, and then I sent a quick group text to the best people on my payroll in Vegas. After I filled them in on what had happened, I asked them to watch the bar, in case Greco's men came back to finish the job. It was tempting to ask them to watch my brother's apartment too, but none of them knew the address and maybe it was best to keep it that way. I trusted these people to an extent, but who could say if they'd remain loyal to me if Greco decided to put the screws to them?

I pulled away from the curb and was deep in thought when Jack said, "Well, shit. That sounded serious."

I'd actually forgotten he was there. "It is."

"So…what are you going to do with me?"

"I'm not setting you free," I told him. "It took me two weeks to find you, and after this you might disappear entirely."

"If you're thinking about leaving me chained up somewhere, I wholeheartedly object."

"Like I'd let you out of my sight. You're coming with me to Vegas." There was so much wrong with that idea, but I really didn't see an alternative. I shot him a look and added, "I need you to not be a huge pain in my ass, though. We have a long drive ahead of us, and believe me when I say I'm in no mood for any bullshit."

"I'll cooperate, I promise. But why are you taking your car? It's a solid eight- or nine-hour drive, as opposed to a ninety-minute flight."

"Because I'm taking a shitload of guns with me, and the airlines tend to frown on that."

Jack whispered, "Oh," before falling silent again.

When we arrived at my apartment, I pulled into the garage, then closed the door behind us and took the keys, the gun, and the garage remote with me as I climbed out of the car. I pinned Jack with a glare and told him, "I'll be back in three minutes. Don't do anything stupid."

"I won't. I swear."

I didn't believe him, but if I hurried, hopefully he wouldn't have enough time to make my night even worse.

7

Jack

I sat perfectly still as I watched Reno go inside his townhouse. But the moment the door shut behind him, I opened the glove box and rummaged around. I found a ballpoint pen and quickly removed the little spring inside it. If I straightened it out, it could be a useful tool. Then I broke off the metal clip and stuck both of those things in an inside coat pocket before tossing what was left of the pen behind a workbench.

Since the convertible's top was down, I climbed over the door and searched the storage cupboard beside me. I didn't dare to open the car door and risk having Reno hear me shut it again.

The cupboard contained a few household supplies like light bulbs and paper towels, which were of no use to me. But there was also a stack of owners' manuals and warranty information for the kitchen appliances, and those netted me two paperclips. I added them to my pocket before climbing back into my seat and pulling up a neutral expression.

With those finds, I could remove the handcuffs any time I wanted to. It might take a minute though, so now wasn't the time to try out my new tools—not with Reno returning at any moment. I'd much rather make the drive to Vegas in a nice, comfy seat instead of the trunk, and I was pretty sure that was where I'd end up if he caught me trying to escape.

Reno returned maybe thirty seconds after I sat back down. He'd put on a black wool overcoat with his charcoal gray suit, and he was carrying a heavy-looking black bag, a laptop case, and a couple of other things. The bags went into the trunk, and after he took a seat behind the wheel, he put a baseball cap and a blanket on my lap.

I asked, "What are these for?"

He pulled his keys and a remote from his coat pocket and opened the garage door with the click of a button. Then he explained, as he started the engine, "The mechanism to put up the Caddy's top is broken, and the desert is cold at night."

"So…did you want me to hold these for you until we get to the desert?"

"They're for you, so you don't freeze."

"I don't understand," I said, as we rolled out of the garage and the door shut behind us. "Why are you being nice to me?"

He shot me a look. "If you make a big deal of it, I'm throwing the blanket out of the car." Then he put the car in gear and began driving down the hill.

"Nope, definitely not making a big deal of it." I put on the black baseball cap, then spread out the white, down-filled blanket and tucked it around me. "Thank you. That was surprisingly considerate. Well, unless you only did it to butter me up, in the hopes of convincing me to return the watch."

"You're making me regret being nice to you."

"I'll shut up now." That lasted all of twenty seconds before I said, "So, I couldn't help but overhear your conversation. What are you going to do about the guy who smashed up your mom's bar?"

"I have no idea. I already temporarily shut down my business and retreated to San Francisco like a fucking coward, because I thought that might defuse the situation. He has a lot more men and resources than I do, so if I go after him, I'm guaranteed to lose."

"What was your business, exactly?"

"Illegal gambling."

I turned to look at his profile, as much as I could anyway, with my right arm chained to the door. "Explain this to me. I get why that'd be a thing in a city like San Francisco, where legal gambling isn't an option. But why would anyone seek out illegal gambling in Las Vegas?"

"People flock to Vegas to gamble, legal or otherwise, so it's the perfect location. There are a lot of reasons why they might choose my high-stakes poker games versus gambling in a state-regulated casino. For example, maybe they've been banned from the legal venues. Maybe they have no interest in informing the IRS about their winnings. Maybe they prefer to remain incognito and are uncomfortable with the high level of surveillance at the legal joints. Or maybe they just like the speakeasy ambience of my establishment."

"Yeah, I'm sure it's definitely the last thing, and not that they're all a bunch of tax-dodging criminals."

Fortunately, he grinned at that instead of taking it as an insult. "Those things aren't mutually exclusive. You can be a tax-dodging criminal *and* enjoy the ambience."

"True enough. So, how'd you end up in the illegal gambling biz?"

"It's a long story. How'd you end up as a thief?"

"It's a short story," I said. "It's just been Ma and me since I was eight years old, and what was I going to do at that age, get a job? Instead, I developed my skills as a shoplifter and a pickpocket. Later, I moved up to small-scale burglary."

"Burglary? Is that what you call it when you let some guy take you home and fuck you, followed by stealing from him? Because it almost seems like a form of prostitution, except that your mark doesn't realize he's paying for you until after the fact."

I sighed and muttered, "Go ahead, get the insults out of your system. I know you're angry."

"Damn right I am! Not that you give a shit, but do you know what it felt like to realize the only reason you'd come home with me was to rip me off?"

"No, it wasn't! I let you take me home because I was attracted to you, and I wanted us to have sex. But then I saw that mahogany chest sitting out in your bedroom and just had to look inside. Curiosity got the better of me. I would have left it at that, if it wasn't for the Rolex."

When he didn't say anything, I pressed ahead with, "I never planned to steal from you. Didn't you wonder why I left all the other stuff in that box? I knew what it was worth, but I didn't take it. I just took the watch on impulse, because it was so special. I planned to enjoy it for a while, and then I was going to sell it. That money could've made a real difference, for both my mom and me. But I regretted taking it and decided to give it back. I know that sounds like total bullshit, but it's the truth."

"I want to believe taking the watch was an impulsive decision," he said, as he pulled up to a stoplight. "I'd also like to believe we fucked because you wanted to, not because it was part of a scheme to get into my home and steal from me. The problem is, you totally destroyed my trust in you, Jack. Because of that, you're right—it does sound like bullshit. In fact, every word out of your mouth sounds like a lie."

It shouldn't have mattered that he thought I was a liar. I'd learned a long time ago to brush off other people's opinions of me.

Except it did matter…a lot. Hearing him say that cut like a knife, and I was desperate to make him believe me. How could I though, after I'd shown him he couldn't trust me? Was there any chance of coming back from that?

I found myself saying, "I promise I'll never tell you another lie, Adriano. You don't have to believe that. In fact, I know you won't. But it's all I can think of to make this up to you."

"You want to make it up to me? Give me the watch."

"I will. I meant it when I said that had been my plan, even before you found me. It's currently in the possession of a punk who lives in my building." No fucking way was I going to admit that punk was about eleven years old. Talk about humiliating. "He's been wearing it to show off, and it should be relatively easy to get it back from him, once my ankle fully heals and I can chase him down. I hurt it when I was running from you, and I've been pretty incapacitated ever since." I pushed the blanket aside and hiked up my pant leg, so he could see the compression bandage I was wearing.

"The only part I can believe is that you hurt your ankle, because there's proof."

"Fine, but that was all true."

He glanced at me and said, "If you're suddenly committed to the truth, then tell me—what's your real name?"

Damn it. I hadn't fully thought through my honesty pledge, but I owed him that much. I sighed and admitted, "It's Jackson Granger. Nobody knows that, except for my mother and my best friend. My birth name was Jackson Caldicott, but after my mom left my dad she changed it to her maiden name."

"Are you still in touch with your dad?"

"No, because he's an evil fucker. To escape from him, my mom picked me up after school one day and just kept driving. She didn't even pack a bag, because she was terrified about what he might do if he found out she was leaving.

"Her plan was to drive to California from Virginia, but we only made it as far as Kansas before the thug my father hired caught up to us. After he slapped my mom around, he confiscated the car, all her cash and credit cards, and her wedding ring. Then he left us where he found us, because my dad didn't want either of us back. He just wanted the stuff he'd paid for, out of spite. He was a multi-millionaire, by the way, so it's not like he needed those things."

I pulled the blanket up to my chin and turned away from Adriano. Why had I told him that? Every word was true, but I wasn't in the habit of spilling my guts to people.

"I'm sorry. That's truly awful." After a moment, he added, "I bet that's why you target men you perceive as wealthy, because they remind you of your father."

"That's great, please psychoanalyze me some more." Not that he was wrong.

We drove in silence for a while, as I stared out at nothing in particular. Then he said, "I never knew my father. He was separated when he started dating my mother, but by the time Mom realized she was pregnant, he'd gone back to his wife and kids. She got in touch with him to let him know he was going to have a son, and he returned to Vegas one last time to see her. He gave her a hundred grand in lieu of child support, which she used as a down payment on the building that houses her bar. He also left her with something to give to me when I turned eighteen, but he never came to see me after I was born. Then he was killed when I was four."

I turned to look at him. "Please don't tell me the gift he left for you was that Rolex."

"It was."

I'd been wondering why he was opening up to me, but now I got it—that story was meant to make me feel guilty, and it worked. In fact, I felt like absolute shit. "I'm so sorry, Adriano. I didn't know."

"Remember what I said that night, when I came upstairs and realized you'd taken the watch?"

"You said something along the lines of 'anything but that.' It's a bit of a blur, since I was in a state of panic."

"I did say that. I also told you I'd give you money if you needed it. That offer still stands. The watch is priceless to me, but its resale value is probably fifty thousand dollars. I'll give you that amount in cash if you return it to me when we get back to San Francisco."

"That's not necessary. I already told you I planned to give it back."

"I know what you said, but come on. It's more likely for a thousand monkeys to come flying out of my ass than for that to be true."

"Thanks ever so much for that visual." Why was I even bothering to explain myself? He didn't believe anything I said, and really, why would he? This whole situation was completely hopeless. I glanced at him one more time and asked, "How long do you suppose we'll be in Las Vegas?"

"My best guess? Somewhere between two days and two months."

I muttered, "Fucking awesome," and turned my head to stare at nothing some more. I really needed to escape as soon as possible and run far, far away from Adriano Dombruso.

8

Adriano

Jack fell asleep maybe an hour into our drive, which left me alone with my thoughts. This wasn't a good thing, because my mind was reeling.

The fact that I was doubting myself was a real problem. I was someone who usually moved through life with a lot of swagger and confidence. It was a requirement in my line of work. To call the people who frequented my poker games a tough crowd was putting it mildly, and the only way to maintain control was to get everyone to believe you were even tougher.

It helped that my mom had given me my father's last name. There was a time when the Dombruso crime family had ruled the west coast. They were the stuff of legend, and nobody dared cross them. The name still carried weight with the old timers, but the problem was, every year saw a new crop of young upstarts, out to make their mark in the criminal underworld. They played by their own rules and respected nothing and no one.

Mario Greco was one of these men. He was fearless, hungry, and impatient, and he wanted to make a name for himself *now*, without paying his dues like the rest of us had. Unfortunately, he had a lot of money, which put limitless resources at his disposal.

Where I could afford to hire ten men as my enforcers, he could hire thirty. And instead of building an enterprise for himself from the ground-up the way I had, he preferred the shortcut of trying to step in and take what others had made.

Okay, yes, I'd had an advantage when I was first starting out. Almost twenty years ago, when I was an ambitious kid right out of high school, the Dombruso name gave me credibility. It also meant most people weren't willing to fuck with me, for fear of incurring the wrath of the Dombruso family.

Even so, I'd gotten where I was through hard work, patience, and perseverance. The Dombrusos didn't even know I existed, which meant they didn't have my back like everyone assumed.

As far as I knew, my dad had taken the secret of his bastard son to his grave. In fact, after he and his wife reconciled, he seemed to forget all about me. They had more kids and had probably been very happy together—until both of their lives were cut short during a home invasion by a rival crime family.

But I still had the name, even though it clearly didn't mean what it used to. If it carried any weight, I probably wouldn't be dealing with Greco right now, and he was a real problem. He was violent and unpredictable, and he'd crossed a line by trashing my mom's place of business.

I'd always gone to great lengths to keep my personal and professional lives totally separate. In fact, most people didn't even know I had a mom and a kid brother in Vegas. So, I really had to wonder how Greco had managed to find out about the bar, which was right downstairs from my mom's apartment.

What the hell was I supposed to do about this? Greco was a loose cannon, and there was no reasoning with him. I'd tried repeatedly before deciding to step back and spend some time away from Las Vegas. I'd even temporarily shut down my business, thinking that would help defuse the situation. But he was still coming for me, in the worst possible way—by involving the people I loved.

So now, I was heading back into a hornet's nest with no plan whatsoever, and to make matters worse, I was doing it with Jack in tow. I glanced at him, sound asleep in his blanket cocoon. Dragging him to Vegas with me was such a terrible idea, but what else was I supposed to do? It wasn't like he would've waited around for me to return.

I glanced at him again. He was a stunningly beautiful man, and I couldn't deny I was still wildly attracted to him.

But right now, that was really just a distraction. Plus, there was no way anything could develop between us, because I didn't trust him. He'd said all the right things earlier, but I felt stupid for believing a single word that came out of his mouth.

And what, like he'd want to date me? I currently had him chained to a car door, and I was dragging him across state lines against his will. Even though he was being cooperative, what choice did he have? He probably thought I'd shoot him if he didn't play nice. There was no doubt in my mind that if he found a way to escape, that'd be the last I ever saw of him.

The blanket slipped off his shoulders just then, and I pulled it up and tucked him back in. Then I sighed and muttered, "What the hell are you doing, Adriano?" Nothing good could come from caring about Jack Granger…or whatever his name was.

About two hours later, I pulled into a gas station that was so brightly lit, it felt like midday instead of eleven p.m. The moment I cut the engine, Jack sat up and looked around as he mumbled, "Where are we?"

"Somewhere on the I-5. Sit tight for a few minutes while I buy some gas, and then I'll uncuff you so you can use the restroom."

He rubbed his eyes with a balled up fist. Then he took off the baseball cap and absently fixed his hair while I filled the tank. Even at this hour, there were a lot of people around, since the gas station was right off a busy interstate. I really didn't know what I'd do if he decided to make a scene or call for help, but he just sat quietly and waited.

When I finished fueling up, I pulled into one of the parking spaces in front of the convenience store and walked around to the passenger door. Then I frowned at Jack and said, "Don't make me regret this."

He looked up at me with those soulful green eyes of his and sounded sincere when he told me, "I won't. I promise." This guy could get away with murder, that was how sweet and innocent he seemed. When I hesitated, he added, "Besides, where am I going to go? We're in the middle of fuck-all, and you've got my phone, money, and ID."

He had a point. Even so, I scowled at him as I reached over the door and unlocked the cuffs. He got out of the car and stretched, and then he made a quick move and pretended he was about to dart out into the night.

My reaction time was painfully slow. By the time I responded, he'd already reversed direction, smiled at me, and began to stroll into the shop. I grabbed his elbow and whispered, "Don't fuck with me, Jack."

He paused and turned to me, his eyes sparkling with mischief. "What're you going to do Daddy, spank me?"

He'd started out the evening contrite but had woken up spicy. I really didn't have the energy to deal with Spicy Jack right now though, so I growled, "There's plenty of room in the trunk and another six hours of drive time ahead of us. Do you really feel like pressing your luck?"

That was definitely the wrong thing to say, and I instantly regretted it. He straightened his posture and glared at me. "I was just playing," he said. "You don't have to be a dick."

I let go of his arm and muttered, "Look, I'm sorry." Jesus, was I actually apologizing? "It's been a long fucking night, and it's only going to get longer."

His expression softened, and he dipped his chin. Then he looked up at me through his thick lashes and asked, "You wouldn't really put me in the trunk, would you?"

"Of course not." I grinned a little and added, "How would I even get you in there? It'd be like trying to get a cat into a tub of water. You'd probably bite me."

That brought out his smile. "I'd definitely bite you. Now come on, I need to pee." With that, he turned and went into the convenience store.

After we used the facilities, I started to pour myself a cup of coffee. "You took all my money," Jack said, "so how am I supposed to buy something?"

"I'll give it back later. For now, get anything you want. It's on me."

"Anything?"

When I nodded, he used both arms to scoop up every bag of chips from one of the shelves. Then he watched me to see what I'd do. Instead of calling him on being ridiculous, I asked, "Hungry?"

"I'm in survival mode," he informed me. "I've been taken hostage, and who knows if my captor will remember to feed me? You strike me as the kind of man who can't even keep a goldfish alive."

"Calling yourself a hostage is kind of dramatic."

"Well, how would you describe this situation?"

"Keeping an eye on you until I get my watch back."

"I'm right about the goldfish though, aren't I?"

"No comment." I changed the subject with, "Would you like a cup of coffee? I'll make you one, since your hands are full."

"Yes please, with obscene amounts of cream and sugar."

I doctored up his coffee with three times the amount of cream and sugar I'd consider reasonable and asked him, "Is that obscene enough for you?"

"It'll do."

On the way to the register, he grabbed a pack of snack cakes—awkwardly, since his arms were totally loaded up with chips. Then he picked up a bag of peanuts in the shell, which I plucked out of his hand. He frowned as he reminded me, "You said I could have anything I wanted."

I replaced it with a bag of shelled peanuts and said, "You can have these. What are you, a circus elephant? It's bad enough you'll be eating in my car. I'm not letting you get shells all over it, too."

"Fine."

All of this felt like a test, and I wasn't sure if I passed.

Jack stood by patiently while the cashier rang up our items. I half-expected him to make a comment about being kidnapped, but instead he just raised a brow when I glanced at him.

Once we were back in the car, he settled in with the blanket on his lap and took a sip of coffee. Then he turned to me and asked, "Will you be chaining me up again like a common criminal?"

"You know you literally *are* a criminal, right?"

"As are you."

"I'm aware. And no, I'm not going to cuff you to the door unless you give me a reason to."

He maintained a pretty successful poker face, but I saw a look of relief in his eyes. "Good, because that was absurd. What did you think I was going to do, leap from a car barreling down the interstate at eighty miles an hour? I'd wreck my suit. I'm already down one from when I landed in those murder bushes beneath your balcony."

"Yeah, those hurt like hell when I went to chase you. Thank you for running away like that, by the way."

"I had to. You were about to shoot me."

"No, I wasn't."

"You pointed a gun at me!"

"It wasn't loaded."

"How was I supposed to know that?"

"Just FYI, when a normal person finds themselves in that situation, they put their hands up and surrender," I told him. "Not you, though."

"I was afraid of you, and my fight or flight response kicked in. Obviously, I went with flight."

"How'd you manage to disappear like that?"

"I hopped over a few fences but stalled out when I twisted my ankle. I was in the back yard of a house that belonged to this amazing LGBT family, and they took me in and nurtured me for a week while my ankle healed." After a pause, he said softly, "It was really nice, actually. I like to think I don't need other people, but… I don't know. Spending time there made me question some things."

"You're not alone though, right? You mentioned a mom and a best friend. Where are they?"

"Back home in Kansas."

I glanced at him and asked, "So, you actually stayed in the Midwest after your mom's trip to California was cut short?" Of everything he'd told me, that part really hadn't felt like a lie.

"We didn't have a choice. We had no money and no car, so we ended up in a homeless shelter for a while, until Ma found a job and got on her feet."

"There wasn't a friend or relative that could help?"

"She tried asking for help," he said, "but people suck, and ultimately you can only rely on yourself." I thought that belief summed up a lot about him. "It turned out we didn't really need them anyway. Manhattan, Kansas was a perfectly fine place to grow up, and Ma and I took care of each other."

"Did she know what you were doing to contribute to the household income?"

"Of course not. I told her I was earning money by doing odd jobs around the neighborhood. I did get caught shoplifting once when I was ten, though. It made her cry, and I swore I'd never do it again. What I actually meant was that I'd never get caught again, and I learned to become a better thief.

"Now she thinks I work as an assistant to an interior designer, and that I move around a lot because he's always getting jobs in different cities. I even went so far as to make a fake website for my fictitious employer. I feel bad lying to her, but I'd feel a thousand times worse if I broke her heart with the truth."

I asked, "Why'd you tell her you're an assistant, and not a successful interior designer?"

He grinned at me and shrugged. "I'm not sure. Maybe because it seemed more believable?" After he took another sip of coffee, he asked, "Does your mom know about your illegal gambling operation?"

"She does, but she's willfully oblivious to the fact that I'm a criminal. She likes to think of it as an anti-establishment, stick it to the man type of thing—screw the big casinos and the government, power to the people."

"Hey, whatever helps our mothers sleep at night."

"Exactly."

Jack glanced at me and said, "Look at us, actually having some stuff in common."

"I'm not surprised. In fact, we probably would have been great together."

That seemed to throw him off. He looked away again and stayed quiet for so long that I ended up starting the engine, leaving the gas station, and merging onto the highway.

After a while, he turned back to me and said, "We could still fuck, even if you despise me. Hate sex might actually be fun."

"I don't despise you. Sex takes trust, though."

"How much trust did it take to get your dick sucked in that Starbucks parking lot?"

For a moment, I had no idea what he was talking about. But then I remembered the lie I'd told him the night we slept together and admitted, "That never happened."

"What do you mean?"

"I lied about some random encounter to make it seem like casual sex was no big deal to me. I didn't want to admit you were the first guy I'd hooked up with since my four-year relationship ended."

He shifted around so he was facing me and asked, "How long ago did it end?"

"It's been about six months."

"And I was the first guy you slept with? What were you waiting for?" When I shrugged, he asked, "Are you still in love with him?"

"No."

"You sound really certain."

"I am."

"So, who did the dumping?"

"It was a mutual decision," I said. "We fought all the time and made each other miserable. It was painful when it ended, but in a lot of ways it was also a relief."

"But then, why did it take you six months to get back out there?"

"I'd been out of the game for several years, so at first, getting back into it felt awkward. Later on, I was dealing with Greco and the threat to my business, so my sex life got pushed to the back burner."

"For the record," he said, "I wasn't being truthful either when I told you I'd had sex with someone the day before you and I hooked up. It had actually been a few weeks. But I didn't want to tell you that, not after you mentioned you'd gotten a BJ six hours earlier."

I shook my head and muttered, "You're as ridiculous as I am."

We finally reached Las Vegas around five a.m.

My brother had texted me a couple of hours earlier to let me know our mom had finally fallen asleep at about three in the morning. I wanted to let her get some rest, so instead of going to see my family as soon as I got into town, I drove to Mom's bar.

It took up the ground floor of a simple, light blue building in an older part of town. Planters full of colorful flowers framed the entrance, and the sign above the door read Mandy's Place. It simultaneously broke my heart and filled me with rage to see sheets of plywood where the big plate glass window used to be.

Jack had dozed off again, but he woke up when I cut the engine, and we both got out of the car. Two of my men were parked out front in a black sedan, and after they checked in with me and reported nothing else had happened during the night, I sent them home.

Then I used my key to unlock the front door, and when I stepped inside I told Jack, "Be careful. There's glass all over the floor."

He followed me into the bar, and after I locked up behind us, we carefully picked our way across the debris. "We should have come in through the back," I muttered. "I didn't realize it was this bad."

Finally, I reached the switch and turned on the lights. That was when I saw the full extent of the damage. In addition to breaking the front window, they'd used their bats on some of the tables and chairs, and then they'd gone behind the bar and smashed up the bottles of alcohol.

I told Jack, "This place has been my mom's pride and joy for thirty-seven years. She opened it right after I was born, and my brother Romy and I grew up in the apartment upstairs. She still lives there, but it wasn't safe for her tonight, so she's staying at Romy's place." I sighed and pushed my hair off my forehead as I looked around me. "Seeing it like this feels like a knife to the heart, which I'm sure is exactly what Greco intended."

"I don't get it," Jack said. "You left town and shut down your business. What more does he want?"

"To make an example of me, because I pushed back when he tried to take over. This is a warning to anyone who might even think about crossing him."

"That's not right!" I turned to look at him, because he sounded so angry. "It's even worse that he involved your mom."

"I know." I took off my overcoat and suit jacket, and as I rolled back my sleeves I said, "I'm going to be busy here for a while, but there's a comfortable couch in my mom's office at the back of the building. Go get some sleep. It's not even light out yet, and you must be tired."

I opened the utility closet and pulled out a large push broom while he went through the door marked "Employees Only." I was fully aware that he might keep on going right out the back door, but I didn't have the energy to try to control Jack right now—not when I was feeling defeated, exhausted, and overwhelmed by all this destruction.

Shockingly, he returned a couple of minutes later. He'd taken off his suit jacket and rolled back his sleeves, and he was carrying a broom and dust pan while dragging a big garbage can behind him. "I put two trash bags in the bin," he said, as he left the can by the door and went to scoop up the pile of glass I'd formed. "I hope that's enough. I was worried about the shards cutting through, so I almost went with three."

"What are you doing?"

"Isn't it obvious? I'm helping you clean up."

"Yeah, but why?"

He straightened up and turned to look at me. "This isn't for you, it's for your mom. As someone who was raised by a single mother, this hurts my heart. I want to help make it right."

That stirred up a lot of emotions in me, but I just nodded and said, "Thanks, Jack." Then we both went to work.

9

Jack

Adriano had to be completely exhausted after driving all night, but he and I worked on the bar for three solid hours. He didn't sit down until every last shard of glass, piece of broken furniture, and drop of alcohol had been cleaned up.

Even then, he didn't relax. He retrieved his tablet from the car and started shopping for alcohol, replacement furniture, and a new window. The fact that he wanted the replacement glass to be bullet-proof was chilling.

Meanwhile, I brewed a pot of coffee and put together a simple breakfast of toast and scrambled eggs in the kitchen. He thanked me when I put a plate in front of him, but he didn't look up from the tablet. I removed it from his hands as gently as I could and said, "Please eat something. We've been together about twelve hours now, and all you've put in your body during that time was a cup of gas station coffee."

He muttered, "I'm too tired to argue," and tucked into the breakfast.

I sat down with the tablet and started looking through the local furniture wholesaler's website that he'd pulled up. After a minute, I showed him the screen and said, "These chairs are nice, and they're similar to the old ones."

"They're the ones I liked, too. I suppose I should ask my mom before I order them, though. She's very particular about this place."

"She's done a beautiful job on it," I said, as I looked around.

The walls were a soothing shade of deep blue, the ceilings were high, and the floor was polished wood. The best part, though, were the clusters of black and white photos on the walls. There were different themes. One set had been taken in the bar, with gorgeous portraits of the customers and a beautiful woman that had to be Adriano's mom. Another set had probably been taken around the modest neighborhood, and a third consisted of artistic shots of old neon signs in various states of disrepair.

"Thank god those men didn't get around to smashing the photos," I said. "They're really something special."

"Thanks. I could have reprinted them if they'd gotten damaged, but I'm glad I don't have to."

"Wait, did you take those pictures?"

"Yeah, a long time ago. They're all at least ten to fifteen years old."

"You have an incredible gift, Reno."

He shrugged and said, "It's a fairly useless talent, that and drawing. Though the latter did come in handy recently." He grinned a little as he pulled what looked like a journal from his laptop case. Then he took a folded sheet of paper from between its pages and handed it to me. It was surprising to come face-to-face with myself when I unfolded it. "That's how I found you," he explained. "I left those flyers at every bar in San Francisco."

"I'm sorry to make you go through that. This drawing is amazing, though. I'm just surprised you drew such a flattering likeness, since you had to be furious with me."

His grin got a little wider. "What was I going to do, add a pair of horns? That's exactly what you look like."

"On my best day and in very flattering lighting, maybe." I glanced at him and asked, "Is it weird that I want to keep this?"

"Go ahead. I don't need it anymore."

"Thanks." I put down the flyer and ended up knocking the journal off the small table. It had fallen open to a page with a list of names and addresses, and I picked it up and asked, "Who are these people with your last name? Dante, Vincent, Gianni, Michael—"

"They're my half-brothers."

"I thought you just had one brother named Romy."

"He's the only one I grew up with. Technically, he's a half-brother, too. Mom dated Romy's dad for about a year, but then he took off when she told him she was pregnant. Needless to say, she has pretty terrible taste in men." Reno took a sip of coffee before continuing, "Anyway, they're my half-brothers on my dad's side. He was with his wife before and after the few months he spent with my mom, so two of them are younger than me, and two are older."

"Are you close?"

"I don't know them at all," he said.

"Most of these addresses are in San Francisco. Were you planning to go see them while you were in town?"

"Actually, I hoped to avoid them. Remember when I gave the valet a fake name, the night we met? There are a lot of Dombrusos in San Francisco in addition to my half-brothers, so I thought it was a good idea to lay low."

"Have you ever actually met any of them?"

Adriano paused before saying, "Don't repeat this to my mom when you meet her, because she'd probably be upset. The summer after my high school graduation, I told her I was going on a road trip and drove to San Francisco. I wanted to meet the other side of my family, and I didn't tell her because I didn't know how it would make her feel. I didn't want her to think she and Romy weren't enough for me, you know?

"Anyway, I managed to track down my oldest brother, Dante. I used a fake ID to get into some club where he was holding court in the VIP section. He seemed like a real big shot, even though he would have only been about twenty-one at the time. I'd had this whole speech prepared, and I went up to him and said something like, 'Paulie Dombruso was my dad. He met my mom in Las Vegas nineteen years ago.' That was as far as I got before Dante leapt up and shoved me.

"He caught me off guard, so I lost my footing and fell on my ass. Before I could get up, he leaned over me and said I was full of shit. He told me his parents adored each other, and that his dad would never cheat on his mom with some whore in Vegas. Before he stormed off, he lifted his lapel to show me the gun in his shoulder holster and told me he better never see me again, or I'd regret it. And that was the end of that."

"That's a pretty extreme reaction," I said.

"He was full of rage. I think that's probably just how he went through life."

"Are you thinking about contacting him again?"

"No. Why give him a chance to reject me a second time?"

"But that happened almost twenty years ago. Maybe he mellowed with age."

"Or maybe he got tougher and meaner. I know I did."

"You could have gone anywhere while things cooled off in Vegas," I said. "Why'd you choose San Francisco?"

"I wanted to do some research on my half-brothers, because I thought it'd be a good idea to keep tabs on them. One thing I wanted to know was whether they still were involved in organized crime. With the same last name, there might be potential blowback on me if one of their business ventures were to go south."

I didn't think he was being totally honest with me, or with himself. There had to be more to it than that, maybe some curiosity about his brothers, but I didn't push. Instead, I asked, "What did you find out?"

"As far as I can tell, they're retired, but it's not like they'd adver-tise it if they were breaking the law. I was worried about digging too deep and ending up on their radar." He scrubbed his hands over his face and muttered, "Am I still speaking in complete sentences? I'm so tired that I barely know what I'm saying."

"I'm sorry. This wasn't the time for a million questions." I got up and collected the breakfast dishes. "Let's get out of here, so you can sleep. I'm going to go rinse these and put them in the sink while you gather your things." He nodded and started packing the journal and tablet into his laptop case while I headed to the kitchen.

Reno was locking the door behind us when the day shift arrived—two big, burly men on his payroll who'd be watching the bar all day and making sure no more harm came to it. I waited in the convertible while he spoke to them. Then he climbed behind the wheel, let loose with a massive yawn, and started the engine.

It took about ten minutes to reach the edge of town from the bar's working class neighborhood. Then we drove another ten or fifteen minutes into the desert before coming to a dusty sign with a dry fountain at its base. It was for something called "Dessert Heights," which made me grin.

"I assume that was supposed to read 'Desert Heights,' not that the idea of a dessert-themed neighborhood isn't appealing," I said. "There could be Cheesecake Lane, Ice Cream Avenue—"

"Nope, not what they were going for. The developer was just a doofus and didn't know how to spell that thing that's all around us."

Reno made a left turn into the residential development, and after we drove for another minute, I asked him, "Um, why do you live in a post-apocalyptic wasteland?"

All around us was a grid of empty roads with sidewalks and street lamps. That was followed by a single road lined with large, two-story houses. Almost every yard was nothing but dirt and dry, spindly-looking weeds, and there was a for sale sign in front of just about every home, except for Reno's.

He paused in the street and fished a remote out of his glove box as he explained, "The developer went bankrupt after his business partner embezzled the investors' money and fled to the Bahamas. Only these twenty-four houses were built out of a planned hundred and forty, and just six were sold. The reason I bought one was because my mom was dating the developer at the time, and the architect's drawings and plans for the neighborhood were beautiful. But you can see what happened after the money was stolen—it all just fizzled out. I bought the house ten years ago and have thought about trying to sell it, but there's no way anyone would ever buy it."

"That's a shame."

He shrugged and opened his garage door with the remote. "It is what it is. At least I never have to worry about noisy neighbors."

"Way to put a positive spin on it."

He parked in the garage beside a big, black SUV and shut the door behind us. Then I collected the bags of convenience store snacks while he grabbed his laptop case and retrieved the large, black bag from the trunk. I assumed it was stuffed with guns, but I didn't ask.

When he entered a code on a keypad to shut off the alarm, force of habit made me take a peek. I idly wondered if the date he'd used was his mom's birthday or his brother Romy's—no doubt it was one or the other, because people were ridiculous with their so-called security.

It turned out his home was actually really nice, with high ceilings, tons of space, and tasteful furnishings and artwork. I left the snacks on the kitchen counter, and as I followed him upstairs he said, "Don't get freaked out if you see a scorpion. I don't know how they get in, but I find one downstairs occasionally."

"That better be a very bad joke."

"We're in the middle of the desert, Jack."

"Right. So, goal number one when building a house here should be to keep the deadly nightmare vermin on the outside."

"They didn't even spell the sign right," he said. "I'm lucky the house is still standing, given the geniuses behind this project."

"My question is, did you see the dessert sign before you bought the house? Because I'm going to go ahead and call that a red flag."

"No, that came later."

"Are your mom and the developer still together?"

He shook his head. "They lasted almost three years though, which was a record for her. She's definitely relationship-challenged."

As long as he was answering my questions, I decided to slip one in that was really none of my business. "Speaking of relationships, did your boyfriend live here with you when you two were together?"

"No. We never lived together."

"How do you date someone for four years and never get to that point?"

Reno glanced at me with an amused expression. "You're very nosy."

"I prefer the word curious."

We'd reached the double doors to the main bedroom, and he changed the subject with, "The guest room is down the hall, last door on the right. There are clean towels and some toiletries in the bathroom cabinet. You can also help yourself to the clothes I stored in the closet, not that they'll fit, but you might find something to sleep in. And please don't run away while I'm asleep."

It stung that he was sticking me in the guest room, but what did I expect? I really liked Reno, and that was only getting stronger the more time we spent together. But to him I was still just the asshole who'd ripped him off. Like he was going to invite me to share his bed?

"I'm not going anywhere, I promise. Can I have my phone back, though?"

He hesitated and asked, "Why do you want it?"

"I'm going to call in a swat team to rescue me from my jailer." When he rolled his eyes, I asked, "What do you think I plan to do with it? I'd like to read one of my ebooks, maybe take a look at the news. If I get really fancy, I might even play a few rounds of Bejeweled."

"You're not going to sleep?" Even though he asked the question, he pulled my phone from his pocket and handed it to me, along with the rest of my belongings. Apparently he'd decided to fully commit to the belief that I wasn't going to leave.

"Falling asleep is a process."

"Normally I'd agree, but I'm dead on my feet. I told my brother I'd be there at lunchtime, so I'll see you in about three hours."

After I said good night, I continued down the hall to the guest room and got naked. I carefully hung up my suit and shirt and moved them to the bathroom, so the wrinkles could steam out. Then I took a long, hot shower. It felt incredible after spending all night in a car, followed by the grungy task of cleaning up the bar.

The potato chips were calling my name, so after my shower I wrapped a towel around my hips and went downstairs. Along the way, I took a detour through the living room and checked out the cluster of photos on the mantel. They were all of Reno with his mom and his kid brother, taken throughout the years. His love for those two was really touching.

I continued on to the kitchen and began browsing through the bags of gas station treats. I'd been acting like a petulant child when I grabbed an entire armload of chips, and I'd wanted to see what Reno would do about it. Much to my surprise, he'd indulged me. Maybe that was just because he was smart enough to pick his battles, but still.

Just then, I detected movement out of the corner of my eye and whipped my head around. At the sight of a scorpion making its way across the kitchen floor, I screamed like the victim in a slasher film and scrambled onto the countertop. Yes, I'd been warned, but the sight of an actual fucking scorpion still freaked me the hell out.

Moments later, Reno appeared in the kitchen and asked, "Are you alright? What's wrong?" He was wearing nothing but a pair of black briefs, and he was holding a machine gun, of all things.

I pointed at the scorpion, who'd frozen in place. Reno's posture relaxed, and he exclaimed, "Fucking hell, you almost gave me a heart attack! I thought Greco's men had found this place and were attacking you." He slung the weapon over his shoulder by its strap and opened a kitchen cabinet. Then he grabbed a metal colander and stuck it over the scorpion, like he was giving the thing its own personal thunder dome.

In the next instant, I shocked the hell out of both of us by bursting into tears. I didn't do it on purpose. In fact, I had no explanation for it, other than a whole bunch of things catching up to me all at once.

Reno muttered, "Oh, shit," and hurried over to me. When he picked me up, I wrapped my arms and legs around him, and he said, "You're shaking."

"I'm sorry. I don't know what's wrong with me. I don't usually cry at the drop of a hat. In fact, I barely cry at all."

He was so kind. Instead of telling me to snap out of it, he carried me out of the kitchen and said gently, "I know this isn't just about getting scared by that scorpion. I made a mistake by pulling you out of your world and dragging you all this way, then putting you in the middle of the shit I'm dealing with."

"I didn't really give you much choice."

Reno ended up carrying me upstairs, and when we reached the second floor I begged, "Please don't banish me to the guest room." I barely recognized this needy, emotional version of myself.

He brought me with him into the main bedroom and said, "I thought you'd want some privacy, but you're welcome to sleep here." After he put me down on the bed, he disappeared into a walk-in closet and emerged a few moments later without the weapon.

I curled into a ball under the covers, trying to take up as little space as possible, while he settled in so we were facing each other. He reached out and brushed my hair off my face, and he gave me a little smile before shutting his eyes.

It only took him a few seconds to fall asleep, but I was pretty wound up. I shifted around carefully while trying not to wake him, pulled the damp towel off my waist, and dropped it on the floor. Then I tried to get comfortable without flailing around like a fish on a hook.

Talking my way into his bed hadn't been the best idea. He was exhausted, and I should have just let him have some space.

I rolled onto my side so I was facing him and tucked my hand under my head. Then I took the opportunity to really study him, from his thick, black lashes to the sensual curve of his full lips.

He really was strikingly attractive, but he was a lot more than that, too. He tried to show the world a tough outer shell, but in truth he was one of the kindest people I'd ever met. I wondered why he tried so hard to pull off that tough guy persona. Was it because he wanted to follow in the footsteps of the father he'd never met? I didn't know the answer to that, and maybe he didn't, either.

Bottom line though, I was grateful he allowed me to see the real Adriano. That was probably reserved for a select few. I just couldn't figure out why I'd made the cut.

When Reno's alarm went off, I hid my face and groaned. Apparently I'd actually fallen asleep, but it felt like I'd only been out for a minute.

He reached over me and jabbed at his phone to get it to shut up. It was a relief when it fell silent. I probably would have drifted off again, except for one thing—I suddenly realized we were all tangled up together, and I was buck naked. The latter only became clear to me when he ran his hand down my back and skimmed my bare ass.

I leaned back a bit to assess the situation. I'd been using his bicep as a pillow, one of his legs was wedged between my thighs, and we were both sporting semis. Whether or not this was super awkward depended entirely on Reno's reaction.

I met his gaze and waited to see what he'd do. Never mind that I desperately wanted to kiss him. Whatever happened next had to be his decision, since I'd destroyed his trust the night we met.

It made me so fucking happy when he slid his hand around the back of my neck and pressed his lips to mine. I had no idea why he'd want this—why he'd want *me*—but I reveled in it instead of questioning it.

I never thought we'd find ourselves here again, and the chance of an encore after this one seemed next to impossible. So, if this was it—if this was the last time I ever got to be with Adriano Dombruso, I was damn well going to soak up every moment. I'd savor it, then store it away, for a time when I was alone again and all I had left was the memory of him.

Everything happened quickly after that kiss. He got naked and pushed me onto my back, and then he explored every part of me with his hands and mouth and tongue. Meanwhile, I did that thing that was always such a struggle for me—I surrendered control.

My nerves kicked in at first, but I soon realized I had nothing to worry about. Adriano wasn't going to hurt me. Just the opposite— he became totally focused on making me feel amazing.

I bucked beneath him as he sucked my cock and sent waves of pleasure rolling up my spine. I was only vaguely aware of the sounds

I was making, or the fact that I parted my legs to offer him more of me. My attention was on the gorgeous man between my thighs, and the way he was making my toes curl.

This went on for a while, until he sat up and told me, "I need to be in you."

I murmured, "Fuck yes," and sat up, too.

He grabbed a bottle of lube from the nightstand, but then he stopped short and said, "I don't have any condoms."

No, of course he didn't. The last person he'd fucked in this bed was his long-term boyfriend. I tamped down the misplaced jealousy which had flared up at that idea and said, "I have some in my wallet. I'll go get them."

I expected him to wait there, but instead he got out of bed with me. As we hurried down the hall, I asked, "Have you had an STD screening since you and your boyfriend broke up?"

"Yeah, I had one as part of my yearly physical last month. All clear." When we reached the guest room, he ducked into the connected bathroom for a towel. He returned just a few moments later and asked me, "Does this really seem like an ideal time to check your messages?"

I'd picked up my phone instead of my wallet, and when I found what I was looking for I held it up so he could read the screen. "I had an STD screening two weeks ago and was negative across the board. I don't expect you to believe me, so here's an email from the clinic with my results. I'd be fine with skipping the condom since we've both been tested, but it's your call."

He asked, "Are you really willing to take my word for it with my test results?"

"You wouldn't lie about that. You also wouldn't lie about only sleeping with two men in over four years, so I figure you're pretty low-risk to begin with."

Even though I was trying to act like I was indifferent to his decision, this was actually a big deal to me. I never had unprotected sex, but if this was our last time, I wanted…what exactly? The same thing he'd had with his ex? That wasn't quite it, and I couldn't really explain why it mattered to me to take this step with him. It just did.

It made me happy when he told me, "I'm definitely down for that."

"Great. Now, where were we?"

He pulled me to him and said, "Right about here," before claiming my mouth with a passionate kiss.

Everything revved right back up in a matter of moments. We climbed onto the bed and began kissing and jerking each other off while Reno worked me open. Once I was ready, he slicked his length before wiping his hands with the towel and tossing it aside. I tried to roll onto my hands and knees, but he picked me up and positioned me on my back, so there was no place to hide.

I held my legs apart for him, feeling vulnerable and exposed. Despite myself, I tensed up when his tip pressed against my hole, but just like our first time he was so patient. "Let yourself relax," he said. "You've got this, baby." I met his gaze, and he smiled at me as he reached up and brushed my hair back.

I fought back a little whimper when the tip of his thick cock finally slipped inside me. He held still to give me time to adjust and murmured, "That's it, beautiful. You're doing great."

He kept up the gentle pep talk while I concentrated on relaxing my muscles. I didn't know why I found it surprising that he was exactly the same—just as kind and considerate as the first time we'd done this. What did I think, that he was going to treat me like shit because I'd ripped him off? He wasn't like that.

Eventually, I opened up enough to take all of him. He slid in balls deep, then almost all the way out again before he began to fuck me. Pretty soon that moment happened, the one where pleasure took the place of discomfort and I was finally able to let go. He began nailing my prostate on each upstroke, and I wrapped my legs around him and rasped, "Harder."

Reno startled me by picking me up, climbing out of bed, and pushing my back against the wall. In one fluid movement, he impaled me on his cock. And then he gave me exactly what I'd asked for.

I wrapped my arms and legs around him, holding on for dear

life as he pounded my ass. There was no question I'd be feeling this for days afterward, but it felt so damn good that I just didn't care.

When he said, "Look at me, Jack," I did as he asked. Everything intensified when I met his gaze. I'd never experienced such an overpowering connection with another person, and it flooded me with emotion. I almost didn't know what to do with everything I felt in that moment. I wanted to laugh and cry, and then I wanted to punch myself in the face, because what the fuck was even happening to me? I needed to get a grip.

Fortunately, my weird little emotional upheaval was quickly overshadowed by the fact that we were, in fact, right in the middle of fucking. Adriano reached between us and started jerking me off, and I stopped thinking about much of anything.

After a while, he muttered, "I'm close," and started thrusting harder still while using the wall for leverage.

He bit back a yell when he started to come, the muscles in his shoulders flexing under my hands as I held onto him. I blurted, "Fuck, Adriano," and tumbled over the edge right after him, thrusting into his palm while driving myself even harder onto his cock.

By the time it was over, both of us were shaking. He pivoted around and sat on the edge of the bed with me on his lap, and then he held me securely while we caught our breath.

I didn't want to let go. Once I did, when would I ever be able to touch him like this? We obviously couldn't stay this way forever though, so I gave myself thirty seconds to be clingy and needy, and to commit as much of this moment as I could to memory.

Before I climbed off his lap, I took Reno's face between my palms and kissed him. I put everything I had into that kiss—all I was thinking and feeling, all my needs and wants, just everything.

Then I forced myself to climb off his lap. "We should get going. I know you don't want to keep your family waiting," I mumbled, "so I'm going to get cleaned up." I didn't look back at him as I walked to the bathroom on unsteady legs.

10

Adriano

Jesus, that kiss.

Everything over the last hour had been intense and unexpected, but that just blew my mind. It reminded me of a kiss between a soldier and his one true love in wartime, right before shipping out with little chance of ever returning.

Was that what it was, a goodbye kiss? It wouldn't surprise me if Jack was planning to bolt. Being dragged into the life of a stranger like this had to be so fucking weird and uncomfortable for him.

The fact that we'd just slept together made the whole thing doubly confusing. I hadn't intended to go there again, but he was just so damn irresistible.

I sat there staring at the bathroom door for a full minute before finally making myself get up and leave the guest room. As much as I wanted to figure out what was happening between Jack and me, there was a lot to deal with here in Vegas, and I had to get my head in the game.

And I couldn't neglect my family, who'd gotten dragged into the middle of this situation. I'd told them I'd be there at lunchtime, so the first thing I did when I reached my room was send Romy a text. Then I called a local deli and placed an order.

After a quick shower, I put on a nice suit. I'd be meeting with some of my men after I saw my family, so I needed to look the part. The gun and shoulder holster concealed under my jacket were included just in case, not that I expected trouble. Greco tended to be most active at night, like the rodent he was.

Once I was dressed, I went downstairs and made some coffee. While it was brewing, I slipped a large envelope under the colander, carried the scorpion out the back door, and set it free. It was a tiny little thing, but it squared up and flicked its tail anyway, just to remind me who was in charge.

Jack joined me in the kitchen as I finished putting the lids on two travel mugs. He was dressed in his blue suit again, because what choice did he have? "I know you prefer cream and sugar in your coffee, but I'm out of almost everything, so it's black," I said, as I handed him one of the mugs.

"That's fine, thanks," he muttered, as he scanned the room. When he noticed the colander in the sink, he asked, "What happened to the alien invader?"

"I set it free."

"In here?"

"Out back. Let's get going," I said, as I draped the laptop case's strap over my shoulder. "I told my brother I'd be there at one, and we need to pick up lunch on the way."

I started to head for the door to the garage, but Jack hesitated and asked, "Are you sure I should come with you? I feel like I'm intruding on your time with your family."

"You're definitely not intruding, and you'll love my mom and brother. Everybody does. Besides, the only food in this house is the junk you got from the gas station, and you must be hungry. I placed a huge order at my favorite deli. They make the world's best potato salad, hands down." That was a pretty weak sales pitch, but what else was I going to do, order him to come with me?

He stood up straighter and managed to hide the hint of vulnerability in his eyes. "Fine," he said, "let's go. But don't blame me when this all turns terribly awkward."

"Why would it?"

He frowned as he asked, "How are you going to introduce me, Reno? As far as I can tell, you have two choices. The first is, 'hey, fam, I'd like you to meet the asshole who stole my father's irreplaceable watch. Lock up your valuables, because he's about as trustworthy as a fox in a henhouse.' I'm sure that'll go over big."

"What's my second choice?"

"Lying to them and introducing me as a friend."

"I can always introduce you as just Jack." I made jazz hands and said the last two words with a little extra flair, which accomplished my goal of making him smile.

"You went way back into the archives for that 'Will and Grace' reference."

"Yes, I did."

Jack followed me into the garage and started to head to the convertible, but I said, "We're taking the SUV, because it's a lot less conspicuous than the Caddy. I'm not sure what Greco has planned, but I don't want to make it that easy for him to find me."

Once we both climbed into the Land Rover, Jack said, "You told me Greco wants to make an example of you, because you pushed back when he tried to take over your business. Do you think he plans to kill you?"

"Yeah, but probably not right away. Word on the street is that he's into torturing his victims, really dragging out their suffering. Just shooting someone isn't enough for him."

Jack muttered, "Lovely," and turned his head to look out the passenger window as I raised the garage door and started the engine.

He was quiet on the drive into town and opted to wait outside while I went into the deli to pick up my order. I was surprised to discover he was still in the SUV when I returned, and he appeared to be sulking. "Hey, look at you," I said, in a feeble attempt at humor, "not running off at the first opportunity."

He muttered, "I promised I wouldn't do that."

After a pause, I asked, "Are you worried about something?"

Jack finally met my gaze, with something that looked a lot like anger burning in his green eyes. "No, of course not. I'm thrilled that you came back to Vegas and put yourself in the crosshairs of a psychopath who wants to torture and kill you. That was definitely the smart thing to do, instead of giving up on your illegal gambling bullshit, moving your mom and brother someplace safe like San Francisco, and trying to stay alive!"

Oh. So, he was worried about *me*.

"My brother might be willing to relocate, but my mom's stubborn as hell. She loves her bar and her regulars, and she's been building that business for close to four decades. There's no way she'd just walk away from it."

"Even if staying here ends up costing you your life?"

"It's not that cut and dried."

"It is from where I'm sitting," Jack told me. "If that bar is the only thing tying your family to Vegas, I'll go burn it down myself to save Greco the trouble! Then you can pack up your family and get out of harm's way."

"A word of advice? Maybe don't lead off with burning down the bar when you meet my mom," I said, as I turned the key in the ignition. He just sighed at that, and as I pulled out of the parking lot I told him, "I'm doing the best I can here, Jack."

"But you don't even have a plan. Greco was obviously trying to lure you back to town when he sent his people to smash up the bar, and what did you do? You took the bait."

"I never should have run away in the first place. It made me look weak and cowardly, so now Greco thinks he can walk all over me," I said. "And actually, this conversation is making me realize I do have a plan. I need to strike back, as hard as I can. It's what a man like Greco understands, and it's the only thing that'll get him to back down."

Jack muttered, "That's literally the worst plan ever in the history of plans," and went back to staring out the window.

When we reached my brother's apartment, I dodged the awkwardness of defining Jack's and my relationship by not even trying. Instead, I said, "Mom and Romy, I'd like you to meet Jack Granger. I brought him with me from San Francisco, and he helped me clean up the bar this morning. Jack, please say hello to my mother, Amanda Russo, and my kid brother Romeo Russo."

During the introductions, I studied my family. Romy was his usual sunshiny self, but Mom seemed a bit off. I tried to figure out why and looked closer. Her long, light brown hair was still damp from a shower, and she was wearing one of Romy's UNLV T-shirts with her usual jeans and boots. The shirt was big on her, so that might have been why she seemed so thin. She looked tired too, not surprisingly after being up most of the night. I felt guilty for the stress this had caused her.

"Everyone calls me Romy," my brother was saying. He smiled and shook Jack's hand while he did a quick assessment of his unexpected houseguest. Jack had managed to put himself back together flawlessly, and no one would ever guess he'd spent the night in that suit.

"And you can call me Mandy," my mom chimed in, as she took a turn looking Jack over and shaking his hand. By their reactions, it was obvious they assumed we were a couple, and I wasn't going to correct them—not right now, anyway.

Jack had stopped sulking and instead was laying on the charm and charisma. He smiled at them and said, "It's an absolute pleasure. Reno goes on and on about you both, especially you, Romy. I've never met a prouder big brother."

My mom beamed at him, and then she said, "Thanks for cleaning up the bar. I was going to tackle it this afternoon, but I'm glad it's done."

"Yeah, it's all taken care of," I told her, as I shifted a heavy shopping bag in my arms and led the way to the kitchen. "I brought lunch from Martino's, and after we eat I want to show you some tables and chairs to replace the ones that were broken. Jack and I selected a nice set, but I want to make sure you like them before I set up delivery. I also placed a liquor order with your usual distributor, and the front window is being replaced as we speak. A couple of my men are at the bar overseeing the installation, and I've scheduled teams around the clock to keep an eye on the place."

"That's great," my mom said, as Romy grabbed some plates

from the cupboard and we gathered around his vintage kitchen table. "But you don't really think it's necessary to have people watch the bar, do you? That man you're feuding with already sent his message, so to speak. Why would he come back?"

"I'm not sure he will, but my people might as well keep an eye on things. They're all still getting paid during this temporary pause in my business, so why not give them something to do?" Someone knocked on the front door just then, and I stopped unpacking the deli containers and asked my brother, "Are you expecting someone?"

Romy looked guilty as he told me, "Ford said he'd drop by. He heard about the bar and called me to make sure Mom was okay."

I frowned at that and called after him as he went to answer the door, "Why would my ex call you and not me to ask about Mom?"

My mother answered for him. "Maybe because the last time you spoke to him, you called Ford a stuck up prick."

"I've spoken to him since then and called him worse."

My mom ignored that and said, "Besides, why wouldn't he call Romy? You know those two became good friends while you were dating, and just because you broke up with him doesn't mean we all did."

"Yes, it does. That's exactly what it means." I shot my mom a look and added, "Don't tell me you've been palling around with him, too."

She shrugged at that and began peeling the lids off the takeout containers I was lining up on the table. "I wouldn't describe it as palling around, exactly. He comes by the bar once or twice a week to say hello, and last Sunday he took me to brunch, because a new place opened up that we both wanted to try."

I muttered, "Fuck my life," under my breath as Ford breezed into the kitchen. He looked like he'd just stepped off a yacht in his pink polo shirt, white pants, and expensive sunglasses, which he moved to the top of his bleached blond head.

He went straight to my mom and gave her a big hug as he asked, "Are you really okay, Mandy? Romy said you were, but I wanted to see you for myself." He was such a suck-up.

"I'm perfectly fine, sweetie," she said, as she patted his back. "Don't worry about me."

I was struck by the extremely immature thought that my mother liked my ex better than me. Well, why wouldn't she? He was every parent's dream son-in-law, a rich, handsome doctor.

When he finally let go of my mother, he turned his attention to Jack and flashed his perfect smile as he said, "Hi, there. I'm Doctor Stanford Gaines, but my friends call me Ford. And you are?" I'd been right to call him a fucking stuck up prick, dropping his title like that for literally no reason.

Jack's response was priceless. He still oozed charm, but there were daggers in his eyes as he squared his shoulders, shook Ford's hand, and said, "Hi, Stanford. I'm Jack. Just Jack." I cleared my throat to cover a laugh. It was such a subtle way of calling out Ford for title-dropping, while letting him know they weren't friends and weren't about to be.

My nosy ex started to ask, "And are you and Reno—"

"We're lovers," Jack informed him, raising his chin defiantly, as if he was daring Ford to question it. He was barely five-foot-nine to Ford's six-one, but he held himself like a king indulging a peasant with the pleasure of his company. God, I loved his bravado. If he found anything even remotely intimidating about Ford, he sure as hell wasn't showing it.

"Anyway," I cut in, "as you can see, my mom is fine. Now I'm sure you have important doctor business to get to, like a round of golf or a three-martini lunch at the club." I turned to Jack and added, "Ford's a plastic surgeon, so it's not like he needs to get back to work saving lives or anything."

Only then did Ford even acknowledge I was in the room. His ice-blue eyes narrowed just a little as he turned his gaze to me and said, "Hello, Reno. You're looking well."

"I know." If he thought I was going to pay him a compliment in return, he was dead wrong.

My mom cut in with, "Why don't you join us for lunch, Ford? Reno went to Martino's, and it looks like he bought enough for ten people. I know how much you love their potato salad."

Oh, fuck no. I tried to keep my expression neutral because I didn't want to piss off my mother, but if he agreed to stay I'd have to leave. I just couldn't do this right now.

Before my ex could reply, Jack circled the table and cuddled up to me, and I put a protective arm around his shoulders. He was probably just doing that for show, but then again this all had to be incredibly uncomfortable for him, so maybe he really did want a little reassurance.

The muscles in Ford's square jaw tightened, but only for a moment. Then he smiled at my mom and said, "Thanks for the offer, Mandy, but I need to get going. I'm meeting a client at the clinic in half an hour. Poor dear lost both of her breasts to cancer, so I'm helping her regain some of her confidence through the use of implants."

Oh, nice try, Ford. Way to make it sound like his job was all about doing god's work. I asked, "Did you have to special order a believable size? I know most of your clients go for the double-Ds at a minimum, or as I like to call them, the trophy wife special."

"Be kind, Adriano." That was from my mom, who shot me a warning look.

Ford said, "Anyway, I'm off. Mandy darling, call me if you need anything at all. Reno, good to see you. And Jack, it was a pleasure meeting you." Then he turned to Romy, who'd been watching all of this with a frown, and asked, "Will you walk me out, kiddo?"

When the two of them left the kitchen, I sat down and exhaled slowly, and Jack sat beside me. "Sorry," I whispered, so Ford wouldn't overhear us from the other room. "I had no idea we'd be running into my ex today, and I know that was awkward."

"It was fucking hilarious," Jack whispered in reply, while my mom took a pitcher of iced tea from the refrigerator. "What a complete tool. 'I'm Doctor Stanford Whatever.' And then it turns out he's a plastic surgeon! I mean, I guess I get what you saw in him since he's conventionally handsome, but I don't think I've ever instantly disliked a person quite that much." I loved the way he sprinkled the word "conventionally" in there. No way was he going to pay my ex an out-and-out compliment.

I teased him with, "Maybe you're jealous," which earned me a scowl.

Romy returned to the kitchen a minute later, and as he grabbed some silverware he said, "You should really make the time to talk to Ford, bro. I know you're with Jack now, but there's no reason you and your ex can't be friends."

There was *every* reason we couldn't be friends, starting with the fact that we were completely toxic together. But I didn't want to get into that right now, so I told him I'd think about it.

As soon as we all sat down at the table, my mother flashed me a hopeful smile and asked, "So, where did you and Jack meet?"

I answered truthfully. "In a bar." Then I redirected the conversation with, "What's new with you, Mom? You've been so busy the last couple of times I've called that we've barely had a chance to catch up."

Romy answered for her. "She's dating someone. His name's Chet, and he's really nice."

My first thought was *oh no*, because this never ended well. But I said, "Oh yeah? Tell me about him."

Over lunch, I discovered that Chet was forty-eight (so, fifteen years younger than my mom, not that I was judging…much), an artist (red flag—that usually was a code word for unemployed), and divorced. When I pressed, I discovered he'd actually been divorced three times. Fucking hell.

"Please be careful," I told her. "I know you have a tendency to jump in with both feet, and I really don't want you to get hurt." She actually sighed at that, as if her track record proved me wrong somehow.

Toward the end of the meal, I brought up a topic I knew would go over like a lead balloon. I chose my words carefully as I turned to my mom and said, "Even though the bar's going to be put back together by this afternoon, I'd feel a lot better if it remained closed for a few days—just until I get this situation under control."

"I can't do that," she said. "My regulars depend on me. For some of them, it's all they have, and they count on me to be there. I can't turn my back on them."

"But if it's not safe for you—"

"It is, though," she insisted. "You have people watching the place, and like I said, that Greco fellow already sent his message. Why would he do it again?"

"I don't know. Nothing he does is predictable."

"Also, those men didn't target me or any of my customers. They just broke stuff. If they actually wanted to hurt me, they could have done that easily, but it wasn't their objective," she said.

That wasn't reassuring. I tried a few more arguments, but of course it ended exactly like I'd thought it would—with my mom digging in her heels and being stubborn. Finally, I just had to let it go, and trust that my teams of armed guards would keep her safe.

After we ate, I took out my tablet and showed Mom the table and chairs I'd selected. She browsed through the entire selection before finally settling on the style I'd picked out. As I placed an order and added rush delivery, Jack's phone buzzed. He took it from his jacket pocket and glanced at the screen before telling us, "It's my best friend, Wyatt. Please excuse me while I message him back."

He got up and went into the living room, and as soon as he was out of earshot Romy whispered, "Why didn't you tell us you're dating someone? Jack is absolutely gorgeous! And I'm sorry about inviting Ford over. I had no idea you were bringing your new boyfriend to meet us."

"I don't know what Jack is to me at this point, but he's not my boyfriend."

"Yet," my mom whispered. "You brought him with you from California, so he obviously means something to you."

"It's complicated."

"Isn't it always," Romy murmured, before finishing the last of his iced tea. Then he added, "I like Jack. He doesn't say much, but the way he looks at you is really sweet."

"How does he look at me?"

"Like you fascinate him."

I thought about that before asking, "Is that how Ford used to look at me?"

"No. He usually seemed like he was irritated." That was from my mom, and it sounded about right. She added, "Now he seems like he's full of regret."

"He still cares about you," Romy said. "When I walked him to the door, he had a million questions about you and Jack. He wouldn't ask if you didn't matter to him. But just to be clear, I'm not telling you this because I think you two should get back together. You were pretty terrible as a couple. That doesn't mean you can't be friends, though."

"Maybe, but Ford's way down at the bottom of the list of things I need to worry about right now."

"Oh, I know, and I'm just saying," my brother told me. "Between dealing with the thug that smashed up the bar and your new relationship with Jack, your plate's obviously very full."

It wasn't a relationship, but I definitely had a lot to figure out where Jack was concerned. Was it more than a mutual attraction? Did I want it to be, and if so, could I actually trust him? I hadn't been kidding when I told my mom it was complicated.

11

Jack

I sat down on Romy's dark blue, L-shaped sofa and looked around me. The apartment was definitely on the modest side, really just a box with white walls, but he'd obviously tried to make it feel like home. There were house plants and framed photos clustered around the room, and the furniture had been selected with comfort in mind.

Even though they looked nothing alike, it made me think of the pink Victorian. Oddly, a tinge of homesickness accompanied that thought. I'd only spent a week there, so that didn't make sense. But there it was.

I pulled my thoughts back to the present and took another look at the text I'd just received. Wyatt had written: *Hey J, it's been a minute. What are you up to?*

Where should I start?

Wyatt and I had been best friends since high school, and I thought of him like a brother. But just like with my mom, I didn't tell him everything. I was sure he strongly suspected I was a criminal, but we coexisted with this don't ask, don't tell unspoken rule between us.

It was just that Wyatt was this sweet, innocent guy, and I thought the truth of who exactly he'd been friends with all these years would hurt him, just like it would hurt my mom to find out what her only child had amounted to. So, while I never lied to Wyatt, I deliberately kept things vague.

That meant I was now faced with the dilemma of how to explain Adriano. I ended up writing: *Hey W, I'm currently in Vegas with a hot guy. Long story. How've you been?*

Since I'd never had a relationship, he didn't automatically assume this person and I were dating. He responded: *Forget that how've I been business. You know I need details about this hot guy. How else can I live vicariously through you?*

I worried about my friend. I didn't know if it was because he was deaf or because he was Wyatt, but he tended to live a pretty isolated existence. Most of his time was spent alone in his apartment, either playing video games or drifting around the internet. He even worked from home as a programmer, so there was very little to get him out of the house.

I told him: *He's tall, dark, and Italian, and sexy beyond words. His name's Adriano.*

I could have left it at that, but I really wanted to talk about this, so I sent another text: *I'm currently at his brother's apartment, and I just met Adriano's ex-boyfriend. Now I feel like a slug by comparison. The ex is a doctor. As if that's not enough, he's also tall and muscular with blond hair and blue eyes. He looks like a giant Ken doll.*

Wyatt replied: *Gross. I hate the Ken doll type.*

I grinned and texted: *Me, too. But how am I supposed to compete with Dr. Perfect?*

My friend's response was: *First of all, you're smoking hot. You may not be Dr. Perfect, but you're your own brand of sexy. You're like a Midwestern David Tennant.*

I laughed out loud at that as another text popped up: *Besides, who says you need to compete with this guy? He's an ex for a reason, right? The fact that you're thinking about this stuff suggests this is more than a hookup, though. So, did a miracle happen? Did you finally start dating, at the ripe old age of 34?*

I had no chance of lying about how old I was with Wyatt, since we were the same age. I wrote: *No, we're not dating. I do like him though, but I've already given him plenty of reasons not to trust me, so I doubt this'll go anywhere.*

Wyatt answered: *Think positive, dude. You never know. I'm going to let you go in a minute, since you're busy with this guy. But first I'm going to call you for proof of life.*

This was an old joke with us. We did most of our communicating by text, but then he always liked to end with a quick video call, so we could see each other and make sure the other person really was okay—like in those TV crime shows where the kidnappers sent the victim's family proof their loved one was still alive.

A few seconds later, I answered the call and my friend appeared on the screen. Wyatt was a stocky redhead with a lot of freckles, and he currently looked a bit like a mountain man, since he'd grown a full beard and was way overdue for a haircut. We waved at each other, and I signed, "Love you, bro," before we ended the call.

Reno came into the room during that last bit and took a seat at the other end of the big sectional. I snapped a photo of him, and when I sent it to Wyatt my friend replied with a string of fire emojis.

As I returned the phone to my pocket, Reno said, "So, you really do have a deaf best friend."

"Like I'd lie about that. Also, when did I tell you about Wyatt?"

"You explained why you knew sign language and demonstrated a little of it the night we met. You were saying something about being able to keep talking while giving me a blow job."

He grinned at me, and I said, "Oh. Now I remember."

"Was your friend born deaf?"

"No. He lost his hearing when he was eight years old."

"That must have been tough."

"I'm sure it was."

"So, you've been friends a long time?"

"Since we were fourteen." I tilted my head and asked, "Why all the interest?"

Reno shrugged and told me, "You don't seem to have ties to very many people, so I'm curious about the few who made the cut."

I didn't really know what to say to that, not that he was wrong. I changed the subject with, "What are we doing now?"

He turned his gaze to his hands, which were splayed out on his knees. "That's up to you. Here are your two choices. Option A is to continue allowing me to drag you all over Vegas and potentially put you in harm's way while I deal with Greco. Option B is where I drive you to the airport and buy you a first class ticket back to San Francisco."

That felt like a kick in the gut, and I muttered, "A."

He glanced at me and asked, "You're actually choosing to stay with me?"

"Yes."

"Why?"

"Why not?"

"How about the fact that it could become dangerous?"

"I'll take my chances." Reno stared at me for a long moment. To break the silence, I asked, "Why would you even suggest sending me back home? Aren't you worried I'll disappear forever with your Rolex?"

"I'm more worried about you getting hurt if Greco tracks me down."

"But that's like saying I matter more to you than your most prized possession."

"You do."

"And yet, you were willing to shoot me when you caught me stealing it."

He sighed and told me, "That gun was empty, Jack. I'd never point a loaded weapon at you. I was just trying to scare you, so you wouldn't run off. It obviously had the opposite effect, which goes to show I have no idea what I'm doing when it comes to you."

I got up and told him, "No, you really don't. Now, are we still visiting with your family, or are we moving on to our next destination?"

"Moving on. I want to see how the bar's new window looks, and I also want to be there when the furniture and liquor are delivered. Mom wanted to handle it, but I managed to convince her to take a nap and open later than usual this afternoon. It's a small victory, but I'll take it."

We went back to the kitchen, where his mom and brother were deep in conversation. They stopped talking and smiled at us, and as Reno packed his tablet back in his carrying case, he asked, "We're going to take off in a minute, but do either of you need anything before we go?" He was definitely the caretaker for his family, no doubt about it.

Romy told him they were all set, and Reno turned to his mother and said, "I think you should pack a bag and stay here for a few days, Mom. I don't like the fact that the bar's on Greco's radar now, and with your apartment directly above it—"

"I'll be fine," she said. "You even have a couple of people watching it, which is probably overkill. What could happen?"

He muttered, "I really don't want to find out. At least think about it, and I'll see you tonight."

I told Reno's family it was nice to meet them, and we started to head for the door. But Mandy called, "Jack, could you please hang back for a second?" When Reno turned to her with a raised brow, she said, "Never you mind what I have to say to your boyfriend. Go on outside, he'll be there in a minute."

He shot concerned looks at both his mom and me before muttering, "Alright," and leaving the apartment.

Romy waited until we heard the front door close before saying, "We want to give you our phone numbers, Jack, so you can keep us updated on this situation. We also want to ask you to please take care of Reno for us. We know he's downplaying his conflict with that thug, and we're worried sick about him.

"We didn't want to say that in front of him, because he'd feel terrible about worrying us. But you're with him all the time, so you'll know if he gets into trouble and needs help. That might mean calling the police on Greco if there's a confrontation, which is something Reno would never do. As an EMT, I work with the police all the time, so I've never understood why my brother thinks of them as the enemy."

Because Reno was a criminal, like me. It was obvious. I didn't know what to say to that, and I only got as far as, "I…um—"

Then Mandy chimed in, "Just keep us in the loop, Jack, and do whatever you can to make sure he's okay. That's all we ask."

I said I'd do my best and handed over my phone. Romy typed in his number, his mom's, and the bar's, which nearly doubled my total number of contacts.

Then they both walked me to the door. "It was great meeting you," Romy said with a smile. "And again, I'm sorry about inviting Reno's ex over. I never meant to make you uncomfortable."

I said, "I know, and it's fine," as I took a moment to study him. He was twenty-seven—the age I usually pretended to be—and I now realized I definitely couldn't pull it off. Romy just seemed so innocent and trusting, and I hadn't been either of those things in a very long time. If that was typical for twenty-seven, then forget about it.

He and his mom took turns giving me a hug before I left the apartment. When I got outside, I found Reno pacing in the parking lot. He stopped in his tracks when he saw me and asked, "What was that about?"

"Romy asked if I wanted to go clubbing sometime, since we're both in our twenties," I joked, and he rolled his eyes as we climbed into the SUV. "I'm obviously kidding. They just asked me to take care of you and make sure you're okay."

"How are you supposed to do that, exactly?"

"Don't ask me. I can't even take care of a house plant, let alone a big, surly gangster." He grinned as he started the engine, and I added, "I'm prepared to get very annoying and lecture you if you start skipping meals and missing sleep, though. They both gave me their phone numbers, so I can rat on you if you don't take care of yourself."

"Thank you."

"For what?"

"For being patient with all of this, and for being so charming with my family."

"I'm naturally charming, so it's not like I had a choice." That made him chuckle.

It was a five-minute drive to the bar. A worker was just finishing up the window when we arrived, and two of Reno's men were sitting in an SUV drinking coffee.

While he checked in with his people and sent them on a break, I paused on the sidewalk and asked the glass installer, "Is this window actually bulletproof?"

The guy said, "Nah, there's no such thing. This is the best product available, but it's only bullet-resistant. A single shot will penetrate the outer sheet and get stopped by the polycarbonate layer in the center. Nothing's going to stop multiple shots from a high-powered weapon, though."

I muttered, "Well, that's great."

After the lookouts and the worker took off, I followed Reno into the bar, which was hot and stuffy. He said, "Make yourself at home while I turn on the lights and the air conditioning."

I stood around awkwardly while he went in the back. A few moments later, about a third of the lights came on, illuminating the bar area and bathing the rest of the room in a soft, golden glow. Then some retro Rat Pack-style music began to play.

I took off my jacket and rolled up my sleeves, since it was going to take the air conditioner a minute to do its thing. When Reno came back, he was carrying a large bowl of lemons and limes. A random thought occurred to me, and I asked, "Why wasn't your house six thousand degrees inside when we arrived?"

"I have everything running off an app, and I turned the air conditioning on an hour before we got there. I keep trying to convince my mom to let me install the same thing here, but she's not big on technology. It's about the only way she shows her age."

He stepped behind the bar, and I took a seat and said, "Speaking of your mom, I was going to mention how odd it is that you and she are the same age."

He smiled and told me, "She's actually sixty-three, but you're right that she doesn't look a day over forty. Don't tell her I let that slip."

"Me? Never. As you know, I'm a big fan of lying about your age."

While we were talking, he took off his suit jacket and hung it on a hook behind the bar. A sick feeling welled up in me, and I froze at the sight of his gun. When he saw my expression, he removed the shoulder holster and stashed it and the weapon beneath the bar. Then he said, "You really hate guns, don't you?"

I nodded. "The first time I ever saw one, I was eight years old. The thug my father hired to track down my mom waved it in her face and made her cry. I've hated and feared them ever since. Every time I see one, it takes me right back to that moment."

Reno muttered, "Shit," and took my hand. "I'm sorry, Jack. I—"

"There's no need to apologize. I know why you're carrying it, and I wouldn't want you to be defenseless if Greco catches up to you."

When I looked up at him, he let go of my hand and gently ran his knuckles across my cheekbone. Then he took a step back and cleared his throat before asking, "Want a drink? I can make just about anything…well, as long as it involves gin or vermouth. Those were the two bottles that didn't get smashed up last night, and the liquor delivery's still about an hour out."

"Did the beer survive?"

He grinned and poured two pints, and we clinked our glasses together before taking a drink. After that, he pulled out a cutting board and a knife and started making quick work of the citrus fruit as he explained, "I thought I'd get some of the prep work done while we're waiting on the deliveries, just to make tonight easier on my mom."

"You're surprisingly good at that."

"I've been helping out here since I was a kid—back in the kitchen at first, obviously, so we wouldn't get shut down for allowing a minor in a bar. I did most of the cooking for our family too, after Romy was born."

"But you were only ten at the time."

"Yeah, but Mom was busy trying to keep this place afloat, and I wanted to help."

My heart went out to Reno. I knew what it was like to want to contribute to the household at a young age, but he'd had the added pressure of a younger sibling in the mix. That was a lot of responsibility for a kid.

I asked, "So, how'd you go from being the world's youngest barback to running an illegal gambling empire?"

"While I was in high school, I started working for the neighborhood bookie to earn a few bucks. Then in my early twenties, I started working at one of the big casinos on the strip. Pretty soon, I started running poker games out of my apartment, and it grew from there."

"That reminds me—are you worried about Greco going after your place of business?"

He shrugged and explained, "I moved to a new location every month, so there isn't a building for him to target. It was how I stayed ahead of the police. Only established patrons would be informed of the new address."

"It sounds like a pretty complex operation."

"It was," he said. "There were a lot of moving parts, coupled with the constant threat of law enforcement catching up to us."

"So, when is it enough?"

He paused what he was doing and looked at me as he asked, "What do you mean?"

"You've obviously made a lot of money. The signs of your success are written all over you, from your pair of high-priced cars to those custom-made suits. Over lunch, your brother mentioned you put him through college, but now he's a grown man with a full-time job. Your mom seems like she's doing well with her business too, so it's not like you need to support either of them. Given that, when do you decide you've had enough of the illegal gambling game and walk away? Because sooner or later, your luck's bound to run out. Either the cops or the FBI will catch you, or Greco or some other thug will decide to eliminate the competition once and for all. Is it still worth the risk?"

He put down the knife and leaned on the edge of the bar as he said, "I'd actually decided months ago that this was going to be my last year. You're right that I've made a lot of money, and I was smart enough to put away plenty for the future—including a retirement fund for my mom, if she ever decides that's something she wants to do.

"So now, I'm ready to walk away, but I can't do that until this situation with Greco is resolved. I have no idea how I'm supposed to do that, though. I don't even know where to find him." After a pause, he met my gaze. There was raw emotion in his eyes when he admitted, "I hate this so much, Jack. I can't stand feeling helpless, and I hate the fact that the choices I've made could come back to harm my family. I hate letting you see me like this, too. My whole life, I've been confident and in charge. I built an empire from literally nothing, and I was proud of it. I wanted to show you that version of me, not this pathetic husk of a man."

"Why do you care what I think?"

He broke eye contact and muttered, "I just do."

"For what it's worth, I believe you're a strong, intelligent, capable man who's been put in an impossible situation."

Just then, someone knocked on the door, and I jumped. "It's okay," Reno said. "It's just the liquor wholesaler."

"You sure?"

He nodded and stepped around the bar. "My mom's been using the same guy for nearly twenty years."

I turned around and saw a blue delivery van parked out front. Reno let in an old man with a clipboard and a hand cart, and over the next few minutes, they brought in several cases of liquor. I offered to help, but they both told me they had it under control.

Once the guy took off, Reno transferred the sliced fruit to some lidded containers, then began unpacking the boxes and lining up the bottles on the wooden shelves behind the bar. He also kept refilling my beer glass whenever I hit bottom, so I was feeling no pain.

After a while, he said, "I love this song," and turned up the music. He was obviously making an effort to lighten the mood, and I was more than happy to let him.

He started singing along to "Mack the Knife" and swaying his hips, and I grinned and told him, "You were born in the wrong era."

"Oh, I know." He hurried around the bar and pulled me to my feet as he said, "Dance with me, Jack."

I laughed as he swung me around and went back to belting out the lyrics. I had no idea how to dance to this type of music, but it didn't really matter. Reno didn't need me to impress him with fancy footwork. He just needed me to enjoy the moment with him.

A Sinatra song was up next, and he serenaded me with, "The Way You Look Tonight." He knew every word, and he had a great voice. That was followed by a slower song I didn't recognize. Reno stopped singing and pulled me close, and I rested my head on his shoulder as we swayed to the music.

When he nuzzled my hair, I looked up at him. We watched each other for a few moments, and then he leaned in and kissed me tenderly. I'd never experienced a kiss like that, one that sent a sensation all the way down to my toes.

I whispered, "What are we doing, Adriano?"

"Honestly? I have no idea. All I know is that I like you, and that being with you feels really good." He ran his knuckles down my cheek and asked, "Can we just enjoy this, without trying to label or explain it? Everything in my life is complicated right now, so it'd be great to keep this simple."

I said, "Sure, we can do that," but there wasn't anything simple about it. I was falling for Adriano Dombruso, and I was falling hard. I'd never felt like this about anyone before. It was scary and overwhelming, and it was also totally undeniable.

12

Adriano

I really didn't understand why Jack opted to stay with me instead of returning to San Francisco. He spent the entire day letting me drag him from one place to another, and that couldn't have been very interesting for him.

We started with lunch at my brother's apartment, followed by a return trip to the bar to finish getting it back together. In the late afternoon, I had a meeting with my inner circle—the five people on my payroll I trusted the most. I was hoping one of them had some ideas about how to deal with Greco, but ultimately I was left without any solutions.

From there, Jack and I went back to the bar for a while. My mom arrived and rearranged all the liquor bottles I'd set up for her, and she closely inspected the tables and chairs that had just been delivered before finally deciding they'd do.

I left four armed men guarding the bar, two in back and two out front. They were fairly conspicuous, so I hoped that would deter a repeat performance—not that I really expected Greco to smash up the bar again. He'd definitely try to lash out at me, no doubt about it. But by now he probably knew I was back in town, so I assumed he'd try to come for me directly.

That worried me, not because I was concerned for my own safety, but because of Jack. He was constantly by my side, and I hated the thought of him getting hurt if and when Greco finally tracked me down.

Then again, Jack was a survivor, and he definitely knew how to take care of himself. When the shit hit the fan, I fully expected him to run and hide and keep himself safe. Besides, I really didn't think Greco was just going to gun me down, not when he could have the fun of capturing and torturing me. That meant Jack was probably okay by my side, but I worried about him anyway.

In the early evening, we made a quick stop for some groceries before returning to my house out in the desert. As I set the alarm system, Jack asked, "Do you think Greco knows about this place?"

"No. I think if he did, he would have burned it down while I was gone, just out of spite. I bought it through a holding company that's impossible to trace back to me, so I assume we're pretty safe out here."

He nodded at that, and after we piled the shopping bags on the kitchen counter he said, "You mentioned some clothes up in the guest room closet. I'm going to go change, because I'm getting pretty sick of this same suit and shirt."

"I'll take you clothes shopping tomorrow, but help yourself to whatever you want in the meantime. My closet's fair game, too."

He thanked me before leaving the kitchen. Once he was gone, I took off my jacket, then removed the holster and gun and stashed them in a drawer. Now that I knew why he had such a negative reaction to guns, I really didn't want to keep traumatizing him.

I'd finished putting away the groceries and had started on dinner when he returned to the kitchen. He was wearing one of my light gray T-shirts, which was enormous on him, along with a pair of gym shorts, and he looked adorable. I ran my gaze from his bare feet to his slightly tousled hair and grinned. Meanwhile, he scanned the floor, probably on the lookout for another scorpion.

When he sat down on one of the barstools at the kitchen island, I put a glass of white wine in front of him and said, "I'm making pasta primavera with cream sauce. I wanted comfort food tonight, and to me that means carbs. If it doesn't sound good to you, I can make you something else."

"It sounds great. I'm always grateful for a homecooked meal, and I'm definitely not picky."

"I'm the same way," I said. "The bar went through a rough patch when I was about six or seven, and my mom and I were barely scraping by. Living on a grocery budget of ten dollars a week taught me to be grateful for whatever was put in front of me."

"We were lucky, because my mom found a job in a mom and pop grocery store after we got settled in Kansas. In fact, she still works there. It was great, because she got first dibs on the clearance bin. Some nights, we'd play mystery meal with cans that didn't have labels. Would it be corn with a side of peaches for dinner? Or green beans with a side of even more green beans? Nobody knew until the cans were opened. Maybe that should have been depressing, but as a kid I actually enjoyed it. Ma played it up and made me think it was a fun game."

I told him, "She sounds like a good mom."

"She is. She's also a good person. She tries so hard to make the world a better place and is always doing volunteer work in the community, on top of her fulltime job. She devotes her time to dogs, kids, the elderly—if there's a way to help, she's all over it." Jack looked like he was getting emotional, so he took a sip of wine and changed the subject. "Speaking of helping, give me something to do, so we can get dinner on the table."

"If you want to, you can chop the vegetables that are drying beside the sink. First though, why don't you put on some music?" I opened an app and handed him my phone as I explained, "The house has a built-in sound system that's linked to my online Spotify account, so pick a playlist."

He took the phone from me and chuckled as he scrolled through the list. "Oh, of course. We've got Rat Pack, Rat Pack in Vegas, Rat Pack Live, Dean Martin, Sammy Davis Junior, Sinatra, more Sinatra—you, my friend, are stuck in a rut."

"Yeah, but I like my rut."

"I'm logging onto my playlists," Jack said. "Not that I don't enjoy your stuff, but I think it'd be good for you to branch out a little."

A moment later, the Spice Girls started playing in surround-sound, and Jack flashed me a huge smile. I shook my head and said, "No way," as I tried to take my phone back, but he leapt up and held it out of reach.

"Yes! This is happening, so stop being uptight and enjoy it."

"Don't tell me you actually like this."

"Of course I do," he said. "Why wouldn't I?"

"Because you're not a twelve-year-old girl."

"And you're not a seventy-five-year-old senior citizen, but look at your musical taste!"

"I have great taste," I insisted.

"So do I, and if you stop being biased and listen, you'll realize this is such a good song." With that, he turned up the volume and proceeded to dance around the kitchen while singing along to "Wannabe," loudly and badly.

It made him so happy that I decided to let him have his fun. I even ended up tapping my foot to the beat at one point, and when he discovered that he yelled, "Ah ha!"

"Okay, so it's actually a really catchy song," I conceded, which delighted him.

He turned down the volume a bit when that song ended, but he kept shaking his hips to the rest of his Spice Girls playlist while we stood side-by-side chopping vegetables. Once that task was done, it only took me a few minutes to get the rest of the dish completed, and then we sat down to big bowls of pasta at the kitchen island.

There was something touching about the way Jack ate. He savored every mouthful and heaped it with praise, as if it was the best thing he'd ever had. Then he grinned at me and asked, "Would you judge me if I licked the bowl?"

I got up and cut a slice of French bread for him as I said, "No, but maybe this is a better approach." He beamed at me before using the bread to mop up the last of the sauce.

"I'm way too full now," he said, when he finally sat back and patted his stomach, "but wow was that good. Thank you for dinner."

"My pleasure."

Jack helped me clean up and load the dishwasher, and then he glanced at me uncertainly and said, "You must be really tired, since you barely slept last night. Are you going straight to bed?"

I shook my head. "I need to unwind first."

"Want some company?"

"Definitely. Let's go upstairs, so I can change into something more comfortable."

I took his hand as we left the kitchen, and he held on tightly. Along the way, I scrolled through the app on my phone with my free hand and shut off the lights on the first floor, then the sound system.

When we got upstairs, he asked to borrow a phone charger. I found a spare in my nightstand and handed it over as he asked, "Will I be sleeping in the guest room tonight?"

"Only if you want to. I'd prefer it if you slept here, with me, but it's your call."

"So you can keep an eye on me?" He seemed so young at times, especially when he forgot to hide his vulnerability under his usual swagger.

"So we can keep each other company."

He smiled at me and plugged in his phone while I went to change. When I returned a couple of minutes later dressed in sweats, a T-shirt, and a hoodie, he was sitting primly on the bench at the foot of the bed with his hands folded in his lap.

I asked, "Can I show you something?"

He said, "Sure," but when I handed him the sweatshirt I was carrying, his expression turned suspicious. "If this thing you want to show me is outside with the scorpions, I'm changing my answer to no thank you."

"It's outside, but not at ground level." He still looked skeptical, so I said, "Trust me, Jack. I think this is something you're going to like."

Ultimately his curiosity won out, and he put on the sweatshirt and followed me to the den at the back of the second floor. One wall was lined with bookshelves, and there was also a TV, a large sofa, and a built-in wet bar.

Jack made a bee-line for the books. He plucked one from the shelves and began reading the back cover, and I grinned and said, "That's not actually what I wanted to show you, but if you want to, we can spend some time here when we come back inside."

With that, I opened the sliding glass door at the back of the room and wheeled an upholstered chaise lounge out onto the large balcony. Jack followed me as far as the doorway, but he raised a brow and said, "It's cold out there. Why not stay in this fabulous room, which has books and a couch and far less chance of anything horrible flying at us?"

"Scorpions don't fly."

"No shit, but moths do. I bet you get nice, big mutant ones out here in the desert."

"We'll be safe from the moths. I guarantee it."

"How can you possibly guarantee that?"

"Because I'm planning to turn off every light in the house, so there won't be anything to attract them."

He looked even more skeptical. "So, your plan is not just to sit in the cold, but the cold and dark?"

I collected a blanket from the back of the couch, then went out onto the balcony and said, "Exactly. Come join me, and close the door behind you."

I pulled my phone from my pocket and turned down the lights in the den. Then I got comfortable on the chaise with the blanket over me and waited. Jack stalled and grumbled for a minute before finally doing as I asked.

"Where am I supposed to sit? You're taking up the whole fainting couch."

"It's a chaise, but sure, call it that if you want," I said. "And I was thinking you'd sit on my lap, if that's okay with you."

He lifted a corner of the blanket and straddled me, and as he buried his face in my shoulder he said, "I didn't know there'd be cuddling. Next time, lead off with that."

"I will."

I turned off all the lights before putting the phone beside us on the lounge chair. Then I wrapped my arms around him and let myself relax. After a moment, Jack raised his head and muttered, "It's pitch black."

"Yup."

"I mean, like, alarmingly so."

"You're fine, doll face. I've got you."

"Okay, but why are we out here recreating a scene from a horror movie?"

"I'll show you in a minute," I told him, as I held him securely. "We just need to give our eyes a little time to adjust."

He tucked his head beneath my chin, and as I rubbed his back I could feel him start to relax. After a while, I kissed the top of his head. One of his hands slid to my face, and he patted all around it to get his bearings, which I thought was pretty funny. Once he located my mouth, he sat up a bit and kissed me. I grinned against his lips before deepening the kiss.

Then I said softly, "Turn around and look up at the sky, Jack."

He shifted around so he was sitting between my thighs, and then he leaned against me and murmured, "Oh, wow." The back of the house faced the open desert, so there was nothing to dim the jaw-dropping view of the night sky. He reached out and traced the river of stars above us as he whispered, "I've never seen the Milky Way before, except in pictures. It feels like I'm dreaming."

I wrapped my arms around his shoulders and said, "This is my favorite thing about living out here, and a big reason why I haven't abandoned the house and moved back to the city."

"I get it. This is extraordinary."

We both fell silent as we took it all in. After a while, I told him, "I want to bring you back here to see the meteor showers. There's one in December, but the one in summer is even better."

When he shifted around to face me, he bumped my phone and lit up the screen. In its faint glow, I saw his look of surprise as he asked, "You think we'll be together then?"

I'd said more than I'd intended. It wasn't like me to just put it all out there, so I tried to reel it back in with, "I hope so."

Instead of replying, he hugged me tightly. The phone powered back down, and once again, we were in darkness. After a moment, I felt him shiver, so I said, "Maybe we should go back inside."

We both got ready for bed, and once we were under the covers I drew him into my arms. He was uncharacteristically quiet, but that was probably because he was tired. Lord knew I was, too.

I settled in and said, "Good night, Jack."

He whispered, "I want you to know this time with you has meant the world to me." I kissed his forehead, and then I closed my eyes and let sleep pull me under.

When I awoke the next morning, I was alone in bed. A glance at my phone told me it was nearly nine a.m. Since I'd slept in, I figured Jack was probably in the kitchen, making himself some breakfast.

I used the bathroom and brushed my teeth before going downstairs. But instead of finding Jack, I found a note on the kitchen counter. All it said was:

I decided to go back to San Francisco. You're going to think I stole your Cadillac, but I only borrowed it. I'll leave it with valet parking at one of the hotels on the Strip before I take the bus home. I don't know which hotel yet, but I'll message Romy and let him know, since I don't have your number. The valet ticket will be at the hotel's front desk, in an envelope with your name on it.

Also, I swear to you I'm going to get your watch back. It's the first thing I'll do when I get home. I'll send it to your Vegas address by certified mail, since it looks like you might be there a while.

Please stay safe, Adriano. You mean more to me than you'll ever know.

I didn't care about the car or the watch. All I cared about was Jack, and I needed to know why he'd suddenly decided to slip out in the middle of the night like that. Why didn't he tell me he was going? And did he ever plan to see me again? The note left me with a million questions and an ache in my chest.

The thought occurred to me that maybe he'd only left a minute ago, so maybe I could still catch him. I rushed to the front door and threw it open, which set off the alarm. It kept shrieking as I ran out into the middle of the street and looked all around.

But he was long gone. Of course he was. He'd probably left hours ago.

I pushed my hair out of my eyes and yelled, "What the fuck, Jack?"

13

Jack

The pre-dawn sky was just beginning to turn pink as I let the big convertible roll down the driveway and out into the street. I ran back into the garage and entered the alarm code, which I'd noted when we first arrived. Then I hurried to the Cadillac, shut the garage door with the remote, and started the engine.

I drove out to the main road and made it about a mile before I started freaking out. It was so bad that I had to pull over, for fear of driving into a ditch.

Part of me wanted to go back, right the hell now. Adriano was a sound sleeper, and he probably had no idea I'd taken off. I could tear up the note and climb back into bed. He'd never know.

But then there was that other part of me, the one that had kept me up all night, worrying—about getting too attached to Adriano, about making myself vulnerable, about setting myself up to get not just hurt, but devastated if he didn't want me the way I wanted him.

Whenever I really wanted something, it always ended in disappointment. In fact, most of my life was nothing more than one letdown after another. Over the years, they'd chipped away at me, until my thick skin was worn down to nothing more than the flimsiest veneer. I acted like I was strong and tough, but in reality I was fragile and terrified of getting hurt.

I took a few deep breaths before pulling back onto the empty stretch of road. Okay, so it had been cowardly to leave like this, but I'd been too scared to be up front with him and talk about my fears. I'd only end up admitting how hard I was falling for him.

And then what? There was no way he'd want me. Right now, he was distracted and stressed out from this situation with Greco, and he was probably reaching out to me just because I was there. That had to be the explanation.

Once his life returned to normal, he'd wonder what the hell I was doing in it. He'd remember the way I'd betrayed him on the night we met, and he'd realize he couldn't be in a relationship with someone so untrustworthy.

Either that, or he'd just realize I wasn't good enough for him, plain and simple. And then where would I be? How could I pick up the pieces after something like that?

It was all too much to think about, so I tried to just concentrate on driving.

When I got back into town, I drove down the Strip with its surreal landscape—past a fake Egyptian pyramid and its huge Sphynx, a castle, a pretend New York skyline with its own Statue of Liberty, a mock Eiffel Tower, a pirate ship—all of it as out of place here as I was.

It was so quiet. There were still people gambling inside those giant casinos, unsure if it was night or day, but out here there was almost no one. The only vehicles on the road were a street sweeper, a cab, and me in this giant boat of a convertible. At least the Caddy looked right at home.

When I ran out of casinos, I turned around and started making my way back up the Strip. After a while, I randomly pulled into the driveway for Caesar's Palace, with its fake coliseum and towering, flashing billboard. But instead of heading to the valet station, I pulled into the labyrinth of underground self-parking, found a space, and cut the engine. Then I climbed into the back seat and curled into a ball.

I felt nauseous, and exhausted, and like I really wanted to cry. I hated this part of myself—the part that got scared so easily and ran like a startled bunny when I thought I might get hurt. I'd worked hard over the years to make myself into a survivor, someone so much tougher than this. But it was all an illusion.

～

I ended up falling asleep, waking abruptly when a noisy group of revelers hurried past on their way to the casino. I sat up and scrubbed my palms over my face before taking my phone from my pocket and turning it on. I'd decided to power it down before I left Reno's house. If he decided to call and yell at me, I really wasn't up for it.

When the screen lit up, I saw it was almost ten a.m. I also saw I had fifteen calls from the same unknown number starting around nine, and one voice mail. Obviously Adriano had gotten my number from his brother.

Might as well get it over with. I played the voice mail and was surprised by the tenderness in Adriano's voice. He said, "I don't know what made you run off, Jack. I also don't know what time you left or how far you've gotten, but please come back. Let's not wait until we're both in San Francisco to talk this out. I'll be at my mom's bar starting at about ten a.m. She was tired, so I'm doing her lunch set-up for her. Anyway…please just come talk to me. I really care about you, and I need you here with me so we can fix whatever's wrong."

That was completely unexpected. I thought he'd be pissed off about his car, and that he'd totally assume I'd stolen it—especially because it had been a few hours, and I hadn't messaged his brother with instructions on where to find it.

He was such a good person, but I already knew that. It actually made this a lot harder. If he'd yelled at me and gotten upset about the car, it would have been infinitely easier to run away.

With a sigh, I sent a text—not to Adriano, but to my best friend. It said: *I've totally blown it with that guy I told you about.*

Wyatt responded moments later with: *How do you think you blew it?*

I wrote: *I got scared and ran away.*

His reply was simply: *So, run back.*

I told him: *I'm still scared, though.*

The three dots on my screen bounced for half a minute before I received the next message: *So what? Everything's scary—life, relationships, caring about people. But you're strong enough to face your fears.*

I replied: *Am I, though?*

His answer surprised me: *You're the strongest and bravest person I know, Jack.*

I wrote: *Okay but to be fair, you're kind of a hermit and don't really know a lot of people.*

He sent me an emoji that was rolling its eyes, but then he added: *Okay, you're right. But still, you're stronger than you realize. Also, you obviously really like this guy, or you wouldn't be concerned about running away. So, go fix it, and report back.*

He made it sound so simple, and maybe it was. Maybe I hadn't done irreparable damage yet. I wrote: *Thanks, Wyatt. I'm going to go talk to him. I'll let you know what happens.* I climbed into the driver's seat and started the engine as a final text popped up. It was a string of clapping hands, cheer emojis, and thumbs up.

I had no idea what I was going to say to Adriano, and as I drove to the bar, no brilliant ideas suddenly presented themselves to me. I ended up parking around back to buy myself some time and checked my reflection in the rearview mirror.

If only I didn't look so ragged. After I tried finger-combing my hair, I brushed at my wrinkled suit and shirt, which had definitely seen better days by this point. None of this could be helped though, and I needed to quit stalling.

My heart was pounding as I walked around to the front of the building. Adriano's SUV was the only car in the parking lot. I paused in front of the tall picture window and watched him for a few moments as I took a deep breath.

His back was to me. All the chairs were upside down on the tabletops, and he was mopping the floor. I noted absently that he was wearing jeans and a black T-shirt. This was the first time I'd ever seen him out in public in anything besides a nice suit.

Adriano flinched and spun around when I tapped on the glass. Then his expression turned to one of relief. He dropped the mop into the bucket before hurrying to the door and unlocking it for me.

When I stepped inside, he drew me into an embrace. Despite myself, I stiffened up a little, so he let go right away. We stood there awkwardly for a moment, until he said, "Come in. Be careful, the floor's wet and slippery."

He locked the door behind me as I wandered into the bar. I felt ridiculous, embarrassed, and guilty for running off the way I had, and I kept my back to him as I whispered, "I'm sorry."

"It's okay."

I gripped the edge of the bar top and shook my head. "It's not, though. I should have stayed and talked to you, but running away is my default. When I get scared, I run."

"What scared you, Jack? Was it the situation with Greco? If so, I totally get that. It's why I offered to send you someplace safe until this blows over. But that doesn't explain leaving without saying goodbye."

"It's not that. I just…I don't know how to do this."

"Do what?"

How could I explain this? I didn't know how to do any of it— how to allow myself to be vulnerable, how to be in a relationship, how to take a chance and risk heartbreak.

I turned to face him as I searched for the words. Reno was standing about five feet away, and there was so much pain in his eyes. I wanted to run to him and grab him in a hug and apologize. But just then, I noticed something behind him and shifted my gaze to the picture window.

Four huge men were right out front. They were dressed in black, and they were armed. Fear and panic slammed into me as they raised their weapons. Then time seemed to slow down.

When they began to fire the guns, it didn't sound the way it did on TV. Not really. It was more of a popping sound, followed by the crackle of glass. The first three shots hit and created concentric circles in the window, like drops of water making ripples in a pond.

That window wasn't going to hold, and Reno was just starting to react. He flinched, and then he began to turn toward the sound.

He was right in the line of fire.

I lunged at him and shoved him to the floor, a split second before the window shattered. Suddenly, there was searing pain, and I was falling.

Then there was nothing at all.

14

Adriano

At first, I didn't know what was happening.

Jack was standing with his back to me, trying to explain what was going on, why he'd left. Then he turned around, and a moment later there was pure terror on his face. That was followed almost immediately by the sound of gunfire and a weird, crackling sound I couldn't place.

In the next instant, he lunged forward and shoved me to the floor—right before the front window shattered. I covered my head as glass rained down on us.

When I looked up again, Jack was face-down on the floor. There was blood, and he wasn't moving. *Oh god.*

I yelled his name and tried to go to him, but two men grabbed my arms. I shook them off and punched one of them in the face.

The last thing I saw was a third man swinging the butt of his gun at my head, right before everything went black.

15

Jack

As near as I could tell, I'd ended up slipping, falling, and knocking myself unconscious. When I came to, I was all alone.

I got up and staggered to the broken window. There was no sign of Adriano or those men with the guns. Fucking hell.

My head and my arm were pounding. I touched a spot on my bicep that felt like it was on fire. There was blood on my fingertips when I pulled my hand away.

I took a few shaky steps back into the bar and dropped to my knees. The room was spinning, but I couldn't pass out again. Not when Adriano needed help.

I pulled my phone from my pocket and called the first person I could think of. Romy answered on the second ring with, "Hey, Jack. Did you and Reno kiss and make up? He called me this morning, and—"

"Romy, I need help. They took Reno."

His tone of voice changed in an instant, from cheery to dead serious. "Who did?"

"They had to have been Greco's men, four big guys with guns. I think…I think I was shot." My arm hurt so bad. Blood was running down my hand and dripping off my fingertips.

"Where are you?"

"Your mom's bar."

Romy spoke to someone who was there with him. Then he came back on the line and told me, "I'm on my way, and Mom's dialing 911. Stay with me, Jack."

"Okay."

"Was Reno shot, too?"

I looked around and said, "The only blood I see is coming from me, so I don't think so."

"Where are you injured?"

"My arm. It really hurts."

"Listen to me, Jack," he said. "I need you to put pressure on the wound. Can you do that? Grab a towel or something and tie it around your arm if you can, or at least press it to the spot that's bleeding. I'm going to be there in five minutes, and Mom says an ambulance is on the way."

I struggled to my feet and mumbled, "Okay, I'm up and getting a towel. I hit my head, so everything's kind of swirly. Hang on, I'm going to put you in my pocket while I go do this."

I dropped the phone into the pocket of my suit jacket and clutched my injured arm as I made my way behind the bar. Once I found a dish towel, I sat down on the floor and wound it around my bicep. I had to use my teeth to cinch it, but I finally managed to get it tied.

That had taken a lot of effort, and I slumped against the shelves beneath the register. Then I noticed Reno had brought his laptop case with him. It was sitting open on one of the shelves, and his journal was sticking out.

As the sound of sirens became audible in the distance, something occurred to me. The cops probably weren't going to be able to help Reno. If they knew where to find a criminal like Greco, wouldn't they have done it already? Adriano's men didn't know where to find him, either.

So, maybe it was going to take someone more powerful, someone with better connections, who understood the workings of the criminal underworld.

I pulled the journal from the case and got blood all over the pages as I leafed through it. Finally, I found the information he'd gathered on the Dombruso family. There were addresses and phone numbers to go with most of the names.

I grabbed my phone, hung up on Romy, and dialed the first number on the page with shaking hands. It was for someone named Stana Dombruso. The note beside her name said, "Paulie's mother."

The room started spinning, and I pressed my eyes shut and tried to will myself to remain conscious as a recording played. It was a woman's voice, but I was too out of it to pay attention. When I heard a beep, I said, "You don't know me, but I'm Jack Granger, and I'm calling because of a man named Adriano Dombruso. I don't think you know him either, but his dad was Paulie Dombruso. I don't have much proof of that, except that Paulie left him a real nice watch, a platinum Rolex. The back was engraved with three initials in a diamond shape, P-D-A.

"I hope I'm making sense. I've been shot and I'm probably going to pass out soon, so it's hard to think straight. The thing is, Adriano needs your help. He just got abducted by this awful gangster named Mario Greco, and he's going to be killed if we don't do something. We were at his mom's bar when it happened. It's called Mandy's Place, and it's here in Las Vegas."

I paused for a moment and took a shaky breath before continuing. "I think the ambulance is pulling into the parking lot. The siren's really loud. Please help us, Ms. Dombruso, I'm begging you. Don't let Adriano die. I just can't lose him. He means everything to me."

Tears were streaming down my face as I clutched the phone and the journal to my chest. Right before I lost consciousness again, I whispered, "Please hang on, Adriano. Please, just stay alive."

16

Jack

When I awoke sometime later, I knew right away I was in a hospital. I could tell by that horrible smell of disinfectant and misery. Fuck, I really hated these places.

I blinked a few times, and as my eyes started to focus I sat up and mumbled, "Adriano?" The dark-haired man sitting in the corner looked up from his magazine, and I slumped against the pillow and muttered, "You look so much like him. That's really weird."

As he set aside the magazine and stood up, I noticed he was wearing black-on-black, from his suit to his shirt to his tie. He looked…well shit, he looked like a mafioso. I sat up again and grabbed the first thing I could find. Then I held it up like I meant to hit him with it and snarled, "If you're one of Greco's men, you can fuck right off. I won't let you take me prisoner, too."

His dark eyes crinkled at the corners as he smiled at me and asked, "What's the plan here, to bludgeon me with a plastic bed pan?"

"If I have to."

He chuckled at that. Then he ran a hand over his short beard as he studied me. "So, Jack, is it?"

"That's right. Who the fuck are you?"

"I'm Dante Dombruso."

I lowered the bed pan and asked, "For real?" When he nodded, I exclaimed, "Holy shit, you actually came!"

"I didn't have a choice. You left a message for my grandmother, telling her a long-lost grandson none of us had ever heard of was in trouble. Of course, she insisted that we fly to Vegas immediately. Right now, she and my brother Vincent are downstairs at the vending machines, undoubtedly buying a bunch of shit she's not supposed to eat."

"Well, thank god you're here," I said, as I threw back the covers and swung my bare legs out of bed. "We need to go save Reno, before they kill him."

"Reno?"

"That's Adriano's nickname. Try to keep up."

When I tried to stand, I was yanked back by my left arm, which was tethered by a bunch of tubes. I gathered them in my hand so I could pull out the IV and whatever else was happening there, but Dante blurted, "Shit, don't do that," and grabbed my wrist to stop me.

"Didn't you hear me? I need to go save him, and I can't do that if I'm stuck in a hospital bed."

"Just relax for a minute, and let's talk." Dante sat down on the edge of the bed and asked, "Can I let go of you, or are you immediately going to yank out your IV?"

"I'm definitely going to yank it out, but not this minute so you can let go."

He released my wrist and sat back before saying, "I know you're worried about your boyfriend, but I have four teams on the ground here in Vegas and two more back in San Francisco, and they're all working on tracking down this Greco douchebag. At the same time, they're spreading the word that Dante Dombruso is looking for him. My name doesn't carry the same weight here as it does back home, but if Greco has half a brain and does a little research, he'll realize he's in deep shit. He'll also realize the only way to save his ass is to return Adriano unharmed."

"Okay, great. I still need to help, though."

He looked skeptical. "What're you going to do, find the bad guys and bleed on them?"

"I can knock on doors, chase down leads, ask questions. The more people we have out there digging for information, the sooner we'll find him."

"You're not well enough to do any of that. Also, the police are going to want to speak to you."

"All the more reason to leave. I don't have time to answer a bunch of questions."

"If you don't want to tell them what happened, tell me instead."

"Four big men in dark clothes showed up at the bar and shot out the window so they could get in. I shoved Adriano to the floor to get him out of the line of fire, and then one of the bullets hit me. I remember falling, and I hit my head and passed out. The floor had just been mopped, so maybe I slipped. Anyway, I think I was out for maybe a minute or two, and when I came to, everyone was gone. I didn't see what they were driving, or what direction they went." I glanced at my upper arm, which was all bandaged up, and asked, "How bad is the gunshot wound?"

"Not very. According to the doctor—who thinks I'm your cousin, by the way—it bled a lot, because the bullet nicked a major artery as it passed through the fleshy part of your arm. They did some minor surgery to patch you up, and you got some stitches. It's going to hurt like hell when your painkillers wear off, but it didn't do any permanent damage."

"Spoken like a man who's been shot before."

"Yeah, once or twice." There was a lull in the conversation, and when I frowned at him, he asked, "What?"

"You met him once."

"Adriano?"

I nodded. "He came to find you right after he graduated from high school. I guess you were about twenty-one at the time. You cussed him out, flashed a gun, and told him to stay the hell away from you. Do you remember that?"

Dante looked surprised. "That actually happened? I was really drunk that night, and the next morning I wondered if I'd dreamt it. I'd forgotten the name he gave me…"

"It happened, and you broke his heart. I guess you didn't want to hear about your sainted father splitting up with your mom for a while—and they *were* split up, by the way. Paulie wasn't cheating on his wife when he and Mandy got together."

"I listened to the message you left for Nana, and the bar where you got shot was called Mandy's Place. I assume that's not a coincidence."

"Right. Adriano's mom owns it. She's a really good person, and if you're mean to her when you meet her, I swear to god I will kick your ass. Like I said, she wasn't the other woman."

He smiled at me and said, "I like you, Jack. You're like a tiny, overprotective chihuahua."

"Whatever. Do you know where my pants ended up? I need to get out of this hospital gown. I also need my phone."

Dante retrieved a plastic bag from the closet and peered inside it. "Your clothes are covered in blood and pretty much ruined. Here's your phone, though. I'll text Vincent and ask him and Nana to try to find you something else to wear, not that I think bailing out of the hospital is a great idea."

He grabbed a paper towel from beside the sink and used it to fish out my phone, which he handed to me before putting the bag on the nightstand. When I peered inside, I saw what he meant about the clothes. There was no way I'd make it very far dressed like an extra in a slasher film.

While I used some tissues to wipe my bloody fingerprints off the screen, he took his phone from his pocket and started composing a text. Then he glanced at me and asked, "What size do you wear, extra small?"

"Medium. Dude, just because you and your brother are built like professional wrestlers doesn't mean everyone else is miniature-sized."

He raised a brow and asked, "How did you know Vincent's the same size as me?"

"Your other brother, Adriano."

"Oh. Right. It's going to take me a minute to get my head around that one."

"He mentioned four brothers. I guess two of you are older than him, and two are younger."

"How old is he?"

"Thirty-seven."

"My brother Gianni's thirty-seven, too," he said. "This is all pretty wild. My parents died when I was seven, and I never knew they split up for a while. I guess I must have been about three or so when it happened."

"That sounds about right."

I fished the journal from the bag and wiped the blood off the cover before offering it to him. "He was curious about you, so he did some research. That's how I had your grandmother's phone number. When things with Greco got bad, he went to San Francisco. Even though he denies it, I think he did that because he really wanted to reach out to you. He was just afraid you'd reject him again."

Dante returned the phone to his pocket and took the journal as he said, "I wish he'd tried again to contact me, on a night when I wasn't drunk. Or even a couple of years later, when I'd had a chance to mature a bit."

"Tell him that, once we find him." I pulled up his photo on my phone, the one I'd snapped when we'd been in Romy's apartment, and showed it to Dante. "This is Reno, by the way. He has a kid brother who's ten years younger, and that's where the nickname came from. Romy couldn't say 'Adriano' when he was a toddler."

He took the phone from me and muttered, "Jesus, he really does look like me."

"He probably did when he was eighteen, too, but you turned him away."

Dante handed the phone back and frowned as he asked, "Are you going to keep holding that against me?"

"No. I just wanted to make sure you felt really guilty about it before I let it drop."

"I do."

"Perfect."

He started to flip through the journal, but then a tiny little old lady bustled into the room, followed by a tall guy who looked a hell of a lot like Dante, except that he was wearing glasses and was clean-shaven. "Nana and Vincent, meet Jack," Dante said, with a sweeping hand gesture.

Nana's white hair was up in a bun, and she wore a pink track suit and round glasses that made her look like an owl. She was carrying a shopping bag, which she thrust at Dante before grabbing me in a tight embrace. "You poor little thing," she said, as she squeezed me. "Your message broke my heart, so I called Dante and made him charter a plane, and we got here as soon as we could. Now, don't you worry. We're going to find your boyfriend." She let go of me and pulled a huge handgun out of her purse. "Then we're going to put the fear of god into the son of a bitch that kidnapped him!"

Dante swore under his breath and plucked the gun out of his grandmother's hand. She scowled at him as he tucked it into the back of his waistband, and I said, "I guess they don't make you go through a metal detector for a charter flight."

"No, they don't, not when you reserve the whole plane. Then they treat you like a VIP," she said. "Good thing too, because Dante and Vinny brought a shitload of guns along. Oh, don't look so surprised, boys. What do you think, that I was born yesterday? I know what that funny-looking luggage is for, and it ain't pool floaties."

"Well, good. We might need them," I said.

Nana started pulling things out of the shopping bag she'd handed to Dante. "Now look," she said, "we don't have much time. We've got to spring you from this hospital. Fortunately, I have a lot of expertise in this area. We need to do it pronto, too, before the fuzz shows up and starts asking questions. They get real uptight when gunshot wounds are involved." She thrust a baby pink pair of sweatpants at me and explained, "Dante said you needed some clothes, and there wasn't much selection downstairs in the gift shop. See if those fit. We got you some shoes, too, even though I was unclear on whether you needed any. But I got them anyway, because they match the outfit."

She looked pleased with herself as she took a pair of hot pink glittery Crocs from the bag and showed them to me. I thanked her as I pulled the sweatpants on under my hospital gown. Except for being about six inches too short, they were a good fit. "I'm going to need to pull the plug before I can put on a shirt," I said, as I gestured at my IV. "I just hope I don't puke, because the sight of blood makes me queasy."

I started to reach for the IV, but Nana thrust the shoes at Dante and said, "Let me. I know how to do this, too." I pressed my eyes shut while she unhooked me, and then she said, "It's only bleeding a little, and I have a bandage."

Nana dug around in her purse while Dante shifted the bundle in his arms, and I dabbed at the puncture on my arm with a tissue. She handed me a hairbrush, a candy bar, a taser, and a giant hunting knife in a sheath before saying, "Here we go." Then she daintily stuck a rainbow-striped bandage over the spot where my IV had been.

Dante made a small choking sound and tried to snatch the knife and taser, but Nana slapped his hand away and put the weapons back in her huge purse. I glanced at Vincent while all of that was going on. His eyes were closed, and he was pinching the bridge of his nose and grinding his teeth. It seemed like he was about two seconds from shrieking and running away, so I liked him immediately.

"Just so you know, your arm and head are going to start to hurt, since you just cut off your morphine drip," Dante told me.

"He'll be fine," Nana said, as she pulled a pale pink zippered hoodie from the shopping bag, tore off the tags, and handed it to me. "I've got some edibles in my purse, and this is Vegas, so there's hooch everywhere. Hell, there's probably a bar and some slot machines right here in the hospital. Which reminds me, we need to do some gambling after we rescue my new grandson. I haven't been to Sin City in ages!"

I gingerly put on the jacket, trying to be careful of my injured arm, and looked down at myself. It was cropped and exposed about five inches of my midriff. Also, there were three pastel Care Bears on it, but again, it wasn't the worst fit. Maybe it was the boatload of narcotic painkillers talking, but I actually kind of liked it.

As I stuck my feet in the Crocs, Dante asked his grandmother, "What would possess you to pick out that sweatsuit for a grown man?"

Vincent answered for her. "She dressed him like that because she can." It was the first time he'd spoken. "If we allowed her to dress us, that's exactly what we'd be wearing, too."

"Damn right," Nana said, "and Jack looks adorable. Now come on, we're pushing our luck by staying this long. The cops are going to show up any second, and then it might be hours before we can get out of here."

I stuck my phone in my pocket and picked up the bag containing my ruined suit, and Dante collected the journal and the magazine he'd been reading. It was Teen Vogue, and when Vincent shot him a look, Dante said, "Don't judge me. I was reading a surprisingly insightful article, and I want to finish it."

Vincent raised a brow and asked, "Was it about whether Timothee Chalamet or Shawn Mendes is the bigger babe?"

"The answer is Timothee Chalamet. Duh," I said. "Now can we go, please?"

We all stepped out into the hallway, and Nana whispered, "The fuzz is staking out the joint! Everyone hang a left and try to look casual while we make a break for it." Sure enough, a pair of police officers were talking to a nurse at one end of the long hallway, so we went the other direction.

Fortunately, we reached the stairwell without incident. As we made our way downstairs, I muttered, "Shit." When Dante asked what was wrong, I told him, "You're right about the morphine wearing off. My arm's really starting to hurt."

Nana dug around in her purse of wonders again and handed me a bag of gummy bears. "Be careful with these," she said. "They look harmless, but they're actually jam-packed with weed. If you eat too many of them at one time, you'll be tripping balls."

She glanced at Dante and added, "I'm not saying how I know that."

He sounded exasperated as he asked, "Why do you even have those?"

She glared at him defiantly. "Why not? The devil's lettuce is legal in California now, so don't be a square."

I selected a bear before offering the open bag to my companions, who all declined. Then I bit its tiny ear off before wrapping the rest in a scrap of the packaging and sticking it in my pocket. Dante chuckled at that and said, "Woah, slow down there, Snoop Dogg. We wouldn't want you to spiral out of control on your point-zero-zero-one gram of weed."

"I've never had a marijuana edible before. Also, I have no idea what it does when combined with morphine. We have a lot of work to do, and I need to be clear-headed so we can find Reno."

"Oh shit," Nana said, "were we supposed to go to Reno? That's not the same as Vegas."

While Dante explained about the nickname, we exited through a side door and hurried to the parking lot. A minute later, Vincent pushed a button on a key fob to unlock a big, white SUV with tinted windows.

I climbed into the back seat, curled into a ball, and muttered, "Ugh, I feel like shit."

"Yeah, again, that's why you were in the hospital," Dante said, as he took a seat beside me.

While Vincent started the engine and Nana put on her seat belt, I asked, "Where are we going?"

"I got us a vacation rental. A couple of our family members are already there," Dante explained. "According to them, it's a little funky, but it's also big and private, and that's all I really care about."

I forced myself to sit up, which made my head throb. As I pulled my phone from my pocket and jabbed at it, I mumbled, "I need to make a call."

Romy answered on the first ring with, "Jack? How are you doing?"

"I've been better."

"Why does it sound like you're in a car?"

"Probably because I'm in a car."

"They didn't actually release you, did they?"

"Not exactly."

His voice rose in alarm. "What are you doing, Jack? You have a mild concussion and a gunshot wound. You need to go back to the hospital!"

"I can't do that," I said. "I need to help find Reno. It's been five hours since they took him, and every minute counts."

"The police are already looking for him. I filed a report when Mom and I were at the hospital with you. Did you speak to them?"

"No, but I don't have any information to give them anyway. You came to the hospital?"

"Yeah, don't you remember? We rode in the ambulance with you," Romy said. "I guess you were pretty out of it, though. After you came to, you kept trying to get up and go look for Reno, so they ended up giving you a sedative."

"I don't remember any of that."

"We stayed with you for a couple of hours, but Mom was freaking out about Reno, so I ended up taking her home so she could lie down. I planned to come back after I got her settled, but she's still pretty agitated."

"It's okay, I…made some new friends, so I'm not alone. They're helping me find Adriano."

Romy sounded confused. "Just, like, some random strangers?"

I hesitated before admitting, "They, um, they're actually Reno's relatives on his dad's side. I called them and asked for help. I'm not sure how Mandy will feel about this, but I figured they'd have a lot of ideas and resources."

"I think she'll just be glad they're helping find him." After a moment, he said, "Reno looked into them a while back. Aren't they involved in organized crime?"

"Maybe. But isn't that exactly what we need to find a man like Greco, and to get your brother back? Reno always felt outmanned and outgunned, but now we're evening the odds."

"That actually makes sense."

"I need your help, too," I said. "The Dombrusos have people out there gathering information. But this is your hometown, and with your job as an EMT, I bet you know this city better than anyone. Where would a thug take a hostage if they didn't want to be discovered?"

"I can think of several options, including a few abandoned buildings at the edge of town. But if someone really wanted to remain undetected, there are some houses scattered out in the desert that are literally in the middle of nowhere."

"That would make sense."

He paused before saying, "I'm trying so hard to think positive here. If all Greco wanted to do was kill my brother, he could have just shot him at the bar. But instead, he took him hostage. That probably means he plans to keep Reno alive, right? At least for a while…"

"That was Adriano's assumption. He said Greco would most likely want to drag it out and torture him. But I don't think we have days to rescue him. We probably have hours."

Romy swore under his breath. Then he asked, "How can I help?"

"You can come meet us and go over some maps to help narrow the search—as long as your mom's okay with you leaving her."

"Her boyfriend's here so I can leave, especially since it's to help Reno. Where are you headed?"

"I'm not sure, but I'll text you the address when we hang up," I said. "One other thing, do you have any friends at the Las Vegas Police Department?"

"Yeah, I do. One of my good friends is a police officer."

"Could he look up Greco and tell you if they have an address for him? There's a good chance a man like that has been arrested in the past."

"I actually already reached out to my friend, back when Reno first started having trouble with this guy," Romy told me. "We found out there's no record of a Mario Greco—no criminal record, DMV, nothing. That means it's probably an alias. They could identify him if they had some prints to run through the system, but they'd need to find him first."

I muttered, "That would have been too easy." Then I pressed my eyes shut and said, "I'm going to go, because I'm feeling pretty nauseous. But I'll see you soon."

After we ended the call, Dante gave me the address of his vacation rental and I forwarded it to Romy. Then I sent a quick text to Wyatt, because I'd told him I'd check in when we chatted that morning. I didn't want to worry him, so I didn't mention getting shot or Reno's abduction. Maybe I'd fill him in later on, once we got Reno back and everything was okay. For now, I just wrote: *I went back and talked to Adriano, like you said. You're right, that was exactly what I needed to do.* Then I curled up in a ball again and tried not to throw up.

17

Jack

Under normal circumstances, I would have been delighted with the house the Dombrusos had rented. It was big, kitschy, and midcentury-modern, with multiple levels and a lot of period details from the 1960s.

In my current condition though, I barely noticed any of that as I made my way from the front door to the cream-and-mustard-yellow couch in the sunken living room. A pair of college-age guys were sitting on the matching loveseat. They looked up from their laptops and a crackling police scanner when Vincent said, "Jack, this is my son Josh and his fiancé Darwin. We brought them along because they're good with technology, and because they wanted to help. Boys, this is Jack Granger, Adriano's boyfriend." A moment later, Dante called to him from across the very large living room, and Vincent went to join his brother.

"Good to meet you," Josh said. He had shaggy dark hair and glasses, and he looked at me curiously as I curled up in a ball at one end of the couch.

"It's nice to meet you, too. I've been shot and I have a concussion, so forgive my manners. I just need to shut my eyes for a second."

Darwin, who looked sort of goth with his pale skin, black hair, and black T-shirt and jeans, asked, "Can we get you anything? A glass of water, maybe?"

"I'd love that, and about six hundred Advil," I mumbled.

When someone put a blanket over me, I raised a lid and gave Nana a little smile. "I'll get you that stuff," she said. "That way, the boys can keep working."

I thanked her, and after she left the living room I told my companions, "She bought me this outfit. It's not exactly my style, but my clothes were blood-soaked. Compared to that, the Care Bears are a big improvement."

Josh started to say something, but then we all fell silent to listen to a message coming in over the police scanner. Darwin shook his head after a moment and said, "It's just a robbery."

When I thanked them for helping, Josh said, "I wish we could do more. We've been compiling a list of vacant buildings in the city and relaying that information to Dante's teams in the field, but it's a total long-shot. The bad guys probably took your boyfriend to a property Greco owns, but we just don't have any information to go by."

"I have a local expert on the way," I said, as I pulled the blanket up to my chin. "He may be able to help you narrow the search. One thing he mentioned was looking into isolated houses out in the desert, which seems like a good idea."

While Josh started clicking away on his keyboard, Darwin said, "That actually makes a lot more sense to me than an abandoned building, because think about it. If I'm a thug who's just taken someone hostage, I want to be comfortable, right? I mean, I don't care about the prisoner, but me? I want air conditioning. A bathroom. A kitchen with a coffee maker. Guarding somebody around the clock requires a few basic amenities."

"Makes sense to me, too," Josh said. "On TV, it's always an abandoned warehouse. But why not, like, an office building, or a house, or whatever? The only requirement is that it doesn't have a lot of neighbors, because they'll rat you out to the police if they hear someone screaming or see a bunch of dudes with guns."

I sat up when Nana brought me the water and ibuprofen. As I

washed down the pills, Vincent and Dante joined us. "I think we might have a lead," Dante said, as he held up Reno's blood-smeared journal. "Turns out, Adriano is big on research. There's not just stuff on our family in here, there's a whole section on Mario Greco. It looks like he was trying to find this guy before Greco found him, and there are four pages of addresses and business names. I've sent photos of the list to my people, and they're dividing up and heading to the first three locations as we speak."

Josh held out his hand and said, "Let me see." When Dante handed over the journal, both he and Darwin glanced at the list, then began clicking away on their keyboards.

I stood up shakily and asked, "So, what are we waiting for? Let's go check out the rest of those places."

"We're about to," Dante said. "Vincent and I will let you know what we find. Meanwhile, you need to rest and gather your strength."

"No, I'm coming with you."

Dante shook his head. "We can handle this."

I tried to think of a convincing argument for including me, and all I came up with was, "But I have some skills that might prove useful. I'm a thief, so I'm good at getting into places others can't." Never mind that breaking and entering was hardly my specialty. I was reasonably sure I could pull it off if need be.

My argument backfired, though. "Then you really do need to rest up," Dante told me. "We might need to break into wherever he's being held once we locate Adriano, and we'll need you at your best." With that, he and Vincent headed for the door, and I sat back down with a sigh.

I awoke with a start a few hours later. It was getting dark out, and the starburst clock on the wall told me it was almost six p.m. I'd never intended to fall asleep, but it just showed how much my injuries had taken out of me.

When I sat up, Romy said, "Hey there, Jack." He was curled up in one of the mustard yellow club chairs, and his red eyes told me he'd been crying.

"Did they find Reno?"

"Not yet, but they're narrowing their search."

"Where is everyone?"

"Nana's taking a nap upstairs, and Josh and Darwin are in the kitchen, eating pizza. I can bring you some if you're hungry."

"I don't know about that. I'm still kind of nauseous."

"I brought along my medical kit," he said. "Can I do a quick exam to make sure you're okay?"

When I agreed, he moved to the couch and put a canvas tote on the coffee table as he asked, "How do you feel?"

"I have a headache, but it's not terrible. My arm is throbbing like crazy, though."

After he asked a few more questions and checked my pupils with a small flashlight, he turned his attention to my arm. I took off my jacket, and he carefully peeled off the blood-spotted bandages before gently cleaning the wounds—entry and exit, it turned out—with some type of antibiotic solution.

While he was doing that, I said softly, "This was my fault."

He looked up at me and asked, "What do you mean?"

His eyes were eerily similar to Adriano's. I broke his gaze and told him, "This morning, I got scared and left before Reno woke up. I was going to take the bus back to San Francisco, but I just couldn't do it. No matter how terrified I am of getting hurt if this doesn't work out, I care about him way too much to run away.

"I ended up going to the bar to talk to him, and to apologize for leaving the way I did. I'd only been there a minute when Greco's men showed up. Now that I think about it, maybe I even led them there. Maybe they spotted the convertible and followed me to the bar."

Romy shook his head. "You don't know that."

A tear tumbled down my cheek as I said, "No, but I know I was distracting him. Reno was facing away from the window when those men arrived and started shooting. If I hadn't been drawing his attention, maybe he could have gotten away—"

"Or maybe he would have tried shooting back, and maybe they would have killed him. He probably had a gun with him. He started carrying one when this mess with Greco started. It's possible you actually saved his life."

"That's a lot of conjecture, but thanks for trying to make me feel better."

As he wrapped my arm with a fresh bandage, he said, "Don't beat yourself up, Jack. Feeling guilty isn't going to help my brother."

"I mean, sure, if you want to be logical about it."

He grinned and started to repack his medical kit. "I did the best I could with your arm, but it's going to start bleeding again if you don't stay still. Also, they gave you a shot of antibiotics at the hospital, but you need to promise me you'll go see a doctor in the next day or two so you can get a prescription."

"I'd promise, but I don't want to lie to you." He sighed at that, and I asked, "What else did they do to me at the hospital?"

"They did a scan and determined you had a mild concussion. They also gave you fluids, painkillers, and a unit of blood intravenously. You actually might have passed out from blood loss, not your head injury."

"The second time, you mean. I passed out from hitting my head before those men took Reno. Then I passed out again after I called you."

Romy's brow creased with concern. "Once we find my brother, you should go back to the hospital. Seriously."

"Eh, I'll be fine."

He sighed and muttered, "You remind me so much of Reno right now." Then he added, "Stop grinning. I didn't mean it as a compliment."

"Well, I'm taking it as one."

He got up and told me, "I'm going to bring you some toast. Even if you're nauseous, you should be able to manage that."

"Thank you, Romy. For all of this." He gave me a little smile before heading to the kitchen.

I found myself alone for the first time since the hospital, and I put my jacket back on and wrapped my arms around myself.

Reno had been in Greco's clutches for about eight hours by this point, and that terrified me. Sooner or later, his time was going to run out, and even though a lot of people were out there looking for him, I was sitting here doing nothing. I hated feeling so helpless.

A few moments later, Josh and Darwin rushed into the room with Romy on their heels. "We need to go meet my dad," Josh whispered, "but we're under strict orders to sneak away without Nana. They might have a lead on where your boyfriend is, and she'd definitely try to go in guns blazing."

I quickly stuck my feet into my Crocs, and Romy grabbed his medical kit before we all slipped out the front door. As Darwin locked up behind us, he whispered, "I feel bad about ditching Nana."

"Me too, but you know she doesn't do stealth," Josh said. "Just the opposite. If we needed a huge parade and a fireworks display, she'd be the first person we called. But we'll make it up to her once we rescue her new grandson."

While the rest of us climbed into one of the rented SUVs, Josh took what looked like a mini helicopter with four rotors out of the trunk. Once he was situated in the back seat with it, Darwin pulled out of the driveway, and Romy turned around in the passenger seat and asked, "Why do you have a quadcopter?"

"I'm studying filmmaking, and I usually use it for aerial shots," Josh explained, as he inspected the machine. "But the reason I brought it to Vegas is because I thought it might come in handy, in case we needed to do a bit of search and rescue. It looks like I was right, too. My dad and uncle got a tip that Greco leases a place out in the desert, so this could be a good way of getting close enough to check it out."

I asked, "Was it one of the addresses from Adriano's journal?"

"No, but the journal led them to an underground gambling parlor, which is where they found an informant," Josh said. "Apparently this guy was on Greco's payroll for a while, but he got sick of working for a douchebag and quit. Once Uncle Dante plied him with cash, he gave up the address of an isolated desert compound."

"A compound? That's not good," I said. "It implies a big fence and guard towers."

Josh shrugged. "I guess we'll find out when we get there, assuming my dad lets Darwin and me come within fifty miles of this place. He's so overprotective. In fact, the only reason he let us come along to Vegas was because we promised to stay in the house."

"Yeah, you don't seem to be doing that," Romy said.

"No, and Dad's going to be pissed when we come rolling up. I was just supposed to tell you and Jack where to meet him, but there's no way we want to sit back and miss all the excitement!"

As predicted, Vincent was livid when we joined him and his brother in a parking lot on the edge of town. He crossed his arms over his chest and said, "No. Absolutely not," as Josh climbed out of the SUV.

"You need Darwin and me to work the drone," Josh pointed out. "We can do that from a half-mile away, so it's not like we're asking to storm the place with machetes and hand grenades." His dad was still scowling, so Josh turned to Dante and pleaded, "Come on. We're not kids anymore, and you know you need us and the quad-copter to do some surveillance. If this place is by itself out in the desert, there's literally no way you can go driving up to it without putting every evil henchman on high alert."

A tall, muscular brunet joined us, and as he took Dante's hand he said, "You know, Josh has a point."

Dante had been scowling as much as his brother, but his expression eased a bit and he said, "Fine. They can come, but they're staying way, way back when this starts to go down."

The brunet smiled at him, and Dante drew him close and nuzzled his cheek before remembering the rest of us were there. Then he said, "Romy and Jack, this is my husband Charlie. He flew in this afternoon to lend a hand."

"I also flew in to keep an eye on you," Charlie teased, with a sparkle in his eyes. "Someone needs to talk you down if you start going all Rambo."

While the adoring husbands grinned at each other and started kissing, Vincent gave Darwin the address of the alleged compound, and the kid pulled it up on Google Earth. "Yeah, that's definitely in the middle of nowhere," Josh said, as he took a look at the satellite image on his fiancé's phone. "If it turns out Adriano's in there, I'm not sure what you're going to do. It's exactly like I said—you'll never be able to drive down that long, private road without alerting everyone in the compound."

I looked around and asked, "Does anyone have a bobby pin and a hundred bucks?"

Dante stopped kissing his husband's neck and raised a brow. "Why?"

I pointed at a retro kids' bike with a long banana seat, which was padlocked to a chain link fence. "I want to steal that and leave the owner some money for it. I don't think I'm well enough for a long hike, but if the drone gives us a reason to believe we're in the right place, I can easily bike up to the compound, sneak in, and find Adriano. Then all I need to do is smuggle him out."

Romy shook his head. "There's no way. They'll shoot you, Jack."

But Dante shrugged and said, "If they caught him sneaking around in that outfit, would they really shoot him? He doesn't exactly look like a threat. Besides, Vincent and I would obviously go along."

Romy remained unconvinced. "Then why would Jack go in at all?"

"Because I'm good at breaking into things." Romy started to argue, but I said, "I know it's dangerous, but it's a risk I'm willing to take."

"Or, here's a crazy idea," Romy said. "We call the police, they send in a SWAT team and a hostage negotiator, and this all gets resolved by trained professionals."

Everyone said, "Nah," and went to work implementing our plan.

Dante handed me some money, and Charlie led me to the trunk of the other SUV and said, "I packed a few essentials before I flew in. Let's see if there's something you can use, not just to steal the bike, but if you end up trying to infiltrate the compound."

We rifled through his go-bag, and I selected a multitool and a pocket knife. Then I picked up a small leather case with a lopsided cat on it and asked, "Is this what I think it is?"

Charlie grinned at me. "It's a Hello Kitty lockpick kit. You're welcome to borrow it, but please be sure to bring it back. It has a lot of sentimental value." I didn't ask.

He went with me to steal the bike while everyone else climbed into the pair of SUVs and started the engines. "You doing okay? I heard you got shot," he said, as he indicated a spot of dried blood on my sleeve.

"I feel like shit, but whatever. I'll rest once we rescue Adriano."

He stood guard when we reached the bike, and as I picked the lock he said, "It's wild—another Dombruso brother. It's even wilder that he seems to be just like Dante and Vincent. One of the first things Nana told me when I started dating a Dombruso was that I just had to accept the fact that danger seemed to follow them."

I freed the bike and closed the padlock again as I asked, "Are their younger brothers danger magnets, too?"

"No, those two have always led normal lives. Dante and Vincent made sure of it by becoming the family caretakers after their parents died. They took all the heat that came with being Dombrusos, so their little brothers could stay safe."

I folded the money Dante had given me—almost three hundred bucks—and stuffed it through the padlock's shackle as Charlie said, "Um, we need to run."

"Why?"

"Because a kid gang is about to beat the shit out of us."

I straightened up and looked down the street. Sure enough, about ten little kids were running toward us, and they looked pissed. Charlie picked up the bike, and he and I booked it across the parking lot as the yells of some very angry kids grew louder. He tossed the bike into the open trunk of one of the SUVs, and then we piled into the back seat and peeled out of the parking lot in a hail of rocks and profanities.

"Wow, those kids had really foul mouths," Romy muttered from the passenger seat, as he turned to look behind us.

"Hopefully they'll forgive us when they find the money," I said, as I gasped for breath.

"Maybe we can put the bike back where we found it when we're done with it," Romy suggested, with a hopeful expression.

Dante, who was behind the wheel, grinned at Charlie and me in the rearview mirror and said, "That was fucking hilarious. You should have seen your faces when the pint-sized mafia started closing in."

Charlie chuckled at that, and I curled up in a ball on the seat and mumbled, "Tell me when we get there. I just need to die for a few minutes."

That made Romy sigh and mutter, "This is all such a terrible idea."

18

Adriano

At first, I thought I was hallucinating. I'd been tied to a pillar in an overheated garage for hours, but all of a sudden, there was Jack, barefoot and dressed in a cropped pink top with teddy bears on it. My mouth was so dry that I had trouble mumbling, "Is that really you?"

His soft hands clutched my face, and he kissed me gently before whispering, "Yes, sweetheart. I'm right here."

Tears tumbled down my cheeks. I couldn't have stopped them if I tried. "I didn't know if you were alive or dead. There was blood, and you weren't moving. I was so scared."

He wiped my tears away and kissed my forehead before saying, "You can't get rid of me that easily. Now, we've got to get you out of here. Can you walk?"

I nodded, and he produced a pocket knife and sawed through the ropes that bound my wrists behind the pillar. My arms burned as feeling began returning to them, and I leaned on him heavily as he helped me to my feet. I had so many questions, starting with, "How did you find me?"

"I had a lot of help from your brothers. I'll tell you all about it later, but right now we need to hurry. Greco and his men don't know we're here, and I'd like to keep it that way."

"Brothers? I only have one."

"You have five, and three of them are part of this rescue operation. I know this is confusing, but I'll explain everything once you're safe."

We rushed out of the garage hand-in-hand, but there were two huge guys with automatic weapons waiting for us. They almost looked like twins, except one had glasses, and the other had a beard. I pulled back a fist to hit the one closest to me, but Jack caught my arm and exclaimed, "No, they're on our side! They're your brothers, Dante and Vincent Dombruso."

I scrubbed a hand over my forehead. I had a pounding headache, but it didn't explain how confusing this was. Just then, we heard shouting in the distance. One of the guys, the one with the beard, said, "I think they just discovered the guard we knocked out, so we won't be able to leave by way of the side gate."

"This way," Jack said, and we hurried back into the garage.

Two of the three bays contained vintage muscle cars. Jack effortlessly vaulted over the door of a black 1964 Corvair convertible, yanked down a bunch of wires from below the dash, and began hotwiring it. I climbed into the passenger seat, watching him closely as I muttered, "That's so sexy."

He grinned and said, "It'll be sexier if I actually succeed. It's been a minute since I hotwired a car, but let's think positive."

The guy with glasses locked the door and slid a large tool rack in front of it, and then he and his brother climbed into the back seat. A moment later, someone rattled the door handle, and we heard them yell, "We need the garage door opener! Hurry up!"

Jack took a deep breath and concentrated on the tangle of wires, and I told him, "You're a fucking rock star, and you've got this."

"Thanks for the vote of confidence." He knit his brows in concentration and kept working as he told the men in the back seat, "I'd suggest calling Romy and his team and telling them to clear out. They should take both SUVs, because we'll either drive out in this thing, or we'll get caught. Either way, they shouldn't wait around for Greco and his men to discover them."

The guy with glasses said, "Good idea," and placed a call.

At the same time, I asked, "Romy? My kid brother's out there with the bad guys?"

"Don't worry," Jack said, without looking up from the wires. "He and Charlie and the boys are about half a mile away, just off the main road. There's no cover leading up to this house, so the three of us hiked and biked in. Shit, why isn't this working?"

"Tell them to hurry! Greco's on his way back from New York, and he'll be arriving any time now," I said. "If he sees someone parked nearby, he might stop to investigate."

"Go now, Josh. Hurry. Take both SUVs, because we found a new ride," the guy with glasses said into the phone.

My heart leapt as the garage door behind us began to rattle open. The guy with the beard turned around and knelt on the seat with his machine gun at the ready, and he said, "Now would be a great time to get that engine started, Jack. Otherwise, this is about to turn into a Quentin Tarantino film."

Jack muttered, "I'm trying," as he stripped a bit of wire with his pocket knife.

Glasses guy dropped his phone back into the pocket of his suit jacket and said, "They're safe and on their way back to town." Then he too turned around in his seat and pointed his gun at the garage door as he told his brother, "I would have said John Woo, or maybe Robert Rodriguez. Their films have a much higher body count than Tarantino's."

"That's a good point," the other guy said. "You know what's funny, though? I recently read an article that claimed the director with the highest body count overall is actually Peter Jackson." How the hell were they so calm?

"No shit."

"Yeah, well, when you think about it, all those Middle Earth armies really stacked up the casualties." He turned his head and added, "We're about three seconds from major carnage, Jack."

The slow-moving garage door was maybe three feet up by this

point, and I could see at least six pairs of legs on the other side. Good thing none of those men were ambitious enough to duck under and start shooting us like fish in a barrel.

In the next instant, the engine turned over and Jack whooped with joy. I smiled at him and said, "I knew you could do it."

He grinned at me, and then he threw the car into reverse and yelled, "Duck!"

All four of us ducked down as the Corvair shot backwards. The windshield tore off with the sound of bending metal and breaking glass as we just barely cleared the garage door. Jack sat up and looked over his shoulder as he sped down the driveway, and I peeked over the hood at the scene back at the garage.

Greco's men had all managed to dive out of the way, and as they staggered to their feet a couple of them started firing guns in our direction. I pulled Jack down so we were both below the dash, and he smiled at me and said, "I'm so happy you're okay."

Then he sat up again, shifted gears, and yanked the parking brake. The car spun around with the smell of burning rubber and the squeal of tires on asphalt. Now that we were pointing the right way, he shifted gears again and slammed on the gas.

He laughed delightedly, and I sat up and yelled over the wind, "Marry me!"

He flashed me a smile and yelled back, "Ask me again when you're not high on adrenaline!" Then he shifted gears once more and accelerated, and we were tossed back against our seats.

I said, "I will," and fished around in the glove box. Then I handed him a pair of aviator-style sunglasses. It was dark out, but the air flow was intense without a windshield.

He thanked me and put them on, and then he said, "Shit, do you suppose that's Greco?"

Another car was dead ahead, barreling toward us on the one-lane private road. "Probably." After a beat, I added, "He's not slowing down. I bet his men called and told him I escaped, so maybe he plans to run us off the road."

Jack asked, "Should I offroad it?"

"Nah, you might flip the car with those ditches on either side of us," one of our companions said, as they both stood up. Without discussion, they started shooting at the approaching vehicle, which was maybe a hundred yards away and closing fast.

Seconds before impact, one of them managed to hit a tire, and the other car careened off the road. As we zoomed past, I caught a glimpse of Greco's startled expression, which made me grin. Then I turned around and watched as he staggered out of the car, which had ended up nose-down in a ditch.

Moments later, Jack made a wild left turn onto the main road and asked, "Is anyone chasing us?"

The guy with the beard looked behind us and said, "I don't see anyone, but I'm not worried. I'll just shoot out another tire if they come after us."

I asked him, "Which one are you, again?"

"Dante. That's Vincent." He gestured at the guy in glasses, who offered me a little salute.

"I hate to break it to you, Dante," I said, "but Vincent shot out the tire. The one on the right blew, and you were aiming at the one on the left."

Vincent smirked and said, "I was just about to point that out."

Dante muttered, "Whatever," and took a phone from the pocket of his black suit jacket. Both he and Vincent were dressed impeccably. I had to admire anyone who decided a perfectly tailored suit was the right choice for a heavily-armed commando raid.

Dante placed a call, yelling over the rushing wind, "Charlie? Is that you?" He listened for a few seconds, then said, "I can't hear a fucking thing, but this went great and we're right behind you. Can you pull over so we can catch up? I think we need to ditch our ride, because it's making my eyes water." He listened for another moment before shouting, "I adore you, angel. See you in a minute." Then he returned the phone to his pocket and reclined casually with his arm draped over the back of the seat, as if he was out for a peaceful Sunday drive.

A couple of minutes later, Jack pulled in behind a white SUV that was parked on the side of the road. Dante immediately vaulted over the side of the convertible, closed the distance to a muscular brunet, and kissed him passionately.

When I caught up to them a few moments later, Dante introduced me to his husband Charlie. Then Romy climbed out of the passenger seat, rushed over, and grabbed me in a hug as he asked, "Are you okay?"

"I'm fine, thanks to all of you."

"Jack's the real hero here," Romy said. "He had the foresight to call the Dombrusos for help."

"It was a team effort." Jack handed Charlie a few things, including a slender case with a lopsided cat head on it, and told him, "Before I forget, here's your knife and tools. The lock pick kit was perfect, by the way."

After Dante and Vincent offloaded about a dozen guns into the trunk, we all piled into the SUV. Dante and his husband began making out in the third row of seats while Vincent started the engine and pulled onto the road. At the same time, I drew Jack into my arms and exhaled slowly.

After a while, I asked him, "How did you know to call the Dombrusos?" I could barely process the fact that they were actually here, especially since I was reeling from the past twelve hours.

"From what you'd told me about them, I figured they'd know how to deal with a man like Greco. I found your grandmother's name in your journal and left her a message, and she enlisted your two older brothers. She's here in Vegas too, by the way. The journal also led us to Greco's house, thanks to a snitch Dante and Vincent found at one of the places on your list."

When a tremor ran through Jack's slender body, I tucked his head under my chin and asked, "Are you alright, doll face?"

"I was doing pretty well with all that adrenaline coursing through my system, but now that it's wearing off I'm not gonna lie, I feel like shit."

"He has a concussion and a gunshot wound," Romy chimed in from the passenger seat, "and earlier today he escaped from the hospital without a doctor's permission. We should really take him back."

"Absolutely not," Jack muttered, as he curled up against me and shut his eyes. "I'm staying with Reno. Also, was that really this morning? This has been the longest day ever."

Romy sighed at the bit about not going back to the hospital, and then he told me, "By the way, I called Mom a few minutes ago and told her you're safe, but she wants to see you for herself."

I asked him, "Where is she right now? We should do a quick detour so she doesn't keep worrying." Romy told me she was at her boyfriend's house and gave Vincent directions.

A moment later, I noticed a growing spot of blood on Jack's sleeve and exclaimed, "You're hurt!"

He shrugged and told me, "That's from this morning. It's where I got shot. I guess I opened up my stitches in all this excitement."

Romy handed me a bandana and instructed me to tie it around Jack's arm, so it would put light pressure on the wound. I almost couldn't manage it, because a fresh wave of rage was making my hands shake. I cupped Jack's cheek and muttered, "That bullet wound is inches from your heart. I could have lost you."

"But you didn't," he murmured, as he snuggled closer.

This thing with Greco wasn't over, and I was overcome with the need for revenge. It wouldn't be tonight, though. Right now, I needed to take care of Jack and rebuild my strength. But it would happen soon. I'd make sure of it.

When we got to our first stop, everyone waited outside to give my mom and me some privacy. I noticed in passing that her boyfriend's house was big, modern, and extremely nice. Maybe I'd been off base with the unemployed artist thing.

It was odd to meet Chet for the first time under these circumstances. He was tall and slim and wore his long, thinning hair in a ponytail, and we shook hands a bit awkwardly when I introduced myself. Then he said, "Dude, what happened to you is a real bummer." There was no question he'd been a surfer at some point.

A moment later, my mom appeared in the entryway. She started ranting, crying, and squashing me in a hug, all at the same time. I'd never seen her so upset, and I felt guilty as hell for scaring her like that. I also felt terrible when I told her just a couple of minutes later that I had to go, because I was about to collapse. Fortunately, Chet stepped in and began comforting her as I hurried out the door.

By the time I got back to the SUV, Romy had moved into my seat and was tending to Jack's wound. It was freshly bandaged, and he was lecturing him about taking it easy for the next few days. Jack promised he would as he pulled his teddy bear jacket back on.

While my brother repacked his large first aid kit, I finally got why they'd brought him along. He was our field medic, and if that rescue operation had gone south, he might have had his hands full.

When we pulled up in front of Romy's apartment a couple of minutes later, I got out with him and gave him a hug as I whispered, "Thank you for helping. But if you ever put yourself in danger again because of me—"

"Try and stop me. I love you, Reno. Get some rest, and see a doctor tomorrow. You look terrible."

I grinned a little and said, "Maybe," as I climbed back into the SUV. He rolled his eyes, because he knew what my version of "no" sounded like.

Finally, we drove to the vacation home the Dombrusos had rented. It was just too much effort to haul ourselves out to my house in the desert, so Jack and I decided to spend the night.

When we got inside, I was introduced to Josh and Darwin, who'd been in on the rescue mission and had gotten home minutes ahead of us. Then I was crushed in an embrace by a little old lady in a pink track suit. After she squeezed the hell out of me, she held me at arm's length and said, "Let me look at you." There were tears in her dark eyes as she nodded and told me, "Yup, you're definitely a Dombruso. You look just like the rest of my grandsons. We have so much to talk about, kiddo."

"Tomorrow, Nana. He and Jack are dead on their feet." Dante handed me a couple of bottles of water and some ibuprofen as he told me, "Go on upstairs and pick out any of the empty bedrooms. We'll see you in the morning."

I paused and took a good look at him for the first time. He was a little taller than me, and his coloring was darker, but he looked so much like me that it was eerie. There was a lot I wanted to say to him, but for now I left it at, "Thank you, Dante. For everything." I turned to Vincent, who could practically be Dante's twin, and said, "Thank you, too. I won't forget what both of you did for me today."

Vincent shrugged and said, "Happy to help." He was so casual about it, as if he'd just helped me carry some groceries into the house, instead of saving my life.

I handed Jack the bottles of water and the Advil, and then I picked him up and carried him upstairs. At the same time, Nana started cussing a blue streak and chewing out Dante and Vincent for leaving her behind on the rescue mission. I liked her already.

Once we reached an unoccupied bedroom, I closed the door behind us with my foot, carried Jack across the room, and sat him on the edge of the bed. After I gave him a few pills and he washed them down with water, I told him I'd be right back and hurried into the adjoining bathroom.

I returned a few moments later with a dry towel and a wet one. Then I knelt in front of him and cleaned his feet one at a time as I asked, "What happened to your shoes, baby?"

He mumbled, "I left them with the bike I used to ride up to the compound. They were squeaky, and I needed to be quiet while I was trying to find you. We knew we were in the right place because Josh flew his camera drone over the property beforehand, and I recognized one of the men who'd shot up the bar. But we didn't know where exactly they were keeping you."

I helped him strip off his soiled outfit before tucking him into bed. He fell asleep almost immediately, and I went and took a long, hot shower.

When I came back to the bedroom, I shut off the overhead light. I could still see Jack in the light spilling from the bathroom, and I moved a chair beside the bed and watched him while he slept.

As tired as I was, I couldn't quiet my mind enough to sleep just yet. Instead, I drained one of the bottles of water and leaned back in the chair with a heavy sigh.

My head was pounding. Since I'd been knocked unconscious earlier that day, I probably had a concussion. Just about everything else hurt too, including my wrists, which were raw and chafed from the ropes. And my bruised ribs ached on every inhale, thanks to a hard punch from one of Greco's lackeys.

But I'd gotten damn lucky today, and I knew it. If Greco hadn't been out of town when I was captured, he probably would have tortured the hell out of me. He might have even killed me.

Instead, the most unexpected thing had happened. I'd thought the situation was hopeless, and that no one would come to save me. I'd thought I was all alone. Then Jack proved me wrong.

I leaned forward and gently brushed a lock of hair out of his eyes. He looked delicate and fragile, but in truth, he was tough and brave and strong as steel. Tonight, he'd shown me he was a warrior, and I was awed and humbled by him.

I'd already known I was falling head over heels for this amazing, beautiful, totally unexpected man. And now, everything I felt for him was utterly overwhelming.

19

Adriano

Jack and I slept in the next morning. He didn't feel great when he finally woke up, so I told him to stay right where he was. Then I got dressed and hurried downstairs.

The Dombrusos were gathered around the big dining table adjacent to the kitchen. It seemed so strange that they were here with me. How many times had I thought about them over the years? But now, in the midst of all that had been happening, I could barely make sense of it.

There was a breakfast buffet set up in the kitchen, complete with catering-style warming trays, and I asked, "Is it okay if I take some of this to Jack?"

"Of course," Nana yelled from the far side of the dining table. "You don't even have to ask!"

I found a tray and started loading it with things I thought Jack might like. A few moments later, Dante came into the kitchen with an empty coffee cup and told me, "Vincent and I led a raid on Greco's compound this morning at dawn."

I stopped what I was doing and turned to him. "Without me?"

"We would've brought him to you if we'd found him, but we figured it was important for you and Jack to rest and heal after the day you had yesterday. Nothing came of it anyway. Everyone was gone, and it looked like they'd cleared out in a hurry. I assigned a couple of guys to keep an eye on the compound, but I'd be surprised if Greco returns. He probably figures you're out for revenge, and now he knows you have backup. He won't make it easy for you to find him."

"Thanks for trying. I should have been included, though."

"You're right. Next time."

He poured himself a cup of coffee, but instead of leaving the kitchen, he stood there awkwardly for a few moments before saying, "Jack told me you came to see me after you graduated from high school. I don't remember much about that. In fact, the next day I wasn't sure if it had even really happened. What I do know is that I was drunk at the time. I was also an angry little shit back then, and I totally fucked it up when you tried to talk to me. I want you to know I'm really sorry, Adriano."

I went back to filling the tray as I muttered, "It doesn't matter."

"Sure it does. I'm your big brother, and—"

"Half-brother."

"That doesn't make a bit of difference," he said. "You're family, and by being a dick, I ended up costing us the last two decades."

I glanced at him, then looked away again and shrugged. "You were young, and I came at you out of nowhere. We both could have handled it better."

"I never knew that my parents split up for a while. Nana talked about it for the first time on the flight here. She didn't know about you, but she knew about the separation. I guess they were apart for six months or so, when I was about three. She said it was my mom's doing, that she got tired of all the danger and drama that came with my dad being in the mob."

"Yeah. That's how my mom tells it."

He lowered his voice, like he didn't want everyone in the next room to overhear him. "I did the math, and it turns out my mom got pregnant with my brother Gianni while she and our dad were separated. Nana said Dad came back to see us a few times during those six months, so maybe my parents hooked up during one of those visits…or maybe my mom was seeing someone else, too. If he had a different father, it could explain why Gianni's the only one of us that ended up with blue eyes and a smaller build."

I asked, "Are you going to tell Gianni about this?"

"I have to, even if it's just speculation at this point. If he has a father out there somewhere, he has a right to know that."

"So, I may actually be one of two half-brothers."

"*No.* You're one of five brothers." Dante's tone left no room for argument. "You and Romy have different dads, but does that make the slightest difference? Do you love him half as much because you only share half the genes?"

"Of course not."

"Okay, then knock it off with this half bullshit."

I grinned a little and said, "Fine. You're really fucking bossy, though."

He grinned, too. "As the oldest brother, it's my job to keep the rest of you mooks in line. Make no mistake though, Nana's the boss and supreme ruler of this family. She's currently sulking, because she got left out of the rescue operation last night. But she'll decide she's bored of that soon, and then watch out."

I fidgeted with the tray's handle, and after a few moments I said, "Your parents were separated when I was conceived, which means there was no cheating involved. So, why was I treated like a dirty little secret?" It was doubly hard to swallow now that I knew Gianni's situation might be similar to mine, but he'd obviously been welcomed into the family with open arms.

"I wish I knew. The only two people who could have answered that died a long time ago. But if I had to guess, maybe your mother and our father were close, and maybe my mom was threatened by that. I've heard she was the jealous type, so maybe she made Paulie promise never to see either of you again. I mean, who really knows? But that's the only thing that makes sense to me."

"I could see that."

"I'm sorry you were shut out of the family," Dante said. "That wasn't fair to you."

"It doesn't really matter. I have a great mom and an amazing kid brother, and I had a happy childhood. I wouldn't change a minute of it." After a moment, I admitted, "Well, except that I would have loved to have met my dad. I was four when he was killed. If that hadn't happened, maybe he would have come to see me at some point. It would have meant the world to me."

Dante paused before saying quietly, "I tracked down the man responsible for the home invasion, years later. He paid for what he did." He didn't spell it out, but his meaning was clear—the man who'd killed my dad had paid with his life.

I met his gaze as the weight of what he'd just admitted settled on both of us. He seemed to be making a point of keeping his expression neutral, but all kinds of emotion churned in his dark eyes.

While I was trying to figure out what to say to that, he broke eye contact and took the plate of quiche and O'Brien potatoes from my tray. "Your food's getting cold," he said. "I'll stick this in the microwave while you finish getting your breakfast together."

In other words, he really didn't want to talk about it.

I turned my attention to assembling a collection of baked goods and heaping a bowl with fruit salad. After Dante returned the warmed plate, he asked, "Do you and Jack need anything?"

"Yeah, we do." I picked up the tray and told him, "I could use some medical supplies so I can change his bandage, and I'm pretty sure he doesn't have anything to wear besides that pink track suit."

As we left the kitchen, he said, "I can track down a first aid kit and see if Josh and Darwin can lend Jack some clothes, since they're close to his size. I'll leave everything outside your door."

Nana overheard that, and she jumped up and asked, "Why didn't you tell me Jack needs clothes? I'll go shopping and buy him whatever he needs! Do me a favor and ask him to write down all his sizes, Adriano."

"That's nice of you," I said, "but are you sure it isn't too much trouble?"

She waved her hand and exclaimed, "Of course not! I seem to remember there's a great, big mall somewhere in Vegas, so it'll be fun!"

"We'll go with her," Darwin said. "In the meantime, Josh and I can definitely lend Jack some stuff." I thanked them before carrying the tray upstairs.

Jack was sitting up under the covers when I reached the bedroom, and he grinned at me and said, "I seem to be naked, and I think the only thing I have to wear is a dirty Care Bears ensemble. My suit got ruined when I was shot."

"I'm on it. Or, technically, the Dombrusos are. Sorry that took so long, by the way. I ended up having a pretty deep conversation with Dante."

"That wasn't long at all, and I'm glad you two are bonding. I have a good feeling about him, and I don't say that about many people."

"I do too."

I positioned the tray in the center of the bed, and while he started packing away the fruit salad, I found a pen and paper and asked him his sizes. Then I stuck the note out in the hall before gingerly climbing onto the mattress.

After a few moments, he glanced at me from beneath his lashes and told me, "I'm sorry for running off the way I did yesterday morning. I got scared and was feeling overwhelmed, but that's no excuse. I came back to apologize, and to talk about it—"

"Right in time to get shot. I'm so fucking sorry that happened to you."

"That wasn't your fault, and you don't need to apologize."

"Yes, it was. If I'd stood up to Greco in the first place, instead of retreating to San Francisco—"

"Then you'd probably be dead now."

I could tell this was upsetting him, so I let the subject drop. I'd handle Greco on my own, and the less Jack knew about it, the better. I didn't want him to get implicated in…

What exactly?

A murder?

Was I willing to go that far to make sure Greco never harmed my loved ones again?

Would anything short of that actually stop him?

20

Jack

Adriano brought us a huge breakfast, and somehow between the two of us we actually managed to polish it off. After we ate, he said, "I'd like to give you a bath. I know that must sound odd, but I have this overwhelming urge to take care of you. So, will you just go with it?"

Normally, I'd insist I was fine and didn't need him to take care of me, but this seemed important to him. Besides, I really wasn't okay. That rescue mission right on the heels of getting injured had taken a lot out of me—not that I would have done a single thing differently.

When I agreed, he moved the breakfast tray to the dresser and hurried to fill the tub. He came back a few minutes later and carefully wrapped my injured upper arm in a hand towel to keep it dry. Then he picked me up and brought me into the bathroom.

After he carefully lowered me into the warm water, I rested my arm on the edge of the tub and exhaled slowly. It seemed like overkill when he soaped up his hands and went to wash me. I wasn't *that* injured. But then he began to rub my shoulders, and I muttered, "Okay, this I can do."

"Hmm?"

I hadn't actually meant to say that out loud, but I told him, "I thought it might be awkward—letting you scrub me down like a dog at a grooming parlor. But this is nice."

He chuckled at that and pushed his hair out of his eyes with his forearm before going back to what he was doing. I groaned with pleasure as his strong hands began kneading a knot of tension. "That right there, that's magical," I murmured, as my eyes slid shut.

"I'm glad you like it."

"I love it. I only have one question."

"What's that?"

I raised a lid and asked, "Why are you out there, and not in here with me?"

"Two reasons," he said, as he kept up the massage. "First, it's a small tub, and I'm a big guy. If I got in there with you, there wouldn't be any room for the water."

"You'd fit just fine. What's your other flimsy excuse?"

He ran his knuckles along my jaw and met my gaze. "You're the most tempting, irresistible man I've ever met, Jack. Getting in that tub with you and feeling your wet, naked body against mine would turn me on, but since we probably both have concussions, we need to abstain from sex for a few days while we heal and recover."

I frowned at that and asked, "Who says?"

"Most doctors, probably."

"Well, what do they know?"

"A lot."

I knew he was right, but I pouted anyway. Finally, I said, "Okay, fine. No sex for twenty-four hours."

"Try a week."

"That can't be right. Sex is good for you. It'll only help the healing process!" He grinned and shook his head. "I want actual scientific evidence," I said. "Clinical trials and double-blind studies with conclusive evidence that it's actually bad for you to do it with a concussion."

He gently traced my chin with a fingertip as he said, "There's no way you feel well enough for sex right now."

"Well no, not right this minute. But I will in a day or two, not *a week*."

"Let's just take it day by day and see how it goes."

"It's annoying how you're all mature and right about things." He smiled at me, and I asked, "So, what're we supposed to do in the meantime? Die of blue balls?"

"I can stand it if you can," he said. "And just think how much fun it'll be once we both feel better and can finally have sex again, without a pounding headache and countless aches and pains."

I looked at him closely and said, "You feel as bad as I do right now, don't you?"

"No. I wasn't shot."

"But you were knocked out, probably beat up, and then held hostage in an overheated garage. That didn't do you any favors."

I pulled the plug and started to climb out of the tub, and he asked, "What are you doing?"

"Switching with you," I said. "You need this more than I do."

He plugged the drain again and gently restrained me with a hand on my chest. Then he ran more warm water into the tub and told me, "Just relax, Jack, at least for a few minutes."

Reluctantly, I leaned back and said, "Fine. But once I'm done, you're getting in here and taking a nice, long soak."

"I promise I'll do that. Tonight though, after dinner."

"What? Why?"

"Because there's a lot I need to do today."

I shot him a look. "Like napping and resting?"

"Like cleaning up the shattered glass at the bar and replacing the front window again. I also need to meet with my men, and—"

"No. Absolutely not."

"Which part?"

"All of it! What do you think, that a double standard applies because you're a tough guy and I'm a little wimp? If I have to rest, so do you!"

He sat back on his heels and said, "I would never call you a wimp. Just the opposite, I think you're incredibly strong. I already knew that, but you reminded me yesterday when you were saving my ass."

"That's actually very sweet, but my point remains. You're spending the next couple of days resting, just like I am."

"But—"

"I'm serious." Bath water dripped onto his black T-shirt when I sat up and cupped his cheek. "You carry the weight of the world on your shoulders, Reno, but don't you see? You don't have to take on everything by yourself."

"I know, but I really need to get the bar operational again. It's important."

"It is, but you have a lot of people on your payroll, so delegate. Assign one of your men to supervise the window replacement and another to hire a cleaning crew to take care of the broken glass. There's no reason to handle all of this on your own."

"Okay, but my crew's numbers are in my phone. I left it behind the bar, so I have to go get it."

"Romy can bring it to you."

Adriano shook his head. "He has to work."

"He took the week off when you were abducted," I said. "He can bring you the phone and whatever else you left at the bar. He was planning to come by later anyway, because as he reminded me, it's not okay to dodge the police when there's a shooting. So, he's bringing his cop friend to take our statements."

Reno sighed and muttered, "That's just great. Then if anything happens to Greco, guess who'll be the first person they haul down to the station?"

"So, we'll keep it vague and play down any sort of feud or rivalry," I said. "We also won't say a word about your illegal gambling operation, obviously. For all they know you're just an innocent victim, so why would you retaliate?"

He raised a brow and asked, "Think they'll buy it?"

"Who knows? It's worth a shot, though."

After my bath, I drained and refilled the tub for Adriano. Then I made him get in and relax while I texted his brother. When he joined me in the bedroom sometime later, I said, "Turns out, Romy already took care of cleaning up the bar this morning. He also picked up your phone and laptop case, which he'll deliver this afternoon. Plus, he found the receipt for the glass company you used last time and is having them come back out to install a new window."

"He didn't have to do that."

"He wanted to, so now you don't have to worry about it," I said. "There's more good news, too. Your mom's boyfriend convinced her to spend the rest of the week in L.A. with him, which means Mandy's Place will be closed for a few days. Hopefully things with Greco will be resolved by the time she returns, so the bar won't continue to be a battleground."

Adriano looked surprised. "I can't believe he convinced her to go. She almost never closes the bar."

"Apparently he has an art show in L.A., so he used it as an excuse."

"That's actually a huge relief," he said, as he opened the bedroom door and picked up a stack of clothes and a first aid kit. "Now I know she's safe, for the next few days at least."

It seemed several Dombrusos had loaned both of us some clothes. After we got dressed in clean T-shirts and sweats, Reno carefully disinfected and rewrapped my wound. Then, by some miracle, I actually convinced him to get back into bed with me.

He stretched out on his side and closed his eyes. But a moment later, his eyes flew open, and he sat up and exclaimed, "You pushed me out of the way!"

"What?"

"It was all a blur, but it's coming back to me now. When Greco's men started shooting, you saw them before I did. You could have ducked behind a table and saved yourself. But instead, you stepped forward and pushed me to the floor, and you ended up taking a bullet."

"You were facing away from the window, so you had no idea what was about to go down. It was the only way to make sure you didn't get shot."

"But why would you save me, instead of saving yourself?"

"Because I care about you so much, Reno, and I needed you to be okay."

He caressed my cheekbone and studied me with wonder in his eyes. When his lips met mine, the kiss was sweet and tender.

Then he held me in his arms and rubbed my back. As I let myself relax, I marveled at how effortless it was to be with him. I'd spent so much of my life afraid to trust, afraid to let anyone in, lying by telling myself I was fine on my own. But I didn't feel afraid anymore. Instead, I felt like I was exactly where I belonged.

I wanted to explain to him how huge this was, but I couldn't find the words. What I said instead was, "I'm so grateful for you, Reno."

His eyes crinkled at the corners when he smiled at me, and he said, "I'm grateful for you too, doll face." That made me so happy.

We spent the next few hours in bed, alternately talking or napping. I knew it was hard for Reno to allow himself to relax, especially while the situation with Greco was weighing heavily on him. But he managed to be present in the moment, and it meant a lot to me.

Finally, in the early afternoon, we emerged from our room to meet with Romy's cop friend. Reno and I were both unfailingly polite to this guy, but there was also a lot of stiffness and formality, which definitely wasn't our norm.

I wondered if the cop picked up on it, and if he actually bought our story, which we tried to spin as a random robbery and kidnapping for ransom. There was no other way to avoid exposing Adriano's illegal gambling operation. Fortunately, Romy wanted to give us some privacy, so he'd left to run an errand after he introduced us. Otherwise, he would've called bullshit on the whole thing.

By the time Romy returned, his friend was putting away his notebook. The cop handed over a business card and asked us to call him if we remembered anything else. Then he paused and looked at us closely before he left. Okay, so he probably suspected we were lying, but since we were the victims of a violent crime, he wasn't going to put us through the ringer.

Meanwhile, Romy was sweetly oblivious. "See? I told you it'd be quick and painless," he said with a smile.

"I'm just glad to get it over with," Reno muttered. Then he changed the subject with, "How'd it go at the bar today?"

"Fine. The new window was installed, and it only took me about an hour to clean up the glass and blood. It's all good as new and ready for Mom when she gets back from L.A."

"Thanks for taking care of that."

"Not a problem."

Reno took a sip from a glass of water, and then he asked, "What do you think of Mom's new boyfriend?"

"I like him," Romy said, as he got comfortable on one of the mustard yellow club chairs. "Once you get past being called 'dude' every three minutes, he's actually a great guy. Best of all, he adores our mom. I think she finally found her other half, and you obviously have, too. That just leaves me, Romeo Fifth-Wheel Russo."

I asked Romy, "You're not currently seeing anyone?"

He tried to smile, but it was unconvincing. "Nope. I've officially given up on finding love."

"At twenty-seven? That seems a bit premature."

"I've been dating for a decade, and I'm over it. I really tried to put myself out there and find someone, but all it got me was heartbreak, over and over again. I've been dumped, cheated on, lied to— it was pretty much a dumpster fire. So, I guess I'm just destined to be single, and I'm okay with that." No, he wasn't. The sadness in his eyes told me otherwise, loud and clear.

"You just picked the wrong guys," Reno said. "You're drawn to bad boys, when what you need is someone nice. What about your friend that was just here, the cop? What was his name, Freddy? He was…"

He seemed to be at a loss for adjectives, so I tried to help. "Not horrible?"

"His name's Frank, and god no," Romy said. "Never mind that he's straight. He's also just so…"

I said, "Boring?"

At the same time, Reno guessed, "Cop-like?"

Romy shot us both a look, and then he said, "I want someone who's passionate—about life…about me. Or I did, you know, when I was looking for love." It made me sad that he was trying to talk himself out of something that clearly mattered to him.

He stopped talking when Dante, Charlie, and Vincent came into the room. The brothers seemed to intimidate him. I really hoped he didn't think they were trying to replace him in Adriano's life, because there was no way that would ever happen.

As they joined us around the coffee table, Adriano asked them, "How long are you guys planning to stay in Las Vegas?"

Dante answered for them. "Vincent will need to head back to San Francisco soon. He has little kids at home, and I know he misses them and his husband Trevor like crazy. Josh and Darwin will probably head back at the same time, since they're both in college and ditching class to be here. And Nana's going to do what she always does—whatever the hell she wants. As for Charlie and me, we're planning to stay as long as it takes to resolve this situation. I brought in eight more men, by the way, so there are now two dozen people out there making waves and looking for Greco. As long as he doesn't skip town, I expect to find him any day now."

"I doubt he'd leave town," Adriano said. "That'd be like admitting defeat, and he's not about to do that."

I asked, "What exactly is the plan, once you find him? I mean, I assume it'll involve threatening him and beating him up, but is that really going to be enough to get him to permanently back off and leave Adriano and his family alone?"

Dante and Adriano glanced at each other, and Dante told me, "That's entirely up to your boyfriend. Whatever Adriano decides, I'll back him up." I wondered just how far Reno would actually take this.

Just then, the front door was thrown open and Dante, Vincent, and Adriano tensed up and leapt to their feet. But it wasn't a raid by Greco, it was the return of the shopping expedition.

Nana led the march into the house, daintily carrying a small, pink shopping bag. Behind her were Josh and Darwin and a short, stocky little old man they'd apparently picked up along the way. All three of Nana's companions were loaded down with shopping bags.

Her face lit up when she saw us, and she exclaimed, "There you boys are! Adriano and Jack, meet my husband Ollie. He's actually my second husband, due to the fact that my first one was a no-good bum. Ollie had to stay behind in San Francisco for a day to finish up a charity auction we're putting together, but he flew out this afternoon to surprise me."

We exchanged greetings and shook hands with Ollie, after he offloaded eight bulging bags onto the coffee table. Then Adriano introduced Romy, who asked, "Was there some kind of clearance sale at the mall?"

Ollie took a seat and put his feet up on the coffee table. "Nah. My girl just got excited, because she had a cute new family member to shop for. While she was at it, she picked up a few things for herself, of course, along with some gifts for the rest of her boys."

I was surprised to discover he actually meant me when he mentioned a new family member. Nana squeezed in between Adriano and me on the couch, pulled some of the shopping bags closer, and began unpacking her finds, which she piled onto my lap. "Thank you," I said, as she thrust a shoe box into my hands. "Please let me know how much I owe you, and I'll pay you back." But I might have to rob a bank first, because the pile on my lap was still growing.

"Don't be silly," she said, as she added something small and sheer to the pile. Oh god, she'd actually bought me sexy underwear. "I don't want you to pay me back! I just want you to enjoy this stuff, as much as I enjoyed shopping for it."

Josh and Darwin added their bags to the pile as Josh said, "And let me tell you, she enjoyed the hell out of this shopping trip. It was all we could do to get her to stop for lunch."

"I tell you what though, I'm about done for the day," she said, as she placed a mesh tank top on my lap. Good lord, Reno's granny was really trying to tart me up. "Jack and Aidie shouldn't be going out anyway, what with needing to recover and all, so let's have dinner delivered tonight." I grinned at her nickname for Adriano, and I was happy when she turned to Romy and asked, "Can you stay and eat with us, kiddo?"

Romy turned his gaze to the gold shag carpeting as he said, "Thanks, but I have plans."

I didn't believe him. He was probably just overwhelmed by all of his brother's new family members, same as I was. In fact, he made an excuse soon after and said he needed to go.

First though, he pulled aside Adriano and me for a quick medical exam. We moved into the quiet sitting room at the front of the house, and he checked our vital signs and shone a small flashlight in our eyes to see how our pupils responded. Then he turned his attention to my arm. As he changed out the butterfly bandages that had replaced some of my torn stitches, I told him, "The Dombrusos could never take your place in Reno's life, Romy. You know that, right?"

He nodded embarrassedly and didn't look at either of us as Adriano asked him, "Were you worried about that?" Romy just shrugged, and his brother said, "Nothing could ever change the way I feel about you, kid. I've loved you since the day you were born, and you're more than my brother. You're my best friend."

"I don't want to make this about me," Romy muttered. "It's fantastic that you finally got to meet your dad's side of the family, and that they're so eager to bring you into the fold. Your new brothers are great, too, and so much like you. It's funny, actually—it's like all three of you were cut from the same cloth. I wonder if the two you haven't met yet are the same."

He was right about that. Besides the fact that they all looked so much alike and were close to the same age, it was as if Adriano and his two older brothers were all throwbacks to a bygone era—a time of gangsters, and Sinatra, and swagger.

I would have assumed they were all emulating their father, but Adriano had never met him, and Dante and Vincent had been little kids when he died. Maybe they were just influenced by the idea of him and had modeled themselves after the kind of man they thought he'd been, regardless of who he really was.

After Romy finished wrapping a clean bandage around my arm,

he packed up his medical bag and took off. Then Reno moved over so he was sitting beside me on the little, avocado green loveseat and drew me onto his lap.

I kissed him before resting my head on his shoulder, and he wrapped his arms around me and buried his face in my hair. After a while, he said, "This is such a strange time. There are all these new family members to get to know, and my mom and Romy to worry about, and then there's you and me. This thing that's happening between us is amazing. It excites me and makes me feel optimistic, and I haven't felt like that in a very long time.

"Meanwhile though, the situation with Greco is still hanging over our heads, and I don't know when or how that's going to get resolved. I'm terrified you'll get hurt again, but I'm also so damn grateful you're here with me. It feels like we're in the eye of a storm —a place where everything is calm and perfect, even though there's chaos circling us."

"There's no place I'd rather be than right here with you," I whispered, as I nuzzled his cheek.

"When this is all over, can we go somewhere? Just you and me?"

There was so much longing in his eyes when I sat up and met his gaze. "Of course. Where do you want to go?"

"Anywhere. You pick. All I want is a hotel with room service and an uninterrupted week with you."

I grinned and asked, "Just a week?"

He smiled at me, which made his hazel eyes sparkle. "For starters."

21

Adriano

The next few days were surprisingly blissful. I retrieved some clothes and a few things from my house, and Jack and I settled into the rental with my new-found family. I figured as long as they were in Vegas, I shouldn't pass up the opportunity to get to know them.

Besides, the house they'd rented was huge, so why not stay with them? It had eight bedrooms, most of which were empty after Vincent, Darwin, and Josh returned to San Francisco. That left Dante and his husband Charlie, and Nana and Ollie. The four of them were treating this like a vacation, and why not? They might as well enjoy themselves while we were all in this holding pattern.

I was trying not to feel guilty about the fact that it felt like a vacation to me, too. Jack and I had both needed these past few days to heal and recover, so I had to accept the fact that I couldn't actively look for Greco.

It probably wouldn't have helped much anyway. Despite having a team of almost thirty people—between my crew and Dante's small army—at work trying to find him, it was as if the man had vanished. If he'd left town, that would explain it. But something in my gut told me he was still around, lurking in the shadows and looking for his next opportunity to lash out at me.

As great as it was to get to know my new relatives, the absolute highlight of that week was Jack. He was just pure joy. I loved the way he got excited about the littlest things, like when I'd surprised him by making his favorite dessert after he mentioned it in passing. You'd have thought I'd bought him a car, given how appreciative he was.

I also loved the fact that he was a voracious reader. He read every chance he got, anything from nonfiction to gay romance to sci fi. Whenever he came across a passage he particularly liked, he just had to share it with me. Each time, it felt like he was giving me a gift.

His eagerness to learn was remarkable, too—whether it was Dante and Charlie teaching him a card game, Ollie showing him how to crochet, or Nana teaching him how to curse in Italian, he soaked it up like a sponge and clamored for more.

My contribution to his ongoing quest for knowledge was to share everything I knew about music from the Rat Pack era, which was one of my only areas of expertise. The rental had a big, kidney-shaped pool in the back yard, and he loved the water, so we'd float for hours and listen to song after song. Then I'd tell him everything I knew about the artists. We spent so much time out there that the blond highlights in his hair intensified, and Jack's skin turned golden brown—except for a pale band around his right bicep that was covered by the waterproof bandages Romy had brought him. He might have just been humoring me, but he claimed to develop a real appreciation for my favorite music.

On our sixth day at the rental, we floated serenely on our inflatable loungers, our joined hands keeping us side-by-side while Dean Martin sang in the background. The sun was setting, bathing the yard and the water and both of us in a warm glow. He was always beautiful, but in that moment with the light turning his skin to gold, he was ethereal.

He wore mirrored, aviator-style sunglasses—actually, the pair we'd taken from Greco's convertible—and in them, I could see the sky's reflection. After a while, his sexy full lips curled into a lopsided grin, and he murmured, "You're staring at me."

"Of course I am. You're the most beautiful man in the world. Why wouldn't I stare?"

He sighed and shook his head, and then he fell silent for a while. Something was on his mind, I could tell.

Finally, he said, "We've been in Vegas for a while now. I was planning to get your watch back as soon as we returned to San Francisco, but now I hope it's not too late. What if the person who has it moved out of my building? Or—"

"No pressure. Once we get back to California, we'll try to retrieve it. But if it's gone, it's gone."

He frowned at that and reminded me, "It's your most prized possession."

"It was. But it's just a thing, Jack."

"I don't understand," he said. "I thought that watch meant everything to you."

"It used to be really important, because it was the only thing my dad gave me. But that's not true anymore. It turns out, he gave me an entire second family, and four more brothers. In a lot of ways, he also gave me you."

Jack raised a brow and said, "The family I get. But how do I fit in?"

"The watch, and by extension my dad, gave us all this time together to really get to know each other, and to build something that's going to last."

He grinned and nodded. "Okay. I can see the logic there."

"For the record, I was planning to ask you out the night we met, after you came back downstairs from taking a shower. Would you have said yes?"

His smile faded. "I would have wanted to. I was wildly attracted to you from the moment we met, but…I don't know what I would have said. I never dated. Literally never. I was afraid of getting close to people, so I might have denied myself the chance to get to know you. That seems so awful now, the thought that I could have missed out on this, and on you—"

"Don't feel bad," I said. "This all worked out exactly like it was supposed to, and here we are." I was glad to see his smile return.

We were still floating and holding hands a few minutes later, when Charlie opened the patio door and called, "Dante wanted me to remind you that we have dinner reservations at eight, and you mentioned grabbing some cocktails beforehand." He was grinning as he said that. I wasn't sure what the Dombrusos were up to, but there was definitely some sort of surprise in the works for this evening.

After we climbed out of the pool, I wrapped Jack in a beach towel before picking up mine and drying myself off. As he scrubbed his hair with a corner of the towel, he asked, "What do you think the Dombrusos are up to? It really feels like they're hatching some sort of surprise for tonight."

"I was just thinking the same thing."

When we went inside, we found Charlie sitting in the living room with his phone, and I asked him, "Where is everyone?"

He told us, "Nana and Ollie wanted to do some gambling, so they headed to the Strip and will meet us at the restaurant. As for Dante, he had an errand to run." There was that grin again.

"So, when do we find out about whatever you and your husband are planning for tonight?"

Charlie's eyes went wide, in an attempt to look innocent. "I have no idea what you're talking about. If something was in the works though, it would be a fun surprise. Nothing to do with Greco, who's still in the wind."

"Yeah, I didn't think it had anything to do with him." As Jack and I headed for the stairs, I said, "We're going to go get cleaned up, and we'll be ready in about half an hour. How are we getting to the restaurant?"

"Nana arranged transportation," Charlie said, with an amused expression. "I'm sure it'll be super understated and tasteful."

Nope.

Nana had, in fact, booked the longest, gaudiest stretch limo she could find. Since this was Vegas, that meant it was the longest, gaudiest stretch limo in existence. The thing was Barbie pink, glittery, and about a block long, with gold rims and pink running lights. In the very back was a hot tub, which was running at full bubble and lit up in bright turquoise.

The driver holding the door for us was a tall, slender guy with bleached white-blond hair. He was dressed in a hot pink chauffeur's uniform, which was form-fitting and included shorts instead of pants, along with matching high heels. He looked familiar, so I paused in front of him and asked, "Pete?"

Color rose in his cheeks as he said, "Hiya, Reno. How's your brother?" He and Romy had been friends in high school, but they'd drifted apart over the years.

"He's doing great," I said. "How've you been?"

"I'm okay. This gig is only temporary," he quickly added. "I was working as a go-go dancer, but the club got shut down. I thought this would be a step up, but boy was I wrong. Turns out bachelorettes are terrifying. They're like a pack of drunk, horny wolves in miniskirts." That was a mental picture I could have done without, but I nodded sympathetically before introducing Jack and Charlie.

He asked if I'd give Romy his number, and while he was writing it on the back of a business card, I told him, "Just FYI, I'm not the person who booked this limo." It probably seemed odd that three men in suits were choosing to get around in a giant party-mobile.

He smiled at me as he handed over the card and said, "I know. I've been driving Nana and her husband around all afternoon. She told me to call her that, by the way. She's a trip. When she found out I was gay, I think she wanted to adopt me."

Charlie nodded and said, "Yup, she does that."

Once we were settled into the black and hot pink interior and headed toward the Strip, Jack took my hand and said, "I know this is tacky. I do. But it's my first time in a limo, and it's actually pretty amazing."

"It's my first time, too," I told him. "Why don't you see what those buttons do?"

He got some music playing with the control panel beside him, and once he managed to open the sun roof, we both looked at each other and grinned. Then we stood up so we were sticking out of the roof, and he laughed delightedly. I loved seeing the pure joy on his face. It made me think I'd do anything to keep him happy.

Charlie stood up a few moments later and brushed his short brown hair back as the wind whipped it around. "I feel like we're on our way to prom," he said with a grin.

It was a fairly short ride, and we spent all of it standing. Dante was waiting out front when the limo arrived at our destination, and he chuckled and snapped a picture of the three of us with his phone.

Our reservation was at a new, celebrity chef-owned restaurant inside a massive hotel and casino. Like the limo, it had been Nana's idea. It was a wonder that they'd managed a reservation on only a few days' notice, but then the Dombrusos had a lot of connections.

As we cut across the glitzy, golden lobby, Dante said, "Let's go upstairs for a few minutes. I booked us a suite so we'd have a quiet place to talk. The restaurant and its bar are so crowded and noisy that you can barely hear yourself think." Then he sent a text as we rode the elevator to the top floor.

We found Vincent waiting for us in the hallway. "Good to see you again," I said, as we shook hands. That felt a little formal, but he didn't really strike me as the hugging type.

He led us into the opulent penthouse suite, where we were joined by a slender brunet. Vincent looked at the man lovingly and said, "Adriano and Jack, I'd like you to meet my husband, Trevor."

After we shook his hand and exchanged greetings, Jack asked, "Are your kids here, too?"

"No," Trevor said, as he took Vincent's hand. "We're just here overnight, and Josh and Darwin are babysitting for us. Mike's three teenage sons are 'helping' babysit, too. That means gorging themselves on pizza and staying up way too late playing video games."

Dante turned to the couple who'd just joined us and said, "Mikey, meet your brother Adriano, and his boyfriend Jack."

Mike looked a lot like Dante and Vincent with his big build, dark hair, and olive skin. He frowned at his older brother, and then he surprised me by grabbing me in a hug as he said, "I'm so happy to meet you. Just FYI, everyone calls me Mike except for Dante and Vincent, because they're assholes and refuse to let me outgrow Mikey."

Then Mike let go of me and introduced us to his husband Yoshi, who was a handsome Japanese-American guy with an intricate black ink tattoo on one arm. He studied me curiously as we shook hands and said, "Wow, this is wild. I could barely believe it when Vincent told us about another brother, but you're definitely a Dombruso. The resemblance is hard to miss."

"There's one more brother to meet," Dante said, as we moved from the entryway into the suite's spacious living room.

I asked, "Is Gianni here?"

Vincent nodded. "He and his husband are in the bedroom. Dante felt it was best to give him the news about potentially having a different dad in person, so he only found that out an hour ago."

I asked, "Is he okay?"

"Yeah. He's just taking some time to process it," Mike said. "I'll go tell him you're here."

He left the living room while the rest of us took a seat on the white leather couches, and Yoshi told us, "Gianni's husband is famous, by the way. I'm just throwing that out there so you don't freak out when you meet him."

Jack asked, "How famous are we talking here?"

Yoshi considered the question before saying, "Well, he was huge about twenty years ago, and then he took a hiatus from his musical career for a while. He's made a comeback in the last few years though, so he's pretty much back to being recognized everywhere he goes. You've probably heard of him. His name's—"

Jack whispered, "Zan Tillane. No fucking way," as the pop star came into the living room. He looked like he was about fifty, with greying, slightly long hair and a beard, and he was holding hands with a blue-eyed brunet, who was eyeing me curiously.

There was another round of introductions. Instead of shaking my hand, Gianni held it between both of his and said, "Dante called and told me about you a few days ago. Apparently there was a bit more to the story, though. I found out the rest earlier this evening."

"I'm sorry I stirred things up like that." I felt guilty, even though I hadn't actually done anything wrong.

"No, don't apologize. I'd wondered about something like that over the years, since I'm the only member of our family with blue eyes. Plus, Mike, Dante, and Vincent look so damn much alike, and I just don't match." He was trying to act casual about it, but there was no question this news had rattled him.

I asked, "Do you think you'll take a DNA test?"

He shrugged. "Maybe at some point, just to satisfy my curiosity. Really though, whether or not Paulie Dombruso was my biological father doesn't change a thing. I'm a Dombruso, and I love my family with all my heart.

"But I don't want that bombshell to overshadow this moment, because holy shit, I have a new brother!" It surprised me when his eyes began to fill with tears, and he grabbed me in a hug. "I'm so fucking sorry it took this long for you to be welcomed to the family. That's not right. Our parents should have told us about you."

I was touched by that outpouring of emotion, and as I embraced him I said, "It's all in the past. What matters is that we're here now, and I'm really grateful for it."

22

Jack

It was overwhelming to find myself with all of Adriano's new brothers and their husbands, so I could only imagine how he felt. Also, my god was there a lot of gay in that family!

As he and Gianni hugged it out, I snuck a glance at the very famous pop star in our midst. That was just surreal. I'd never met a famous person before, and I was actually a huge Zan Tillane fan. But for both my sake and Adriano's—because I didn't want him to seem dorky by association—I tried to play it cool.

One of the husbands, a super cool guy dressed all in black named Yoshi, asked me if I'd like a drink, then handed me a gin and tonic when I nodded. I thanked him before slamming it back in one go, and he grinned and refilled my glass. "This must be a lot to take in," he said, as he took a seat beside me on the couch.

"It is. Everyone's incredibly welcoming, though. It's kind of surprising, actually. It must have been weird for them to suddenly learn they had a new family member, but they seem to be taking it in stride."

"That's probably Nana's influence. She's all about bringing people into the family. Her specialty is gay men who don't really have anyone else. She already has a huge biological family, but that's a fraction of the bigger family she's created back home in San Francisco," he said with a grin.

A few moments later, Adriano sat down beside me and took my hand. That felt good. It was as if I provided a sense of security to him when things felt overwhelming. I smiled at him and handed him my drink, which he tossed back like I had.

Dante and Charlie snuggled up together on the other side of the coffee table, and Dante said, "Just so you know, I invited Romy to join us this evening, but he said he had plans. I didn't want him to think we were trying to exclude him or anything."

I doubted Romy had plans, since he was a total homebody. He probably just found all these Dombrusos a bit intimidating, which I certainly understood. I wished he'd give them a chance though, because these were kind people, and the way they'd welcomed Adriano (and me) to the family was truly remarkable.

Not that they'd just taken our word about who we were without question. Dante was a shrewd, intelligent man, and I had absolutely no doubt he'd looked into both of us by now. He certainly had the resources and capability to make sure we weren't a couple of con artists, trying to get away with something. Good thing I didn't have an arrest record, not that that would necessarily have been a deal breaker. This family clearly hadn't made its money through legal means, and being a thief probably wasn't all that off-putting to them.

Even so, when Yoshi asked me what I did for a living, I hesitated before saying, "I'm currently between jobs." That was literally true —I wasn't robbing anyone at the moment. But in a bigger sense, I was also at a crossroads. I turned to look at Adriano just as he turned to look at me. Now that we were together, I couldn't imagine going back to robbing men who picked me up in bars—not that sex was involved, but still. It just didn't fit with who I was now.

I really wanted to explain all of that to Adriano, but this wasn't the time or place. Instead, I searched his eyes while he gently ran his knuckles along my cheekbone. We both sort of forgot about everyone else for a few moments, until Trevor said, "Aw, new love. I remember those days."

To which Charlie replied, "You're currently sitting on your husband's lap, Trev, and you two were making out like a pair of horny teenagers earlier. Don't make it sound like you're some sad old married couple whose sex life has gone the way of the flip phone."

"Good point," Trevor said with a grin, before planting a big kiss on his husband. It was amazing to see the way Vincent, who was usually so quiet and reserved, lit up around the man he loved.

We were all on our third round of drinks when the hotel room door flew open and Nana exclaimed, "There all of you are!"

She and her husband breezed into the room. Nana was wearing a hot pink sequined dress—which was when I realized she'd actually chosen the limo to match her outfit—along with a headband featuring two pink dicks on springs. Ollie was wearing a tasteful tweed three-piece suit and a headband that matched Nana's, because why not? Her huge, black handbag was slung over Nana's skinny arm, and both she and Ollie were carrying three-foot-tall margaritas in novelty glasses, which for some reason were shaped like very long cocks with a pair of balls at the base.

As soon as Nana spotted Adriano and me, she smiled and rushed over. Then she kissed both of us on our cheeks and said, "Look at you two, all dressed up and so handsome! I did good on that suit, didn't I, Jackie?"

I nodded and said, "You sure did, Nana. Thank you again." Adriano looked devastatingly handsome in his black pinstriped bespoke number, while I was wearing a plum-colored suit that Nana had bought for me on her shopping spree. I'd paired it with a black shirt and black loafers, and all of it was a surprisingly good fit. It was also the least "she works hard for the money" thing Nana had selected for me.

Dante asked his grandmother, "Where'd you get those drinks?"

"We crashed a bachelorette party downstairs," she explained. "They were such a cute group of girls."

Ollie said, "I think Stana might have convinced the bride to ditch the groom for her maid of honor." They both looked quite pleased with that idea.

"She's better off without him. But look at these cute party favors they gave us!" Both she and Ollie vigorously nodded their heads, which made the pink plastic dick antennae flop around wildly, and which also made Dante sigh. Then she asked, "Why are you all holed up in a hotel room? Don't you know what's downstairs? Vegas!"

"We're pregaming," Yoshi told her, as he raised his glass.

"I don't know what that means, but if it's a sporty way of saying you're getting drunk before you get drunk, then I guess that's okay." Nana and Ollie found spots to squeeze in on the couches, and then she kicked off her low heels and put her stockinged feet up on the coffee table as she said, "I hope you're all making your new brother and his boyfriend feel welcome and not boring them to tears with stories about your kids, and grandkids, and blah blah blah."

"Wait," I said, "some of you have grandkids?"

"Dante and I do," Charlie said. "Just one."

"But you look like you're twenty-five." I didn't know why I felt compelled to point that out. Maybe it was the gin and tonics talking.

Charlie grinned and told me, "I'm older than that, but we took a shortcut. Our boys were half-grown when we adopted them. The older one became a father shortly after high school, and now he's crushing college and totally rocking the single dad thing."

"This is exactly what I'm talking about," Nana muttered.

Dante frowned and told her, "You know you adore those kids, Nana."

She scowled at him and snapped, "Of course I do! I'm just not going to go on and on about them tonight, when what we should be talking about is the trouble we're going to get into. I was thinking we could go to one of those all-male revues after dinner, like The Thunder in my Undies. I hear that's a hell of a show."

"The Thunder from Down Under," Vincent corrected, as Trevor bit his lip to keep from laughing. "They're Australian strippers, I believe."

She exclaimed, "Now we're talking! Aussie Aussie Aussie, oi oi oi!" I wondered where she'd learned that.

Yoshi grabbed his phone and said, "I'll check for tickets, but they might be sold out for tonight, Nana."

She asked, "Can't we drop Zan's name, like we did for the dinner reservations?" So that was their secret for getting into one of the hottest restaurants in town.

"Happy to help in any way I can, love," Zan called from across the room, where he and Gianni were snuggled up and sharing a club chair. Nana smiled at him and blew him a kiss.

Dante, who realized he was rapidly losing control of the situation, said, "I'm not sure that's what we want to do tonight, Nana. Vincent and Trevor are heading home tomorrow, so we only have this one night for all of us to be together." Just then, his phone beeped. He pulled it from his pocket and read the screen, then quickly fired off a text as he got up and said, "Vincent and Adriano, I need to talk to you both in the bedroom."

Mike sighed and muttered, "Don't tell me, let me guess. It's super secret older brother stuff and Gianni and I don't get to know what it's about."

Gianni asked, "Wait, is Adriano older than me?"

"Yeah, by two months," Dante said, as he and Vincent headed to the bedroom with their husbands right on their heels. Adriano followed, and since he didn't let go of my hand, I was included by default.

On the way out of the living room, I heard Gianni tell Mike, "Aw, I thought I finally outranked someone, besides just you."

Dante shut the door behind us when we got to the bedroom and held up the phone for Adriano. "Two of my people just spotted someone matching Greco's description. Is this him?" I leaned over and glanced at the photo of a guy with shoulder-length dark hair, climbing out of a silver muscle car.

It looked like it had been snapped from across the street, and it was a bit grainy, but Adriano said, "That's him. Even though the photo's not very clear, the 1970 Chevelle confirms it. That car was parked in the garage where they were holding me prisoner." While Dante sent another text, he asked, "When was this taken?"

"Two minutes ago, in front of a club called Apex. Have you heard of it?"

Adriano nodded, and then he asked, "Did Greco go inside?"

"Yeah, he did. My people followed him, but they're hanging back and waiting for instructions."

"That club had a gang problem in the past, so there are metal detectors at the doors," Adriano said. "He has to be unarmed if he's in there, so this is the perfect time to grab him. Tell your people not to make a move unless he tries to leave. I can be there in fifteen minutes."

When he yanked open the bedroom door, Nana, Gianni, and Mike tumbled inside. Their spouses were right behind them, standing in the hallway and trying to look casual about having been caught eavesdropping. While they untangled themselves and helped each other up, Adriano said, "You should all go ahead and go to dinner, it's almost time for your reservation. I have something I need to take care of, but I'll be back as soon as I can."

"We know what you're doing, and we're coming with you to get the bastard that took you hostage and wrecked your mom's bar." Nana sounded determined.

Dante shook his head and told her, "No way. It's too dangerous." We couldn't actually leave without them though, because there were six people blocking the doorway.

"We just heard Aidie say he's unarmed, so it's not that dangerous." Nana reached into the neck of her sequined dress, pulled her phone out of her bra, and began writing a text. "I'm telling Petey to pull the limo around."

Adriano turned to me with a look of desperation in his eyes, but all I could do was shrug. Short of locking Nana in a closet, there really was no way to stop her. On top of that, Mike added, "I know we're not, like, trained for this or anything, but we can at least come along and act as lookouts. What if this guy slips out the back door? You can't be everywhere at once."

"We appreciate the fact that you want to help," Dante told

them, "but every minute we spend debating this could give Greco time to get away. He's a very dangerous man, and we don't want any of you to get hurt. That's why you're staying here."

Nana spun on her heel and said, "Come on, boys, we can get there ourselves. The club is called Apex, and I'm sure Petey our limo driver knows where it is. Somebody find me some footwear, and hurry up! Not the heels I was wearing, I need some action shoes." Ollie was right behind her as she left the room.

Gianni shot his older brothers a look and pointed out, "None of you drove here, and good luck getting a cab on a Friday night. The limo is the fastest way to get where you're going, so you might as well accept the inevitable."

Adriano turned to Mike and Gianni and said, "I don't understand. Why do you want to put yourselves in a potentially dangerous situation?"

"Because family sticks together," Gianni said. "If you're going to go deal with this thug, then we want to be there to back you up."

"The thing is, Dante and Vincent have always been our family's shield, but they shouldn't be the only ones to bear that burden," Mike chimed in, as they took their argument in tandem. "Our family got out of organized crime a long time ago, but we still have enemies. We know our older brothers have been protecting us from all sorts of things over the years and making sure Gianni and I could lead normal lives. But your enemy is our enemy, and we're not kids anymore. I get that we're not super tough badasses like you guys, but we're not useless, and we want to help."

"Fine. Come along," Dante muttered. "But promise me you'll be careful."

Just then, we heard Nana yell from the other room, "We're going! Get your asses in gear, boys!" That was followed by the unmistakable sound of the hotel room door slamming shut.

Dante swore vividly and hurried for the door. At the same time, Vincent told his younger brothers, "If anyone pulls a gun, your job is to tackle Nana and Ollie and get them on the ground."

As we all ran after Dante, Mike said, "Sure, but Nana will probably be the one pulling a gun."

"All the more reason to tackle her to the ground," Vincent told him.

We caught up to the pair of seniors in time for everyone to pile onto the same elevator. Adriano and I were back in a corner, and he took my face between his hands as he said, "Promise me you won't be a hero, Jack."

"Me? When have I ever been a hero?"

"When you pushed me out of the way and took a bullet for me, and when you snuck into a compound full of people with guns and saved my ass."

"That's not me being heroic," I said softly. "I was just taking care of you, because you mean absolutely everything to me, Reno."

He whispered, "God, I love you," before claiming my mouth in an earth-shaking kiss. My heart skittered in my chest. Had he really just said that?

Before I could reply, Nana exclaimed, "Those two are just so sweet! And don't they look lovely together? Such handsome boys."

Adriano and I both looked up and found everybody grinning at us. I grinned too and ducked my head as heat rose in my cheeks.

A moment later, the elevator doors slid open, and all of us darted into the lobby. I could only imagine how we seemed to the curious onlookers who turned to watch us pass. Here was this big group of men in suits, one of which was a world-famous pop star, and we were all being led into battle by a little old lady wearing a sequined dress, rainbow-striped tennis shoes, and a penis headband. Ollie was still wearing his, too, and he was holding the giant cock cups, one in each hand. Apparently he'd decided this outing would be better with refreshments.

The limo was waiting right out front for us, and Pete was holding the door open. Adriano tipped him with a big fistful of cash and said, "We need to get to Apex as quickly as possible. It's an emergency. If you get a speeding ticket, I'll pay it. And if you lose your job because of any of this, I'll hire you to come work for me."

A huge smile spread across his face, and he asked, "Are you serious?" When Adriano nodded, he said, "Fucking awesome. Just FYI, I'm going to shoot for getting fired." He opened the passenger door and chucked his hat and heels inside before taking off his jacket. Then he ran around to the driver's side barefoot, got behind the wheel, and revved the engine. Once we were all seated, he said, "Hold on to something," and slammed on the gas.

Everyone braced themselves as the huge, pink limo surged forward. Instead of following the curve of the circular drive, he drove over some landscaping and shot through the valet parking lot. "The only way to get there quickly is to stay the hell off the Strip," he called. "Fortunately, I know a lot of shortcuts."

I couldn't help but laugh, because this was fucking epic—and maybe I was a bit of an adrenaline junkie. As he took a wild right out of the parking lot, I looked out the back window and watched a huge wave splash out of the hot tub and soak a hetero couple who'd been arguing on the sidewalk. They stopped arguing after that.

When I turned back around, I noticed Nana's eyes were lit up like it was Christmas. "Hot damn," she exclaimed, as Pete floored it, "now this is what I'm talking about!" Ollie was just as excited. What a perfect pair.

Dante and Vincent looked perfectly calm, while their husbands seemed amused. Meanwhile, Gianni and Mike and their spouses were gripping any part of the limo they could hold onto. Well, they'd wanted to be included in the badassery, and now they were getting a crash course.

When Adriano took my hand, I turned to look at him and asked, "How are you?" It was hard to tell, since he had his game face on.

"Fine."

Yeah, right. He was definitely worried, not about his own safety, but about me and all of his family members. "I'm going to help keep everyone safe when we get there," I told him. "I promise."

He slid his hand around the back of my neck and rested his forehead against mine as he said softly, "That's my job, so please just concentrate on keeping yourself safe. I couldn't stand it if anything happened to you."

"I need you to be safe, too. Catching Greco isn't worth your life, Reno."

When his lips met mine, it was intense and urgent. Did he think that might be our last kiss, because he might not survive this?

Just as panic started to well up in me, Pete called, "We'll be there in two minutes!" Adriano told him to drive slowly past the front of the club and then park out of sight on a side street, and Pete said, "Will do."

Dante passed around his phone with the picture of Greco and said, "My team is on its way to back us up, but they're fifteen minutes out. Adriano, what can you tell us about our target?"

"He's dangerous and unpredictable, and none of you should approach him. When we get there, please just hang back and let me handle this." Adriano looked around at everyone as he said that.

Nana stuck her huge, round glasses on her face and still squinted at the photo on Dante's phone when it was handed to her. "He's sexy," she said. "Too bad he's a dirtbag." Dante sighed at that, just as Pete announced we were a minute out.

Dante's phone came back around to him, and he texted his people inside the bar. Then he announced, "Greco's still there. He's meeting with someone in the VIP section."

I turned to Adriano and squeezed his hand as I told him, "There's something you need to know."

"What is it?"

I smiled at him and said, "I'll tell you afterwards, when we've all made it through this." Then I kissed him again.

Yoshi had an idea just then and pulled his phone from his pocket. "I'm doing a conference call with all of you. That way, we can be in touch while this is going down. Somebody link in Adriano and Jack, because I don't have their numbers."

A lot of phones rang a moment later, and Dante linked in Adriano, who then brought me in. We all answered and dropped the phones into our pockets, as Pete called, "We're here."

We all looked out the tinted windows as he slowly rolled past a bar, which had a flashy neon sign above the door. I asked, "Does anyone have a knife? Greco's car is right out front, and I want to slash his tires in case he gets past us." Several people held out little pocket knives and multitools, and Nana held out a big, scary-looking hunting knife with a pink handle. I went with a folding pocket knife, because I wasn't planning on brutally murdering and skinning the tires.

As soon as Pete rounded the corner and pulled to the curb, I opened the door and said, "Everyone hang back for a minute, especially you, Adriano. If Greco sees you, he'll immediately go on the defensive."

He got out of the limo anyway and said, "I'm not letting you go by yourself."

Everyone was piling out onto the sidewalk, so I grabbed Vincent's sleeve and said, "I'm not. Vincent's coming with me."

Vincent said, as calmly as ever, "Not a problem."

Mike announced he and Gianni were going to stake out the alley behind the bar to make sure no one left by the back door, and they took off running with their spouses right behind them. Dante and Adriano both sighed at that, and then Vincent and I headed for Greco's car. When I glanced over my shoulder, I saw Dante and Adriano holding their arms out to corral Nana and Ollie, who were trying to dodge around them.

I slowed to a stroll just before I reached the bar. Then I casually circled around to the driver's side of Greco's vintage Chevy, crouched down, and made like I was tying a shoe lace, even though I was wearing loafers. There were a few people around, but no one was paying any attention to what I was doing.

When I unfolded the knife and jammed it between the treads, the tire immediately began to deflate. For good measure, I stood up and casually straightened my jacket, then strolled to the next tire and repeated the process.

Vincent had been acting as lookout on the sidewalk, and I joined him and asked, "Are you going to set off the metal detector if we go inside?"

He pushed his glasses further up the bridge of his nose as he said, "No. Dante and I are both unarmed, because we thought we were just having dinner with our family. If we wait for our team though, they're bringing enough fire power to overthrow the government of a small country."

"Let's not wait for that," I said, as I headed for the entrance. "An innocent person could get caught in the crossfire if your people become trigger happy."

"What's your plan here?"

"No idea. I'm making it up as I go along."

There were some shrubs along the front of the building, and I stashed the pocket knife in one of them as Vincent paid the cover charge. Once we were inside, I took my phone from my pocket and told our group, "We're inside the club." Adriano started yelling, so I put the phone on mute and returned it to my pocket. Then I told Vincent, "Wait here in case he decides to head for the door. I'm going to do some recon."

I strode confidently to the room at the back of the bar, which was roped off with a big bouncer controlling entry. Before I could sweet talk my way inside, I spotted our target. Mario Greco was deep in conversation with a heavyset guy whose back was to me, and he was positioned so he had an unobstructed view of the door. That was such a typical mobster move, sitting where he could keep an eye on everyone who came in.

Greco paused to take a drink. While he did that, he scanned the crowd and landed on me in the doorway. He put his glass down slowly, and his eyes narrowed as they locked with mine.

Did he recognize me? The only time we'd been in the same place, I was speeding toward him at night, wearing sunglasses, and blinding him with my headlights, right before I ran him off the road. He couldn't possibly have gotten a good look at me.

Although…

It occurred to me too late that his compound must have had video surveillance, which filmed me and my little raiding party when we went in to rescue Adriano. Greco probably watched it back later to figure out what had happened to his prisoner.

My heart started pounding when he stood up. Fucking hell, he was huge—easily six-three, and a wall of muscle. He started walking toward me, and I took a step back and bumped into someone. It turned out to be Vincent, who'd ignored my instructions and followed me. When I glanced at him, he put a protective hand on my shoulder. Greco stopped in his tracks, probably because Vincent was just as big and scary. Since he'd also been on that rescue mission, Greco probably recognized him, too.

For maybe three seconds, a tense standoff ensued. Then Greco started running—not toward us, but through the VIP lounge. While I was trying to decide what to do, Vincent stepped around me, unhooked the velvet rope, and handed it to the bouncer. Next, he picked up the metal post the rope had been hooked to, swung it onto his shoulder like a baseball player with a bat, and went after Greco—not at a run, but at a leisurely pace. Man, that guy was cool.

The bouncer and I both stared after him, and I asked, "Is there an exit back there?"

"Yeah, but it's marked 'employees only' and you're not supposed to go that way." Like a sign was going to stop them.

"Where does it lead?"

"To the kitchen, which has a side door to an alley."

I grabbed my phone and shouted, as I turned and ran through the bar, "Greco's about to exit through a side door off the kitchen. He recognized Vincent and me. Guys at the back of the building, be ready just in case, but he's probably going to head for his car at the front of the club. I disabled it so he won't be able to drive off, but who knows what he'll do once he discovers that."

I became tangled up in a big, drunk group of revelers on my way through the club, so I got outside just in time to see Greco mug a pizza delivery driver for his keys and drive off in a red Smart car with a big, lit up sign on top, shaped like a slice of pizza. Well, at least he'd be easy to spot. I reported his escape to the group and unmuted my speaker in time to hear Adriano say, "Stay right there, Jack. We're coming to pick you up."

Vincent caught up to me a moment later, dabbing at some sauce on his black suit jacket with a handkerchief. "The kitchen staff was feisty," he said. "I don't think they liked having unexpected company."

The four guys who'd been watching the back of the building joined us, looking like the cast of a low-budget ren faire production.

They were armed with various makeshift weapons including empty wine bottles, some of them wore cardboard armor, and Zan was holding a plastic garbage pail lid like a shield. When I shot them a look, they quickly discarded their alley armory.

Then the hot pink limo pulled up beside us, with Adriano behind the wheel and Dante talking to him through the connecting window. I quickly dove into the passenger seat, and while we waited for everyone else to pile into the back, my boyfriend frowned at me and said, "I thought I told you not to be a hero."

"I wasn't! I just went inside to check out the situation. I really didn't expect Greco to recognize me." I craned my neck to keep the glowing pizza slice in sight. Then I told him, "He just made a left at the light. We need to hurry."

Adriano called, "Hold onto something, everyone," and slammed on the gas. I glanced in the rearview mirror and saw that Pete was sitting with Nana and Ollie on the long bench seat at the back of the limo. One of them had given him their giant cock drink, and he was sipping it happily. While the three of them looked perfectly relaxed, everyone else was bracing themselves to keep from flying out of their seats.

We reached the light just as it turned from yellow to red, and Adriano slammed on the gas and took a wide left. Our tires squealed, and the back end swung so far out that we were practically driving sideways for a few moments. But then he straightened it out, and I grinned and said, "Look at you, driving it like you stole it. That's hot."

He chuckled at that before telling me, "This thing has the reaction time of a drugged giant sloth, so don't expect much."

"You're doing great, and he's in an old Smart car with a huge sign on the top, so I'm sure we'll catch him."

As Adriano wove the huge limo around a few cars, Dante appeared in the pass-through again and held up his phone. "My team's tracking me and converging on our location," he said. "They should be right behind us in a couple of minutes." Adriano did a quick weave, and Dante was flung out of sight. We heard him curse and then mutter, "Next time, anyone but Aide gets to drive."

Whether it was intentional or not, Greco led us to an industrial part of town, which was mostly shut down on a Friday night. Adriano finally got ahead of him in a large parking lot and whipped the limo around to cut him off.

Greco screeched to a halt, stopping just inches from our rear fender, and then he tumbled out of the car and took off running. For some reason, Adriano grabbed one of Pete's hot pink stilettos from the floor before flinging the door open and sprinting after his quarry.

Exiting through the driver's side door was my most direct route, but I had to scramble over the center console before joining the chase. That put me a few seconds behind.

As I ran to catch up, several SUVs started pulling into the lot. I sincerely hoped they were Dante's team, and that Greco hadn't called his people for backup.

When he was within maybe twenty feet of Greco, Adriano hurled the shoe in a side-armed pitch. It was a perfect throw, landing at Greco's feet and causing him to trip and fall. That gave Adriano the time he needed to close the gap.

Greco was back up in an instant. He whirled around, anger flashing in his eyes as he drew back a fist. Before he could strike, Adriano punched him in the jaw and knocked him back. "That's for smashing up my mom's bar," he growled. When Greco lunged at him, Adriano punched him again. Greco landed on his ass, and Adriano yelled, "And that's because one of your dirtbags shot my boyfriend!"

Greco was like a wild animal. He got up and growled as he tried to come at Adriano yet again. But before he could get punched a third time, someone tasered him right in the chest, and he fell to the ground.

We all turned to look at Nana and her taser, and I said, "Nice shot."

She scowled and muttered, "No it wasn't. I was aiming for his nuts."

It took a few moments, but Greco staggered to his feet, pulled the wires from his chest, and threw them to the ground. I thought he might try to come at Adriano once more, because he seemed absolutely feral. But then he looked around, and I did, too.

Dante and Vincent were flanking Adriano and me, and the rest of the family had gathered around us, like the first layer of a shell.

The second layer consisted of about thirty badass men and women dressed in black. Every one of them had a firearm pointed at Greco, and he yelled, "Who the fuck are all these people?"

"This is my family, that's our army, and here's your one warning." Adriano's voice rang with authority, and he took my hand and straightened his posture. I stared at his profile in awe. He was ice and steel, and the sexiest thing I'd ever seen in my life. "If you come for me or any of my loved ones, we'll hunt you down, and we'll show no mercy. You don't cross the Dombrusos. If you were too ignorant to know our name before today, then you just got educated, you fucking prick."

With that, he and I turned and walked away. Our family fell into step with us, including Pete, who'd picked up his pink stiletto and was grinning from ear-to-ear. "Best customers ever," he whispered.

Vincent took a moment to pluck the keys from the Smart car, apparently just for shits and giggles, and we all piled back into the limo as Pete slid behind the wheel. Meanwhile, Dante's army was standing down, but just barely. They all glared at Greco as he turned and went limping off into the night.

Dante told Pete to take us back to the hotel, and Ollie popped a bottle of champagne. Meanwhile, I straddled Adriano's lap and kissed him passionately before saying, "Marry me."

He grinned and repeated something I'd said earlier. "Ask me again when you're not hopped up on adrenaline."

I nodded and told him, "I will."

23

Adriano

Jack kissed me again while I ran my hands up his back. Then he curled up with his head on my shoulder, and I wrapped my arms around him.

Meanwhile, Charlie snuggled up with his husband and asked, "Do you really think it's over?"

"I think we sent a pretty clear message tonight," Dante said. "Unless Greco has a death wish, he'll back off. Just to be on the safe side, I'll leave my team here for the next few weeks. And of course, Vincent and I can be back on short notice, any time we're needed."

"I really don't think he'll keep coming for me," I said. "He thought he had me hopelessly outnumbered and could push me around. Tonight, he found out I'm not alone." I looked around at my family and added, "Thank you, each and every one of you, for having my back. That meant a lot to me."

"There's no need to thank us. That's just what family does," Nana said. Then she asked, "Do you think we can still make our dinner reservation? I'm fucking starving!"

"Probably not, but you wouldn't have liked it anyway," Dante told her. "The portions would have been tiny, and everything would have been way too pretentious. How about going back to the suite and ordering the entire room service menu with extra dessert?"

Nana's face lit up, and she said, "Now, there's a peach of an idea!"

"Sounds great," I said. "We just need to make one stop along the way." I called to Pete and gave him an address.

A few minutes later, we pulled up in front of Romy's apartment building. His light was on, and of course he was home—just like every other night, because the kid was a total homebody.

Jack came with me, and we went up to the second floor landing and knocked on the door. When Romy answered, dressed in gray sweat pants and an oversized UNLV sweatshirt, I tried my best to look serious and told him, "You need to come with us. Grab your shoes, and let's go."

My brother instantly went into paramedic mode. He stuck his feet into a pair of sneakers, then grabbed his keys and first aid kit as he asked, "Is someone hurt? Do we need to call 911?"

"No. It's a different kind of emergency," Jack said. He was maintaining an excellent poker face.

Romy stepped out onto the landing and locked the door behind him. Then he turned around and spotted the pink limo, and he asked, "What the hell is that?"

"Our sweet, sweet ride," I said, with a big grin. "Just a heads up, it's stuffed full of Dombrusos."

Romy took a step back and said, "Oh. Um, I'll pass."

"Like hell you will. We just faced off against Greco, and it was a huge victory. Now I want to celebrate with my family, and that includes you. I would include Mom too, obviously, if she wasn't still in L.A."

"Yeah, but—"

"But nothing. I love you, Romy, and no celebration is complete without you. Also, just in case you need to hear this, the Dombrusos aren't going to replace you. My heart's big enough for five brothers, a shitload of relatives, and a boyfriend." I glanced at Jack and grinned, and he flashed me a gorgeous smile.

Because he was as stubborn as the rest of the family, Romy still tried to resist. "I know, but I wasn't really planning to go out tonight."

"So, change your plans," I said. "Remember Pete, your friend from high school? He's our limo driver, and he's going to be partying with us. So's Zan Tillane."

"The pop star?" When I nodded, Romy raised a skeptical brow and asked, "Are you on drugs?"

Jack leaned over the railing and yelled, "Hey, Zan!" When the singer poked his head out of the sunroof, he called, "Tell Adriano's brother Romy to come with us!"

"Come along, mate," the man called, with a friendly smile. "The more the merrier."

Romy muttered, "This is fucking surreal," but he headed for the stairs.

Around three a.m., when everyone else had fallen asleep, I brought a blanket out to the suite's balcony. Then I got comfortable beside my boyfriend on a cushioned lounge chair and tucked both of us in.

We had an incredible view of the Strip, all lit up and gaudy and actually really beautiful from way up here. Jack was far more gorgeous and fascinating though, and I ran my fingertips along his jaw as he grinned at me and said, "That was a hell of a party."

"It really was. No one parties like the Dombrusos, which figures. They don't seem to do anything halfway." There'd been mountains of delicious food, and the cocktails and champagne had flowed freely. Nana and Ollie were the life of the party, dancing, eating, and drinking with abandon—for about forty minutes. Then they'd fallen asleep, fully dressed and snoring, on top of the covers in the center of Zan and Gianni's king-size bed.

"I'm really glad we picked up Romy. He seems to be warming up to all the newcomers in your life. It also seemed like he and his friend from high school picked up right where they left off."

"Yeah, they did. Hey, how great would it be if I just found Romy a boyfriend?"

"I hate to break it to you, but god no," Jack said. "Those boys are two peas in a pod—and by that I mean two sweet little bottoms in search of big, burly tops. Pete was asking Romy to be his wingman at some new leather daddy bar in town." When I grimaced, he asked, "What?"

"That's just a little too much information on my kid brother's sex life."

"Reno, he's twenty-seven. He's not a kid."

"I know that…mostly. But some part of me will always think of him as a skinny, defenseless little ten-year-old."

Jack sighed, but he sounded amused instead of annoyed. Then he kissed my cheek and said, "It's actually sweet that you're such a protective big brother. And speaking of sweet, I also love the fact that you hired Pete to work in your mom's bar." He'd quit his job earlier in the evening, and his former employer had come by to collect the limo. It actually wasn't any worse for wear, aside from an empty hot tub.

"He's a nice guy, and he has bartending experience, so it was a no-brainer. My mom can't keep working fourteen-hour days forever, it's just too much. And with me paying Pete's salary, there's no reason not to accept some help."

I'd called her earlier to ask about hiring Pete, and to let her know what had happened with Greco. She'd sounded relieved. She also surprised me by saying she and Chet were having such a good time in L.A. that they'd decided to stay through the weekend. I couldn't actually remember her taking a vacation—ever—so it made me happy that she was prioritizing something other than work for a change.

Jack asked, "So, now that Greco's out of the picture, what are you going to do? I know you'd mentioned retiring, but is that still the plan?"

"It is. I have enough money to take care of you and me, and your mom and my mom, and Romy if he ever needs help, very comfortably for the rest of our lives. So, why risk getting arrested, and why keep dealing with men like Greco? It's just not worth it."

He sounded emotional when he said, "You included my mom on your list."

"Of course I did."

He straddled my lap and grabbed me in a hug as he whispered, "That means so much to me. I can't even tell you." I held him securely, and after a moment he said, "I decided to retire too, by the way. Sooner or later, I would have wound up in jail, and I can't stand the thought of getting taken away from you."

I kissed the side of his head and told him, "That's a good call."

He sat up and smiled at me as he asked, "So, what do a former thief and an ex-gangster do, exactly? Do we take up golf, like the pair of retirees that we are?"

"Do you *want* to take up golf?"

"Not even a little."

"Okay, so not that, then. And I guess the answer to your question is that we do whatever the hell we want. Logistically speaking, you'll move in with me, obviously, and I'd love it if we split our time between Vegas and San Francisco. I want to keep getting to know my dad's side of the family, but I also want us to be here for Mom and Romy."

He looked amused. "So, it's obvious that we're moving in together?"

"Of course. I need you with me every minute of every day, and not to be presumptuous, but I think you might want that, too."

"Oh, I do, and that reminds me. Earlier, I told you there was something you needed to know."

"Yes, you did."

"So, here it is." He took my face between his palms and told me, "I love you, Adriano." He was so serious about it, like this was the most important thing he'd ever said.

I grinned and ran my hands down his back. "Yeah?"

He nodded. "With all my heart. And if you want to live in Vegas and San Francisco, awesome. Let's do it. The only thing I care about is that we're together."

My grin turned into a smile. "You're amazing. You know that?"

"Right back at you."

He kissed me deeply before curling up with his head on my chest. When he dozed off a few minutes later, I pulled the blanket up to his shoulders and held him securely, as I marveled at where we found ourselves.

Jack was amazing. He had a hard time trusting, and yet he somehow managed to make himself completely vulnerable—to put himself in my hands and know I'd never hurt him. His faith in me was humbling.

At the same time, I knew I could trust him, too. He truly loved and cared about me, and he'd never hurt me, either. I felt it deep down.

The effortlessness of it all was surprising. We just fit somehow. I could easily imagine us like this a year from now, and ten, and twenty. It was that right, that beautifully inevitable.

24

Jack

When I woke up the next morning, I had a slight hangover and was someplace unfamiliar—outside, on a balcony. It was disorienting, but then I rolled over and saw Adriano beside me, and I knew everything was okay.

As soon as he felt me shift, he reached for me. I loved that. I burrowed into his arms, and he said, in a raspy whisper, "Waking up with you feels so damn good."

We cuddled for a while, and I asked, "Do you think we can go to San Francisco sometime soon? I was renting a room by the week, and I'm only paid up through this weekend. I'd like to get my stuff instead of paying for another week, and I also want to see about getting your watch back. I know you said it didn't matter that much, but it does to me."

"Sure. We can go today if you want. I'll ask Dante if there's room in the plane he chartered to take the family back, and if not it'll be easy enough to buy us a pair of tickets on a commercial flight."

I grinned and asked, "Don't you want to handcuff me to a car door and drive back?" That felt like such a long time ago—another lifetime.

Adriano smiled at me and said, "Next time I handcuff you, it'll be when we're both naked in bed and you're begging me to do that to you." Now there was a good thought.

We lingered in our makeshift bed a while longer, before reluctantly admitting it was time to get up. After we went inside and took turns in the bathroom, we found everyone gathered in the living room with coffee and pastries. I was glad to see Romy sharing a laugh with Gianni and Mike. Last night seemed to have gone a long way toward making him feel like he, too, was part of the family.

About half an hour later, he told us, "I should go, because I picked up a shift at work and need to get ready." Pete, who was also an honorary Dombruso by now, decided he should go, too. After they said their goodbyes to the rest of the family, we walked them out.

Romy gave Adriano a hug and said, "I'm glad you talked me into joining you last night. This was pretty incredible."

"Thanks for giving them a chance." When they let go of each other, Adriano added, "Jack and I are heading to San Francisco later today. We're moving in together, and we decided we're going to split our time between here and there. We'll only be gone a few days this time, and if you or Mom need anything—"

"We'll be fine, and I'm so happy for you two." He gave me a hug and said, "Text me soon, Jack, and take care of my brother for me."

I told him, "You know I will."

After breakfast, we went with the family to their vacation rental and packed up all of our things. Then we borrowed one of the SUVs and headed to Adriano's house in the desert.

Getting naked to take a shower turned into a blow job, then a quick, hard fuck with me bent over the bathroom sink. It was our first time with privacy in a week, and we'd both finally recovered from our injuries, so it was frantic and urgent and neither of us lasted long. There'd be plenty of time for a lot more later on, but for now it was all about that much-needed release.

We showered together, and as we toweled off afterwards I asked, "What are your plans while we're in San Francisco?"

"I want to meet the rest of the family, including my nieces and nephews. I've been collecting a few gifts for them this past week, mostly online, but I also had one of my employees go out and find me some stuff. It's going to be fun being an uncle."

I asked, "Speaking of your employees, what's going to happen with them now that you're shutting down your business?"

"I messaged them last night with an update and told them I'm paying them all six months' salary as severance."

"That's really generous of you."

He shrugged and said, "It was the right thing to do."

We joked and jostled for position in front of the mirror as we both went through our grooming routine. Then, when I turned to go get dressed, he caught my hand.

I hadn't rebandaged the wound on my arm yet. It looked a bit rough at the moment, and it was definitely going to scar. He touched my arm gently and looked at me with so much emotion in his eyes, and I said, "Don't even think about feeling guilty."

"I can't help it. You got that scar saving me, and—"

"And I'd do it all over again, a thousand times," I said. "You'd do the same for me, too."

He drew me into his arms and kissed my forehead before saying, "Of course I would. I'd do anything for you."

I looked up at him and asked, "Even traveling to Kansas to meet my mom and my best friend?"

A smile spread across his face. "I'd be honored."

"Good. I already called Ma a couple of days ago and told her all about you, and she's dying to meet you."

"You didn't tell me that."

"I'm telling you now. Wyatt's dying to meet you, too."

"I can't wait. Let's go next weekend."

"This is exciting," I said. "I've never brought anyone home to meet my family before."

"Will you teach me some sign language between now and then? I know I won't be able to manage much in such a short time, but I'd like to say some basic things, like hi, nice to meet you, and I adore Jack."

I grinned at that and took a step back. Then I signed exactly what he'd just said and told him, "I'll teach you more than that, obviously, but it's a good starting point."

Just then, we were interrupted by a knock at the door. "That's weird," I said. "We're literally in the middle of nowhere out here. Who'd be knocking?"

As I followed him into the bedroom, he said, "It might be one of my three neighbors. They all pretty much keep to themselves, but maybe one of them needs something." He picked up his phone and accessed the app that went with the camera on his doorbell, and his eyebrows shot toward his hairline. When he turned the screen to face me, there was Doctor Ford, his ex, pacing nervously.

"What do you suppose he wants?"

"No idea, but I guess I should answer it."

He quickly traded the towel around his hips for gym shorts and a T-shirt before hurrying downstairs. Meanwhile, I took a seat on the top step, where I was out of sight but could hear everything. I was way too nosy not to listen in.

Adriano answered the door with, "Hey, Ford, what's up?"

"We need to talk. Can I come in?"

"I don't have much time. I'm about to head to the airport."

"I know," Ford said. "I ran into Romy at a coffee house a little while ago. He was on his way to work so he couldn't talk long either, but he mentioned you were about to head back to San Francisco with some guy. He also said you're moving in together."

"You're intentionally being rude by calling him 'some guy.' My boyfriend's name is Jack, which you know because you met him."

"Boyfriend," Ford scoffed. "What are you, in high school?"

"Don't worry. I'll be calling him my husband soon enough." That made me grin.

"I don't understand what's gotten into you! We were together for four years, and everything happened at a glacier's pace. Now all of a sudden you're moving in with someone you've known for a few weeks? It's not like you, Reno."

"No, it's not, and thank god for that. I was just coasting through life before, and I feel like I finally woke up when I met Jack."

"It's exciting because it's new," Ford said, "but once the novelty wears off, what are you left with?"

"My perfect match." Adriano sounded like there wasn't a doubt in his mind about that. "Jack is exactly what I need. In fact, he's what I've always needed. He and I are the same, and we understand each other."

"Meaning what, he's a criminal like you?"

It was obvious Ford was trying to goad him into an argument, but Adriano didn't take the bait. Instead, he asked, "What was your objective in coming here, Ford? Did you feel like picking a fight? If so, you wasted your time, because I'm not doing that anymore."

"No, of course I didn't come here to pick a fight. I came to ask you for another chance." Oh, hell. Now I felt bad for the guy. He pressed on with, "We had *four years* together! That has to count for something."

Adriano's tone turned sympathetic. "It's too late," he said gently. "I'm in love with Jack. He's everything to me, and I plan to spend the rest of my life with him."

"How can you say that, after such a short time?"

"Time has nothing to do with it. You and I proved how irrelevant it is. We were never right, and we were never going to be, no matter how much time we invested. Sometimes I think we stayed together out of habit more than anything, and because it seemed easier than getting back out there and starting from scratch."

"Maybe…"

"Do yourself a favor, Ford. Accept the fact that you and I failed. Actually, that's probably another reason we stayed together so long, and why you're here now—because you feel like you have to succeed at everything. But failure isn't a bad thing. Look at it as a chance to learn and grow."

After a pause, Ford said, "I guess you're right. So, do you think you and I can be friends?"

Adriano told him, "We already are," which I thought was sweet.

They spoke for another minute or two, and after Ford took off,

Adriano appeared at the foot of the stairs. He grinned when he saw me sitting there and said, "I suppose you heard everything."

"I was just being efficient. Now you don't have to tell me what he wanted."

He climbed the stairs and knelt down on one that nearly put us at eye level. Then he pulled me close and kissed me before saying, "I'm sorry if Ford dropping by like that made you uncomfortable."

"It didn't, actually. I was intimidated by him when we met, but I'm not anymore because I'm confident in our relationship. Now, I just feel bad for the guy."

"Why is that?"

"Because a terrible thing happened to him—he had the greatest man in the world, and he let you slip away."

Adriano grinned as he got to his feet and helped me up. "Come on, let's finish getting ready," he said. "We have a fancy chartered plane to catch."

The plane really was ridiculously nice—so much different than economy class, which was what I was used to. All of us drank Bloody Marys, laughed, and told stories all the way to San Francisco, and I was feeling no pain by the time we arrived.

The Dombrusos offered to drive us to our destination, but we opted to take a cab and promised we'd join them for Sunday dinner. Then I brought Adriano to the crappy building that had been my home for a couple of months. Wow, was I ever *not* going to miss this place.

When we pulled up out front and saw a bunch of kids sitting on the steps, Adriano joked, "Oh look, a kid gang."

"For real, though. They're a bunch of baby delinquents. See the one with buzzed off blond hair? That's who stole your watch from me. And look, the little shit's still wearing it! I can't believe no one's taken it from him."

Adriano turned to me as I slid down in the seat to stay hidden, and a huge smile spread across his face. "That's who took the watch? A scrawny ten year old?"

"He's at least eleven. Maybe even twelve." When he started laughing, I said, "See why I didn't tell you? We need a plan. If he sees me, that mini demon is going to take off running, and we might never catch him."

"Let me handle this. You just stay here." He asked the cab driver to pop the trunk, and then he went and got something out of his luggage.

When he approached the group of kids, they eyed him suspiciously. I couldn't hear what he said to them, but then the boy slipped the watch off his skinny wrist and traded it for some sort of large package. The tiny hoodlums were talking excitedly as they all rushed into the building with whatever he'd given them.

I asked the cabbie to keep the meter running before joining Adriano. As we went inside, I asked, "How'd you do that?"

"It was easy. I traded him for something he considered more valuable than the watch." While he was talking, he unraveled a thick bundle of yarn from the Rolex's band. So that was how the kid had kept it from falling off.

"I can't even begin to guess what that was."

"The latest generation PlayStation, which hasn't hit the stores yet. Never mind that it cost a fraction of what the watch is worth. To a kid, it's pure gold."

"Was that meant for your brothers' kids?"

He nodded and said, "I actually have two of the consoles, so I guess my nieces and nephews will have to share the one that's left."

I had a follow-up question. "If they're not in stores yet, where'd they come from?"

"Um…they might have fallen off the back of a truck."

"You stole them?"

"Me? No. The person I bought them from, however…"

I grinned and shook my head. "I thought you were reformed."

"I am now. That was my last official act as a criminal," he said.

The watch face was covered in fingerprints, so he polished it up with a handkerchief. Then he put it on and turned his wrist, examining the watch from different angles with a smile. I was so damn glad he had that back.

When we got to my room, he looked around curiously but refrained from commenting while I quickly packed my things. I knew it was a hovel, and it was nice of him not to point that out.

Soon we were back in the cab, and fifteen minutes after that we stepped into the townhouse's foyer. "Home sweet beige," he quipped, as we piled our things just inside the door.

"This place isn't so bad. A few house plants and some colorful throw pillows, and it might seem downright homey."

"I'm glad you think so. I'd like to hold off on buying a place here for a bit, because there's something I want to do first." He took his phone from his suit pocket and pulled up a real estate listing. Then he showed me the screen and asked, "Do you think your mom would like someplace like this? I obviously plan to ask her when we visit, but I want to find some examples to show her."

Tears welled up in my eyes as I looked at the charming cottage, which was for sale in Manhattan, Kansas. "You're buying my mother a house?"

"That's the plan. Obviously, if we can talk her into moving to Vegas or San Francisco so you can see her more often, I'll buy her something there instead."

That was when I started sobbing. He picked me up and held me securely as he murmured, "Baby, don't cry."

"I can't help it," I managed. "This is all I ever wanted, to make sure Ma was okay. I tried so hard. I sent money home every month, but it was never enough. There was always some catastrophe—her old car breaking down again, or a medical bill, or something else. We could never get ahead. But this, this is going to make such a huge difference."

He carried me into the living room and sat on the couch with me on his lap. It took a while, but I finally got the tears under control. Meanwhile, he waited patiently and rubbed my back.

Finally, I whispered, "This is so much. What can I ever do for you in return?"

"You're already doing it. You're letting me take care of you, and you're taking care of me in turn. That's all I need."

That evening, we walked to the local market and bought some groceries. Then we came home, put some music on, and went to work making dinner together. With our combined playlists on shuffle, we never knew what song was going to come through the speakers next. This resulted in some groans, some cheers, and a lot of laughs.

After we got a big pot of soup simmering on the stovetop, one of Adriano's old-fashioned songs came on. He twirled me under our joined hands before pulling me close. As he sang to me in his rich baritone and we swayed to the music, I was overcome by the most incredible feeling. For the first time in my life, I felt happy, secure, and at peace, all at the same time.

I wanted to explain that to my sweet, amazing boyfriend. But when I looked into his eyes and he smiled at me, I could see he felt exactly the same way.

Epilogue: Jack

Two months later

The weekend before Christmas, the townhouse was overflowing with our friends and family. Holiday music was playing, the tree and the decorations sparkled, and the whole place smelled like vanilla and cinnamon from all the baking we'd been doing.

We'd flown Wyatt in for the holidays, and I'd finally confessed my (now former) life of crime. It felt good to come clean, and he totally took it in stride. I should have known my best friend accepted me no matter what.

At the moment, he and JoJo were seated in front of the fireplace, carrying on a lively conversation about movies. I'd been delighted when the entire Pink Victorian Crew showed up for our holiday party, and discovering JoJo was fluent in ASL was a wonderful bonus.

On the other side of the room, Romy, Mandy, and her fiancé Chet were deep in conversation with my mother. We'd flown Ma in for Thanksgiving, and she'd gone back just long enough to pack and give notice at her job and apartment before returning to the west coast.

She and Mandy had bonded almost instantly at Thanksgiving, and Mandy had been helping her house hunt in Las Vegas. I was so happy my mother had decided she was ready for a change, and that I'd get to see her a lot more often.

About forty Dombrusos, including Adriano's brothers and their spouses and kids, made up the rest of our guests. They were loud and boisterous and just so much fun. At the moment, Adriano and Dante were arm wrestling, and it was completely ridiculous. Both men were turning red, and neither was budging, since they were so evenly matched. Meanwhile, Vincent and Mike were teasing them mercilessly, while Gianni and his famous husband kept up a running commentary.

I paused in the center of the room and just took it all in. A few moments later, Adriano came up behind me and slipped his hands around my waist. As I leaned against him, I asked, "Did you hurt yourself with that display of machismo?"

"My arm feels like it's about to fall off."

"Who won, you or Dante?"

"Neither. Romy stepped in and told us we were going to burst a blood vessel if we kept it up, so we called it a draw." I turned to face him and draped my arms over his shoulders, and Adriano said, "You looked like you were deep in thought."

"I was marveling at how different my life is now, compared to just a few months ago. I used to spend most of my time alone, and now my life is so full. It feels like a miracle."

He kissed my forehead and whispered, "I love you so much."

It felt like a huge understatement when I told him, "I love you too, Reno."

Later that night, when our out-of-town guests were tucked into the boutique hotel up the street and our local friends and family were back home, Adriano and I snuggled on the couch. We were dressed in pajamas and wrapped up in a fuzzy blanket, and the tree's lights cast a warm, golden glow over everything.

All of a sudden, he sat up and blurted, "I can't do it! I can't wait until Christmas to give you your gift. Can we please just exchange presents right now?"

I threw the blanket aside and leapt up as I exclaimed, "God yes! I thought I was going to explode if I had to wait another week."

We ran off in opposite directions and met up in front of the tree about a minute later. We had our hands hidden behind our backs, and the air crackled with anticipation. Then we both held out jeweler's boxes, raised the lids, and said simultaneously, "Marry me."

I stared in awe at the beautiful platinum band he was holding, and he did the same with the nearly identical ring I was offering him. Then we met each other's gaze as we both exclaimed, "Yes!"

We burst out laughing, and he lifted me off my feet and hugged me. I held on tight and whispered, "Just when I thought my life couldn't get any better."

The End

**Next up in the Series:
My Brother's Enemy**

When I first approached Romy Russo, it wasn't with the best intentions.

What I didn't count on was falling for him. Romy is gorgeous, kind, and too pure for this world. For some reason, he sees the good in me—something I don't even see in myself.

He has no idea who I really am, though. He only knows me as Marcus Greene. He's totally unaware of the harm I've caused his family, and he doesn't know his brother will probably kill me if we ever cross paths again.

As this thing between us keeps growing deeper and more intense, I can't help but wonder—what's going to happen when Romy finally discovers I'm Mario Greco?

www.ingramcontent.com/pod-product-compliance
Lightning Source LLC
Chambersburg PA
CBHW061247120726
48001CB00001B/180